What readers are saying about Seasons by th

"**Jane Lovering has that ability to choose exactly** the right **words and images** to make you laugh, with a wonderful touch of the ridiculous, then moving seamlessly to a scene of such poignancy that it catches your breath."

"**Excellent characterisation** (people and dogs!), well worked plot, great descriptive passages, and of course, Jane's hilarious signature one-liners."

"It's **a wonderful story, fully of whimsy and gentle humour**, a terrific story and wonderful characters, all wrapped up in a very satisfying ending."

". . . **total sense of place, unforced humour, slow-burning romance**. Jane Lovering's writing is very strong"

"**It is very difficult to explain just how wonderful this book is.** The power of her words and her descriptive prowess to put it bluntly is amazing . . . the emotional impact it has had on me will be long lasting."

"I enjoyed every word in this novel, once again Jane didn't disappoint with her unique, inimitable writing. Warm, witty, funny characters with interesting histories, set against a beautifully descriptive narrative of a wintery beach landscape. A lot of laugh-out-loud one-liners, **it's a book I have to read again, only slower this time so I can absorb every word.**"

"**What a heart-warming and emotional ride this book was! I loved it!** The cast of characters were so enjoyable and realistic."

A SEAGULL SUMMER

SEASONS BY THE SEA, BOOK TWO

Jane Lovering

This edition published in 2020 by Farrago,
an imprint of Duckworth Books Group Ltd
1 Golden Court, Richmond, TW9 1EU, United Kingdom
www.farragobooks.com

ISBN: 978-1-78842-190-4

To the memory of Tiggy – my dreadful terrier, who was the model (if 'model' is the word) for Brian, and all the little Brianlettes. RIP, little dog.

Chapter One

The house looked like an attractive person caught midsneeze. Nice outline but everything slumped and crinkled, and an atmosphere of 'waiting' for something big to happen. The caretaker looked at me.

'Sorry we couldn't muster up the Hilton for you, but,' he sniffed and, rather noticeably, wiped his nose along his sleeve, 'this is Dorset. We does things different here.'

'So I see.' Actually I'd gathered that from the fact he'd picked me up from the almost terminally inaccessible Crewkerne station in a minibus without a steering wheel. The spanner shoved through the column had needed both of us leaning on it to get round some of the narrow lanes. 'No, the place is fine. I just need somewhere to base myself, it doesn't need to be posh.'

He sniffed again. 'All the good bed and breakfast places gets booked up with people coming to watch all them TV programmes being filmed. You're lucky the university had this place empty, it's where all the students is based when they're doing their coastal research.' His sniff this time was more disapproval than snot-based. 'Coastal research my left buttock. All they does is gets drunk and shags one another.' He stared off across the hilly landscape. 'Lucky bastards.'

I ignored him, but looked down at the rough hand-drawn map he'd shoved into my hand. 'So, we are… here?' I tapped my thumb on the square that I was presuming was the house. 'What's the quickest way to the harbour?'

'Jump off the cliff.' He started a laugh that sounded like a rusty see-saw being coaxed into action, but my lack of follow-up hilarity stopped it. 'Take that path there.' A dirty nail traced a line on the map. 'Takes you down to Steepleton harbour.' Another sniff. 'You're not stopping here alone, are you?'

I blinked slowly. 'Well, yes. Um.' I wanted to add, 'This is the twenty-first century and I'm a research scientist with a PhD, there's no conceivable reason I should need anyone else,' and to turn a laser-pointer glare on him; knew I should challenge his sexism, but my upbringing wouldn't let me. 'Is there any reason I shouldn't?' I finally asked, but it was more questioning than confrontational.

He turned away. 'Well, it takes two people to work water pump.' A last, final sniff and he was off to the minivan. 'Oh, and if you knows anyone who wants to live here full-time, mind the place and deal with the students, my job is vacant as of tomorrow.' He threw a disgusted look at the van. 'I'm off to drive proper taxis and live in Yeovil where there's running water.' He looked around at the field, the house and then up at the relentless bronze sky. 'It's a great job looking after this place – if you're a hermit with no domestic standards.' And he was gone, spanner-steering the van out of the rutted trackway that led a considerable distance off the road. Leaving me, my bags and the house, which looked as though it was trying to creep away from me on an imperceptible level.

The sun was warm and the long, hot spring had dried the grass that surrounded the house until it crunched underfoot. There was no cover, the house stood at the end of the trackway as though it had been plonked out of the sky into the nearest field. Apart from a stone shed, which looked as if it might once have been a stable, and a single, rather tatty oak tree, there was just a field, the sun and the house. Lengthening shadows dressed the scene with solid blocks of black, giving me the feeling that I was in the opening shot to some kind of bucolic movie, and the gulls skirling overhead, apart from bringing a slight 'Hitchcockian' vibe, weren't doing much to dispel it.

Thomas Hardy would have loved it. Then written an impenetrable poem about it.

I picked up my bags and stumbled my way up the driveway, to the massive front door. It hung slightly askew in its frame, which meant that the keyhole and lock were out of alignment, and I had to jiggle the key to unlock it.

'If there are any ghosts, zombies, mummies or other Scooby Doo type monsters resident, you have thirty seconds to get out,' I announced to the dust motes hanging in the hallway behind the door. 'Your spooky janitor has already left.'

Silence, except for a door rattling somewhere upstairs. The sunlight peered over my shoulder into the stone-flagged passageway which released a musty smell of ancient alcohol and Mr Sheen; someone had clearly made an attempt at cleaning at some point. I followed the sunlight inside.

Indoors, the house had less of the Miss Havisham about it than I had expected. A wide hallway with stairs leading to the first floor, two flung-open doors to either side revealed rooms full of mismatched chairs and crumpled magazines left on low sofas. Following the hall took me through another door and into a large kitchen, which seemed to be built mostly of table. A big Rayburn sat sullenly in one wall but the bin bags full of discarded Pot Noodle containers told me that this was rarely lit. The window looked out over the field towards the sea and its ledge held an impressive collection of bottles, which informed me in various languages that they had once held vodka.

I sighed and dropped my bags on the huge table. Student accommodation had been enough of a pain when I was a student; now I was rapidly approaching an age where I prized comfort over style and a really good cup of tea over all-night drinking sessions, and this house was yelling at me about backache and cold feet. But it came with the research job for the summer and beat having to stay in my home town and write papers on algae farming, so I was going to make the best of it.

The other thing that came with the research job was an assistant, and the continuing silence of the house told me that they hadn't arrived yet. I found my phone, swung around the house until I located a signal in the far corner of the pantry, and dialled.

'Yey, oh ruler of my small, and not very interesting, universe!'

Oh, Lord. 'Don't call me that, for heaven's sake. Leah will do, thanks. Look, I'm at the house in Dorset, whereabouts are you?'

'Still in Exeter. On my way soon, I just promised to go to this party, yeah, and I gotta pick up some gear first. See you in the morning?'

Talking to Tass made me feel very old, very tired and so out of touch with modern living that I always subconsciously adjusted my crinoline after a conversation with them. I had no problem with their gender-fluid identification – although the pronouns gave me a headache – or the relentless energy of youth; I did, however, have severe problems with the lack of punctuality and the seeming desire to prioritise absolutely everything other than the job in hand.

'Early, if you can, Tass. I want to get on and we need to get all the programmes installed on the computer to run the spreadsheets.'

'Yeah, yeah, I got the coordinates, I'll beam in around ten, get me?'

The line went dead. I pulled a face that I suspected made me look like my mother, and sighed again. Thirty-four and already feeling that the Tudors had called and wanted me back. Criticising this perfectly ordinary, if somewhat antiquated and architecturally comatose house and my perfectly normal, early-twenties research assistant, when I should be thanking any deity that recognised me that I had a good and paying project, somewhere to stay while I carried it out and any assistant at all. Plus, this was Dorset, it was June, the sun was beckoning like a shy lover and just at the end of the field I could see the flicker of light that spoke of the sea. For about the millionth time I gave myself a talking to. *Stop looking for the bad. Relax, enjoy the moment. Never mind what might happen, look at what is happening RIGHT NOW.*

For about the millionth time, it didn't work.

I dug in the bottom of a bag and found some teabags, some powdered milk and my mug. There was a kettle standing on the wooden worktop under the window, it looked clean enough inside, so I filled it from a tap that made incredible banging noises while it ran, and plugged it in. Tea would make everything look better. Or, at least, it would give my mouth something else to do other than make the downturned lip of vague dissatisfaction which I feared had become my default setting.

I got my laptop out of its bag and, whilst the kettle boiled, I got it linked up to the internet, via the blinking box in the corner and the password written in VERY LARGE LETTERS pinned to a corkboard on the wall. I guessed that this was the first port of call for the students usually resident and, from the wear and tear on the floor surrounding it, the fridge was their second.

Because of the powdered milk, the tea was too hot to drink. I distracted myself by logging in to my emails, while the smell of the Earl Grey tinged the air with bergamot and memories. We had sat in the sun, in a room very much like this one – well a stone-flagged kitchen with a scrubbed pine table, but without the air of decrepitude and past alcoholism – drinking tea like this so many times. Laughing ourselves silly as the sun slanted in through the window and threw the shadows of her flower-arrangement experiments across the table, with the fallen buds and crumpled petals…

I took a deep breath and made myself look at the laptop screen. I pushed the memory away, it was the only way to function – keeping myself running on what was now, rather than looking back to then. *Then* never held anything I wanted to examine too closely.

I hadn't checked my emails while I'd been travelling down to Dorset, so there were a few unread mails. One from my mother, which immediately made me feel a mixture of guilt and dread, so I didn't open it. Another from my ex-husband, telling me that he was travelling out to Patagonia to do something with DNA testing horses, although why he thought I would care was beyond me, and then another from an unknown sender. Out of curiosity and the desire to avoid what my mother had to say, I opened that one.

'Hi Leah
OK, it's been a year, more or less. And I know you, and you'll be dug in deep somewhere, overthinking fit to bust again. Life goes on, and all that, apparently. But you always did have this feeling that, for you, it doesn't, don't you? But everyone needs to move on, there's a fantastic, wild joy out there and I don't want you to lose sight of that.
X'

I sat still for a second, my fingers paralysed on the keys of my laptop. The sun froze the air like a photograph, all the little dust motes in their fairy dance, the stained table top, the wooden work surfaces with their detritus of tens of years of student occupation. *A year. Yes, it's been a year. Almost to the day.* My nose stung at the memory of the smell of antiseptic covered by flowers and clean sheets; the sound of laughter so heavy with grief still rang somewhere like an old bell.

I opened the email from my mother. It was, predictably, a long tirade against my brother and his friends, which was fair enough, and a plea for money, which wasn't. I understood, of *course* I did, but she seemed to think that me being a Doctor meant unlimited funds, wild parties on yachts, fur wraps and the high ringing of champagne flutes and upper-class voices. I'd tried to explain to her so many times that wasn't a PhD, that was a nineteen fifties film, but she just didn't get it.

I gave a hollow chuckle and looked around me again. The floor was slightly sticky beneath my feet in a patch where the stone flags had escaped what seemed to have been a cursory mop and the single-glazed windows let in the smell of the sea and the cows from the further field.

Then I snapped the laptop shut and went for a walk.

* * *

I crossed the field that lay behind the house, towards the herd of Jersey cows which were crowding into the far hedge for shade. At the edge, the ground slumped down towards the sea; not exactly a clifftop, more a series of landslips and slides that had taken the edge of the land and gnawed it down to planes, angles and loose soil. To my left I could see the harbour wall of Christmas Steepleton, guarding a small collection of boats; further beyond that a sandy beach curved away to end in another cliff. The coastline of Dorset was a series of parenthesising cliffs surrounding small bays, like complicated sentences. To my right, the coast rose and fell in a collection of hills. In front of me stretched the sea, blinking with highlights under the lowering sun. The air was heavy with heat and the smell of cows.

When I'd walked off the worst of my emotions, I found I'd got almost right to the point where the ground began to slide away down towards the sea. Below me, piles of bare soil told of recent earth slippage but mostly the land was overgrown with juvenile trees – just gaining a hold at unlikely angles – massed bramble bushes and grass, like a domesticated precipice. I stopped walking and just stood, staring out over the sea, taking big lungfuls of warm air and being divebombed by flies, flicked in my direction by the lazy swish of cow tails. The sun was warm enough to sting, even through my cotton shirt and I wished I'd worn something a bit lighter. This sort of pensive staring over the sea should be done in a linen skirt, clasping a hat to my head and looking wistfully stylish like Meryl Streep in *Out of Africa*. Instead I was wearing an oversized shirt and jeans and looked like I was going to paint the spare room. More like 'Out of B&Q'.

I ought to go and answer those emails. Well, not the one from Darric, he was going off to test those horses whatever, and he was really only telling me out of courtesy, in case I needed him to finalise any of the paperwork for our divorce. And then I thought about the email from my mother, and how she didn't even know that Darric and I were divorcing, because whenever I tried to talk to her she swung the conversation round almost immediately to her financial situation and thence to my brother and his friends and how they made such a mess of the house and never washed up and played computer games into the small hours. If my sympathy didn't sound sincere and I didn't offer to help in whatever way I could, she would accuse me of something, getting 'above myself' usually, and refuse to communicate for weeks. So, OK, maybe I'd leave her email for a bit. Until the follow-up arrived, anyway.

So. The other email. I hadn't recognised the sender, it was an anonymised address, and it wasn't signed. But it sounded as though it came from someone who knew me, someone who knew about Claire – had it really been a year? A whole year? But then, yes, I supposed it had, the hawthorn blossom had just been settling out in the hedges after a long, cold spring and… yes. A year since I'd lost my best friend, my surrogate mother when my real one didn't quite live up to the role. My confidante, my partner in crime. A year. And someone had decided to send me an email to, what? Tell me it was time to get over it? Who would do that? Who even cared enough about how I felt to bother?

Below me in the undergrowth, something moved. Grasses twitched, the fledgling trees bent beneath an unseen weight and my eyes, eager for something to give my brain to think about, focused. Something was coming, moving across the slumped levels of cliff fall, following an invisible path, weaving diagonally until it came into view on an exposed stretch. It was a man.

At first all I could see was his top half, bent forward under the weight of an improbably large rucksack. He looked wiry, the sort of man who's built for walking five hundred miles of coastal path with no backup except for a small dog. Tall, but spare framed, with messy dark hair. Then the bottom half came into view as he cleared a patch of scrub, he was wearing a pair of shorts with a pattern so loud that they could probably hear it in Belgium.

He walked to beneath where I was standing and looked up at the eight feet or so of sheer surface that separated us. 'G'day!' He tipped his head back and squinted up at me. 'Don't suppose you could give us a tug, could you?'

I stared him down. A brief panic rose inside me, but I reasoned that he was a sheer drop below me and therefore, short of levitation, no real threat.

'A *what*?' And I noticed that I rounded my vowels, bringing out my attempts at inner 'posh', as though I could upper-class him out of any attempts at sex talk. A tug? The only thing I could think of known as a 'tug' – courtesy of far too much time spent in the company of students – was sexual. And as I certainly didn't think he was asking me for a small boat to guide him to harbour, that was the only conclusion I could draw. Did he think he was going to get a hand job off a strange woman standing a good room height above him? Unless he was *exceptionally* well endowed that would be a practical impossibility, even had I had the slightest desire to take him up on it.

'A hand? To get up this scramble? Only my pack's a bit heavy for climbing.' The accent was Antipodean – Australian – I thought although I was no expert.

'No, I… I haven't got anything to pull you with,' I said, cringing inside at my word choices, but he either didn't notice or it didn't have the same meaning overseas.

'OK, can you just catch my pack then? I'm going to lob it up the slope.'

I barely had time to step back before the rucksack came swinging out of the air in my direction and landed just on the edge of the cliff, teetering half on and half hanging out over the drop. Almost without thinking I grabbed it and dragged it clear. It was swiftly followed by a flailing collection of limbs which appeared at the cliff edge, clawing and clutching at the grass, a hairy, half-socked leg hooked over and pulled the rest of him up. There was a whirlwind moment of frantic activity, and then there was a body lying panting on the grass in front of me.

'Brendon,' it said, sprawled full length, the shorts causing my vision to strobe at the edges. 'Brendon Macauley.' He sat up, looked at the drop behind him, and shuffled forward a few feet. 'How d'you do?'

'Why were you climbing up the cliff?'

He pulled a face and ran a hand over his hair, which was full of dislodged bits of cliff and greenery.

'Fancied a ramble,' he said. And then, because apparently I wasn't softening in the face of Australian charm, 'I just pitched up in my little boat, looking for somewhere to stay. The whole village seems to be full of a film crew, so I thought I'd try up here. You got any rooms to rent?' He looked beyond me, at the house squatting in the field. 'Just need somewhere to drop my stuff and sleep at the end of the day, I'm no nuisance. Plus I can pay for my keep and I cook a mean chilli.'

'*Bugger off*,' said my brain, but my mouth only came out with 'Ummmm…' In the hope that he'd get the subliminal message I turned away and began to walk back to the house.

There were noises behind me, and then he caught up. 'Sorry, sorry, didn't mean to come across like a homeless Aussie loon. I'm here to do some family research, looking for my great-grandfather, he came from somewhere around here, and I just need somewhere to stay.'

I reassured myself that, for all he knew, the house was full of armed troops all hell-bent on keeping me safe. To reiterate that illusion, I waved at the empty house as though I was greeting someone inside. 'Well, there isn't really room.' It was as close as I could get to 'no' for now. Gave me a run up at saying it next time. Or the time after.

'Fair enough.' He wriggled his arms through the straps of the rucksack. 'OK then. Thanks for minding my luggage for me while I got up the cliff. See you around.' And he overtook me, striding out across the field and off down the muddy trackway towards the road.

Guilt overwhelmed me and I had to take deep breaths. *You don't have to say 'yes' to everyone!* I could almost hear Claire's voice, telling me off after I'd admitted to spreading myself too thinly again. *No is a complete sentence. You don't have to explain why not, just say no.*

But it had been easier for Claire. She took no nonsense and dished none out, it was second nature to her to tell people that she couldn't do something and make them feel sorry for even asking. Whereas I was the opposite, I was almost congenitally incapable of saying 'no'. A 'people pleaser' she called me. She'd done her best but...

'Hang on. There's a shed you can use, if you really need somewhere to stay,' I called after the retreating figure. 'I've no idea what it's like, but if you just need somewhere to sleep and keep your stuff...'

Brendon Macauley stopped walking and turned, the weight on his back making him spin like an ice dancer. 'That'd be great.'

'Hang on. I'll just get the keys.' I shoved open the front door, surprised at the darkness of the hallway, and picked up the bunch of keys the caretaker had left me from the table. 'I'm just showing this man the shed!' I called to my imaginary troops, who would, presumably, be clustered in a bedroom, sniper eyes on the trackway and laser sights following me out of the door. I needn't really have bothered, Brendan just stood outside in the grassy courtyard formed by the house and the old stable abutting one another at an angle.

'I'm sorry it's a bit of a mess,' I apologised, sorting out the only key that could possibly fit the little padlock. 'But I've only just got here myself.'

And you're doing it again. Why should he care if it's a mess, if he only wants somewhere to stick his bedroll? Come on Leah, you just show him the space, he can take or leave it. In fact, you don't even have to show him at all, just let him go on his way. Claire's voice echoed through my head. But he was here now. And he had nowhere to stay. And the shed was just sitting there.

The place was cleaner than I'd expected. Properly roofed too. It consisted of a small loose box, where a pony could have been kept if it had been good natured and didn't like lying down much, and another room, which contained parts of a bicycle and some oil in cans. There was an electricity point in there too, presumably in case the pony had wanted to watch Netflix of an evening.

'This is amazing, thank you.' Brendon dropped his backpack almost possessively onto the floor. 'Brilliant, can't thank you enough. You've saved me from sleeping under a hedge or having to spend nights on my boat, which isn't a great thought. You're living in the house?'

I glanced back at the windows of the house, just checking that my armed regiment was still there. 'Sort of, staying there doing research. With my… research people.' And then, because he didn't say anything and I couldn't let a silence go unfilled, 'I'm being employed to check the seaweed growth off the Dorset coast, with a view to harvesting it as a possible food source.'

He twitched his head as though I'd amused him slightly. 'OK. Sounds bonza.'

No, it sounded as though I was an interview candidate. Like I didn't know how to actually talk to people, but that's me.

'It's a fascinating subject,' I said, stiffly. 'Here's the key for the shed padlock, I have to get back.'

'Doesn't seaweed just kind of lie around and wait for you?' He sounded a bit confused. 'I mean, is it time sensitive?'

This time I let the silence stand, and walked off, back into the house, which I locked behind me, just in case.

Chapter Two

The bedrooms weren't as bad as I'd imagined. I picked one which had a small bathroom attached, and spent the night wrapped in my sweaty sleeping bag listening to the sea's gentle exhalation against the cliff. The night was so quiet that I could hear the cows grazing in the field, and the dawn cacophony of the seagulls came as loud as any alarm clock going off.

Urgh. I sat up in the bed and peeled bits of down off my skin. The temperature hadn't dropped much overnight and however much I'd wriggled and pushed the bag down or pulled it up, I hadn't been able to achieve any kind of thermostasis. My vest top was damp and I really needed a shower. I went into the bathroom but none of the taps would oblige me with more than a groan and a few drops, which was when I remembered the caretaker's words about the water pump and the sheaf of papers the university had sent me about the house, which were still in the bottom of my bag.

'The house uses water from the local spring, which needs to be pumped up into the treatment tank. One tank should be adequate for one day's usage,' I didn't like that word 'adequate'. It made me think of growing up, food that was 'adequate' but never filled the corners, our flat, deemed 'adequate' but where my brother had to sleep in the little loft with no windows and only a pulldown ladder whilst my mother and I shared the living/bedroom. 'Adequate' to me, meant 'just about bearable'.

There was a diagram of the water pump, it seemed to be somewhere in the kitchen. I wandered downstairs, where it was cooler, courtesy of the stone-flagged floors and the air of haunting. The pump itself I found in a cupboard in the corner, but when I finally worked out which bit you were supposed to push and which was the 'sidelocking key arm, adv work mechanism, (Fig B)' I realised that the caretaker had been right. It needed two people, or one person with freakishly long arms, to work it.

'Excuse me?'

The stable door opened cautiously. 'Hello?'

'It's me, from the house.'

'Er, yeah. I can see that. What's up? Something wrong?' Brendon was wearing a vest, similar to mine, and cotton pyjama bottoms. I was wearing pyjama bottoms too, but his didn't have unicorns all over them.

'I need to pump water and it takes two to work the pump. If you could give me a hand...?' I tailed off and shook the kettle I'd brought, either as illustration or possible weapon. 'I could make us both a cup of tea.'

Brendon opened the door a little bit wider. 'All your research people gone off and left you, have they?' He pulled a jacket over the vest. 'Yeah sure. And I could go a cuppa, it's pretty chilly out here.'

Chilly? Was he mad? The sun was hitting the grass and I could practically hear the dew boiling. The cow field was devoid of bovines but the smell that the heat was raising was leaving us in no doubt that they had been there recently.

'Mind you, it's the middle of winter back home.' Brendon, following me across the courtyard, sounded cheerful. 'So this is terrific. At least you get proper summers, we just get cooked out of our socks.'

'Whereabouts are you from?' I asked, trying to ignore the fact that we were both in our pyjamas and my accent had become so plummy it sounded as though I was greeting a visiting dignitary.

'Melbourne. Australia.' He came behind me into the kitchen and shivered dramatically. 'But my gran was born here, in Christmas Steepleton. Like I said, I'm doing genealogy research. This the pump?'

He held the Fig B bit whilst I pumped the pump arm. After a few minutes we changed places, as it had become apparent that filling the tank wasn't the work of a few moments. I tried not to watch the muscles in his arm as he pumped, but then he'd averted his eyes from my chest wobbling about as I'd had my turn, so I reasoned he was that much of a gentleman.

'So, you said you're looking for your great-grandfather?' I took another turn at pumping while he held the arm steady.

'Yeah. I know he was born in Steepleton in 1923, and that he lived here until the early fifties. Next thing I know, Great-grandma's moved the family out to Oz and there's no sign of Great-grandad and nobody seems to know much about what happened.' A grin. 'Figured I'd come over and take a bit of a look round.'

'That. Sounds. Interesting,' I panted.

'You don't have to talk to me like you're trying to make conversation, you know. Why not let me have another turn. You realise I don't even know your name? I can't keep calling you "that woman in the house" can I?'

'I didn't realise you *were* calling me "that woman in the house".' I massaged my bicep and let go of the pump. My face felt very hot and my hair was sticking to my head. 'But my name is Doctor Leah Jones.'

'Well, then, Doctor Leah Jones.' A hand stuck out. 'I am very pleased to meet you.'

I had to shake his hand. I mean, I *had* to, I couldn't ignore it, Claire, could I? That would have been rude and… and… no, I didn't want to seem rude. So I shook the big, sweaty hand even though mine was all floppy from the pumping, and fought the urge to wipe my palm down the leg of my unicorn trousers, while he pumped a bit more, the pump putting up a good deal of resistance now.

'Reckon that must be about full,' Brendon leaned back and wiped his hand across his forehead. 'Not going to get much more up today. Now, about that cuppa.'

I went over to the kitchen sink which, to my surprise, groaned like a mare in labour for a moment and then gushed water into the kettle. I furtively washed my hands and splashed my face, then plugged the kettle in and found my collection of tea bags.

Brendon sat on the edge of the table and squinted out of the window. 'Never expected the light to be different, y'know?' The Australian upward inflection made practically everything he said sound like a question and I had to fight myself not to leap in with an answer. 'I mean, it's the same sun and everything, but over here it looks, I dunno, older, somehow. Like it's recycled?'

I was about to give him an explanation about how Britain was much more populous than Australia and therefore pollution would affect the light, but I managed to bite my lips together. Instead I just said, 'It's another lovely day,' quite brightly for a woman who had a man in his pyjamas in her kitchen.

In the face of my relentless stating of the obvious, Brendon went quiet and carried on staring over my shoulder, while the kettle boiled. I'd just poured the water onto two teabags and

24

was letting the smell take me back to that other kitchen again in the hopes that Claire, even in memory, would have some advice as to what to say next, when there was the sound of a car engine racing up the drive.

Brendon looked at me and frowned. 'Early for visitors?'

'I'm a seaweed research scientist. I don't *have* visitors.' I poked my head out of the back door. 'It's Tass. My assistant.'

'Oh. I was hoping it was sentient seaweed. Y'know, like something out of *Doctor Who*?' Another frown. 'You get *Doctor Who* over here, right?'

'It would have to have evolved past sentience to be able to drive,' I was aware I sounded a bit snappy, and mitigated. 'It would have to have developed arms and legs to work the gears.'

'Could have, like, fronds. Extra-long fronds to press the pedals.'

'But it wouldn't have the body mass.'

'Could be a big bunch—' but his further pondering on the nature of seaweed being able to work a car was cut short by the arrival of Tass into the kitchen, a whirling mass of energy and suitcases.

'Yo, Prof!'

'Leah will do, thanks.'

'Yo, Leah!' I saw Tass's eyes take in me in my pyjamas and Brendon in his, our bare feet and the tea steaming away in its mugs in front of us both. 'Woah, quick work! Where did you find this one?'

I opened my mouth to refute all allegations, even though Tass hadn't made any verbally. I wanted to cut short their train of thought, which was approaching Complete Misunderstanding at warp speed and didn't look set to stop at Anywhere Sensible on the way, but couldn't think of anything to say, other than,

'Brendon was helping me pump,' which really wasn't much help.

'I came up the cliff. Leah offered me the shed.' He was faster than me and also more accurate.

'Shed?' Tass's eyes widened. 'Oh, I get it, treat 'em mean, keep 'em keen, eh, Prof? I mean, Leah,' they added quickly.

'Brendon, this is Tass. Tass, Brendon. He's Australian, over here doing genealogical research. Tass is going to help me sort and dispatch samples.'

'Good one.' Brendon started drinking his tea.

'Why didn't you let Brendon have one of the rooms?' Tass started unpacking electronics onto the table. 'Aren't there about a million empty? Why the shed?'

Over his mug Brendon lifted an eyebrow at me. 'I could be anyone,' he said through the steam. 'Leah wouldn't want some strange bloke in the house when she's on her own, would she? Think about it.'

I could see he'd taken Tass at face-value, as male. I understood the instinct to pigeonhole, and Tass currently had a beard, but I wanted to avoid any awkward conversations about gender identity right now. Besides, it was morning, I only had a finite amount of time to get this research done, and now Tass was here I could get started.

'Well. You can stay in the house if you'd like, Brendon, of course. Now, Tass, would you like a cup of tea, I'm off for a shower. We ought to start drawing up our plan for our days, so as to get the maximum amount covered. Oh, and can you sort out a supermarket delivery – there's hardly any food in the place and we'll need to eat.' My best bet was to be organised. I knew what I was doing when I was organising, keeping on top of things and nobody could query me if I was organising them and *sounding* as if I knew what I was doing.

Brendon looked at me again. 'Think I'll stay in the shed, I'm settled there,' he said. 'And I won't be in the way over there. I can just come and go and you won't have to worry about me treading on your seaweed. Thanks for the tea. I'm going down into Steepleton to check the boat and ask around, might see you both later?'

And on that upward inflection he put down his mug and was gone, giving us both a wide grin.

I went for my shower, while the tank was still full, leaving Tass in charge of the internet. When I came back down, hair wet and feeling a lot fresher, Tass had several screens on the go around the kitchen, utilising practically every power point there was.

'Got it. Delivery on the way later. Analysis lab ready, spreadsheets sorted.' Tass moved from screen to screen. 'Oh, and you've got mail, by the way.'

I liked Tass. They'd been my assistant before, when I'd done a series of talks on seaweed being the future for nutrition, eighty per cent of the earth covered in natural growing medium, that no poisonous seaweed grew off the coast of Britain (although *Desmarestia* species weren't really edible) and, in clean waters, we were looking at being able to harvest enough to make a considerable contribution to feeding the world. I was aware that being able to talk about this made me a very boring person at parties, though. Probably why I rarely got invited. No, scratch that, I *did* get invited, I just didn't go.

'And you look better for the shower. Unicorns aren't really you.' Tass put the kettle on, they'd left one power socket unused for that very purpose – I'd trained them well.

'And you're looking…' I tailed off.

'It's OK. I'm gender-fluid, not The Invisible Man,' Tass said. 'You're allowed to comment.'

And again I felt like a gauche historic figure, beamed into the twenty-first century. 'Sorry. You're looking good. I'm liking the jeans. Everything all right back at base?'

The jeans were of the pre-ripped variety, with so many holes that I couldn't really see the point in wearing anything at all, and getting dressed for Tass must be like wrapping a parcel, but I was thirty-four. Practically a generation away from Tass, with their long hair, beard and improbable clothing choices. I'd had gender fluidity explained to me – sometimes Tass felt female, sometimes male, but their usual clothing choices were resolutely gender-neutral and I wasn't really sure I'd got a handle on it. But now Tass was just Tass, and the whole gender politics thing slithered past me. It probably shouldn't, I should get more involved, but I had enough trouble just trying to keep my life on track at the moment. Who Tass was, was more important than whatever labels people stuck on each other – and Tass was a friend, or as near as I could get to one.

'Yeah, base camp is cool. All waiting on you getting us the samples.'

'OK then.' I tapped in my password and my emails opened. Yep, there was Mum again, laying the guilt on just a wee bit more this time. I always pictured the guilt that lay between us as a bit like a layer of Marmite on bread. Sometimes it was just a scrape, the thinnest possible, just enough to add colour and that smell of salty cupboards. Other times it was black and thick enough to hang wallpaper.

The other email came from that strange address and was unsigned again.

'I know you. You'll have brushed off my last email, pretended it never happened. And yes, of course you can do that, if you

can – hand on heart – say that you are happy now. That
your life is going exactly the way you want it to and that you
honestly aren't using grief as an excuse. Yes, didn't think you
could!'

At this point there was a picture of a puppy. Wherever – *whoever*
– this email had come from, they knew me well. I let myself
stare at the floppy ears and appealing button eyes for a moment
to stop myself from having to read on.

'I want you to be happy. I want to see you smiling. I want
to know that you are living your life, that losing your best
friend hasn't given you more excuses to shut yourself away.
So I thought we'd play a kind of game, something to take
your mind off yourself and stop you overthinking. But I'm
still working out how to frame it, so bear with me.
X'

I snapped the lid shut and heard the fan wind down into sulky
silence. On the other side of the kitchen Tass looked up, but
the expression on my face must have been fierce, because they
kept their head down, doing something technical with one of
the machines.

Who would do this? Who did I know cruel enough to bring
up Claire dying? And then to use that to accuse me of limiting
myself? Was it someone trying to flirt with me?

A moment. Just a momentary image floated into my mind,
but I knocked it out of the air, screwed it up and stamped on it.
No. Absolutely not.

But I didn't need to think about this now. I could treat it
like my mother's emails. Just something, just a little lump
of something scudding about on the surface of the water.

Ignorable. I put my head down, stared at the pitted surface of the table until Tass tapped me on the shoulder.

'You OK, Prof?'

'Leah,' I said, wearily.

'You look a bit shocky. Need a tea? Kettle is on.' Sympathetically, almost as though they'd read not only those words, but also my mind, Tass pushed me down into the chair. 'Hope they haven't withdrawn the funding for this or something. Algae is really hot at the moment, get me?'

'Not even slightly. But, never mind. No, this is personal stuff, our funding is safe. Which reminds me, I ought to go down to the village and find someone willing to take me offshore to pick up samples. There ought to be fishing boats down there, tourist boats, that sort of thing?'

I must have caught the upward phrasing from Brendon, because it absolutely wasn't a question. One of the reasons I'd chosen this location was the proximity to a harbour. Harbours have boats, boats do trips out to sea, I didn't need a PhD to work that out.

'OK. Want me to come with? Only I ought to sort out—'

'No.' Tass's desire to treat me like a cross between an elderly relative and a Big Business Boss could be just a touch annoying sometimes. 'It's fine. I want to go and have a poke around anyway – send a few postcards, that sort of thing. You stay here and wait for the shopping delivery and all that and I'll call you if I need you.' I tapped my phone. 'Always supposing that there's a signal.'

Tass looked horrified. 'No *signal*? How can there be no signal? Have we wormholed into the Dark Ages?'

There was something almost childlike in their horror and it made me smile. 'I got a signal in the back of the pantry.'

Tass snatched at their phone and ran into the back of the walk-in cupboard with almost indecent haste. I smiled again, picked up my bag and the hand-drawn map, and headed out.

Down the track and onto the road, keeping a finger on the map, to where a dotted line showed me the entrance to a footpath which led across the top of the cliffs, brown earth beaten hard by the sun and innumerable feet. I squeezed through a gap in snatchy-brambled hedges and over a narrow gate onto the path. To my left a field of green spears, rapidly yellowing in the sunshine – with the wind running through them like a living thing – smelled like dusty flour. To my right, over a few metres of heat-oppressed grass, lay a drop I didn't want to think about, down to the sea. Every few strides there was a sign warning me of coastal erosion and not to go too close to the edge, illustrated by some scary looking cracks around the base of the signs.

The horizon was a soft line, as though nature wasn't too sure about it and might need to rub it out at some point. A boat pimpled the skyline, surrounded by shifting blue and silver light, but I couldn't appreciate the beauty of it. I was too busy trying not think of those emails.

The footpath joined another road which then branched down at an angle that made me glad I was wearing sturdy shoes. Lining the road were houses, terraced, facing the road, front doors leading straight to the pavement and little notes in the windows showing that they were holiday cottages for rent. I'd tried those when the idea of Dorset was first raised – all booked. Likewise all the bedrooms in the B&B that rose up a vertiginous flight of steps above me now on the right. Believe me, I'd tried practically everything except the local campsite and the caravan park over near Lyme Regis, rejecting those because we needed a lot of equipment and neither a tent nor a caravan had enough electricity sockets.

Now the heat reflected back up at me from the road surface, smelling of hot tar and newly cut grass. Down the hill I went, occasionally clutching the metal rail that had been installed on the steeper sections – I dreaded to think what going down here would be like in winter. Cupping a hand over my forehead I shaded my eyes. At the bottom of the steep hill was a small car park; on one side lay the beach, from where I could hear the giggles and shrieks of children, mostly curtained from my sight by windbreaks. As I walked further down, the harbour came into view, hugged between a breakwater and a curving wall into a near semicircle of tame, rippling ocean. I emerged onto what constituted the sea front from the tunnel of buildings and the full sun hit me, blinding me with a sudden flash of silver and blue as it reflected the water.

The whole scene was so bright and primary-coloured that it looked as though it had been drawn by someone whose access to paint had been limited to a free gift stuck on the front of a five-year-old's comic. Boats were bright red or bright blue, with self-consciously white sails; they were all so pristine and shiny that they looked as though they'd never been further out to sea than paddling depth. Seagulls swept and shrieked among the masts. Men in smocks and deck shoes wandered on the harbour wall, chatting to one another or stood on their boats turning shiny brass handles to, it appeared, very little end. It looked like the Jack Wills website.

I walked the length of the harbour, past the worst offenders, down to the master's office, where at least it looked a bit more genuinely nautical, and asked if I could hire a boat to take me out to the kelp fields. The harbour master, a lady with short ginger hair and very pink cheeks – straight out of a children's story – made a face.

'Not sure, my lover,' she said, in a reassuring Dorset accent. Most of the other accents I could hear were resolutely Home Counties, and were not filling me with seafaring reassurance. 'Most of this lot is holidaymakers right now. Local boats is mostly round to Landle this time of year, letting out their moorings, y'see. Have you tried up to Lyme Regis? They has tourist boats going out most days.'

A seagull wandered in at the doorway to the hut and looked at me with its head on one side.

'Not even a "trips around the bay" type of thing?' I felt the familiar rising of 'out of my depth' – somewhere in the great Manual of Life, I'd got a few pages that had stuck together but everyone else had read right to the end. *Why* hadn't I checked? Why had I blithely believed the university's assurances that 'there's always plenty of boats for hire down there'. I should have known by now that they worked on best guesses and past experiences, and not so much in the here-and-now. 'Really? I mean I don't have to be out for long, just to get some samples offshore.'

The seagull came right up to me and stared up into my face. Its yellow-eyed expression was one of avian inscrutability, it might just have been curious or it could have been about to bite my nose off. I took a step back and the seagull hopped forward a bit further. It had an odd tuft of black feathers on the top of its head which stuck out at rogue angles, like a coquette's headdress. Or, now I came to look at it in more detail than I really wanted to, a chimney sweep's brush popping out of the top of an eighteenth-century flue.

'To tell the truth, I wouldn't trust most of this lot outside a boating lake,' the harbour master sighed. 'They all hires these boats for the summer, lugs 'em round the coast, Lord only knows how they doesn't crash into each other on the way. It's like them dodgems.' She stared out of the doorway at the clothing catalogue shoot taking place outside. 'Big, expensive dodgems. But it's a living.' She sighed and pushed at the seagull with her foot. 'Roger, get out of it.'

'It's got a name?' I was glad of the change of subject to stop me from feeling so inadequately prepared.

'Raised him from a chick, though Lord knows why. Reckon his parents rejected him for having daft markings and now he won't leave me alone. He'm a bit of a bugger, you want to watch your sandwiches with that one about.'

The gull shrugged a peeved wing and wobbled, then turned to the doorway and launched into the sky with an almost audible effort. We watched as it flapped off out across the harbour. 'Mind, you wants to watch your sandwiches with all of 'em. We tells the tourists, but they don't listen.'

'OK.' I wasn't really listening either. I was running alternative plans through my head – could we move? Relocate to somewhere else that had boats running? It was imperative that the samples be as fresh as possible for testing; driving half way across Dorset with a car full of bladderwrack wouldn't work. No, too late in the season, everywhere would be booked. 'Any ideas as to how I could find someone who might be willing? And capable?'

The harbour master looked out in the direction Roger had flown. 'Could try that un,' she pointed at the only scruffy boat in the harbour. It was distinctly lowering the tone with its peeling paint and sagging sails, bobbing gently at anchor off one of the pontoons. 'He pitched up yesterday, saw him come in on the tide. But looks like he knows how to handle a boat. Australian, or summat.'

I found I was resting my forehead against the door. Unless, by some geographical fluke, there was more than one…

I left the harbour master tapping the barometer hanging from the office wall, and went back out. Sure enough I could see Brendon on the deck of the less-than-pristine boat, doing something arcane with a rope, in the glaring light reflected from the next-door yacht. I took a deep breath and squared my shoulders. He might look more *Marie Celeste* than *Marie Claire*, but appearances, as they say, were not everything, and he obviously knew his way around a boat.

'Hello, Leah!' Brendon sounded cheerful. 'Come for a look round the harbour?'

He showed me round his boat with a capability and practicality that was reassuring. I could see why he regarded my shed as a good place to stay though; beneath the immaculately scrubbed deck, with its ropes all carefully coiled and all the metalwork gleaming in a most migraine-inducing manner, the boat was primitive at best.

'You didn't sail all the way over from Australia, did you?' There were a few centimetres of nasty water in several places, and a redolent smell of damp. 'Not in *this*?'

'Hey, cheeky. *This* is a genuine 1910 motor launch. She's an antique!' He slapped the inside of the hull and a small piece of wood came away in his hand. 'Needs a bit of restoration work, but she'll be right. Bought her down in Plymouth and sailed her up.' He tried to hide the lump of wood, and eventually settled for putting it down on a built-in table.

'Can we go up outside again now?' The smell was making me feel slightly sick, although the gentle heaving of the boat was contributing too. There was a dichotomy – the bits that showed all gleaming and polished and bright with the underneath rotting and smelly – that was uncomfortable.

'Sure. Come on.'

I followed Brendon back up the rickety wooden steps, trying not to notice how nicely shaped he was inside those horrible shorts, and burst out into the sun. Beneath the deck the sea moved restlessly, the water clear and sharp with light, and I bent over the edge. There was always something about water that drew me; Claire had always said I was attracted to things that were big and wet, but then, she *had* met Darric.

Deep below the boat I saw the crinkly fronds of sea belt waving gently, reaching up towards us, seeming to move independently of the fidgety slap of the waves. Brendon and I stood, stabilising ourselves with hands against the cabin. The gentle knocking of the waves against the hull and the pinging of ropework was actually quite soothing, once you got clear of the smell of bilge and cockroach. 'Is there any chance – I mean, would you be willing to sail me out to the kelp beds to get some samples?'

'Leah, I'd sail you to the Maldives if I thought the boat would make it. Call it payment.' Brendon stared out across the little harbour. 'For letting me stay in the shed.'

'Oh, I can pay proper money. I've got expenses.' I followed his gaze. From here you could just see the very tip of the roof of the house, a nodule extruding from the greenery of the cliff.

'Nah. Won't charge you for running out a few hundred metres. Especially when you are providing me with top-class accommodation.'

I gave him a hard look. He was wearing a dark blue T-shirt and slightly less conspicuous shorts than yesterday, which showed off an incipient tan, and his bright, brown eyes twinkling above a scattering of beard. It was difficult to tell if he was teasing, joking or being an arse. 'Well, that's…'

'But I might need a hand with some of my research, if you could help at all?' He scratched at his almost-beard, with a disconcerting 'striking a match' sound. 'I mean, if it doesn't interfere with your work, or your fun time.'

'Fun time?' I said as though the words were foreign to me. Which, actually, to be fair, they practically were.

'Yeah, whatever you get up to in your downtime. D' ya dance, at all, Leah? You know what they say about all work and no play…'

'Yes, they say it pays the mortgage.' I stepped up onto the raised area of the deck, preparing to clamber off the boat and onto the floating pontoon thing it was moored to. 'And I will, of course, help you in any way I can, with your research.'

Brendon winked at me. 'Fan-bloody-tastic. I'd like to borrow a computer, if I may. Got a couple of maybes from some guys in the town there. Might like to look a few things up.'

'Well, yes.' I stepped across as the boat went up and the pontoon went down, performing a strange yoga move to stop myself from plunging down into the waters of the harbour. Was Brendon flirting with me? Or did he have this rather intrusive, overfamiliar way of talking to everyone? I felt the weight of my imaginary bustle and corset pulling me in, keeping me rigid. 'I'm sure Tass will be able to set you up with one of our machines.'

Brendon didn't follow me off the boat. He kept one hand on the roof of the wheelhouse, just balancing himself, but with his legs absorbing most of the movement. It made him look as though he'd been born on board.

'OK, right.'

I'd turned around and walked a dozen steps when I heard him swear behind me. There was a shuffling kerfuffle and then

Brendon landed on the pontoon, making it dip and dive in the water. 'Bloody skyrats!'

I faced the boat again. A seagull had landed on the deck and was strutting up and down, tipping its head from side to side, presumably getting a kind of stop-motion binocular vision. 'What's the matter?'

Brendon was backing up towards me. 'Gulls. Hate 'em. I mean, we have 'em over in Oz, but ours – I mean, they're evil bastards, obviously, but I swear your British gulls are some kind of nuclear mutant variety. I mean, look at it!'

I looked. The gull was staring down as though admiring its reflection in a highly polished brass fitting. It pecked, experimentally. 'It's a seagull. I suspect, actually, that it might be Roger.' The black tuft on the top of its head swung in agreement.

At the mention of the name, the bird looked up, threw its head back and let out a sound similar to that which might be made by a large cat getting its tail caught in a door. 'Yep. Pretty sure that's Roger.'

'They have *names*?'

'That one does.'

'Jeez.' Brendon looked up, doubtfully. Several other gulls cannoned around the skies above the harbour, their rusty-barrow squealing competing with the occasional bursts of laughter from the men in blue smocks. 'That adds a whole new layer of horror.'

I turned and began to walk down the pontoon to the harbour wall. There were hasty steps and Brendon came behind me. 'How can you be afraid of seagulls anyway?' I asked. 'Did one drop on your head when you were a baby or something?'

'Nah. Like I said, ours are smaller, bit more domesticated. I wasn't afraid of seagulls until I came over here and met your

British ones. They look like Oz gulls after the Bomb.' He paused. 'That one's not following us, is it? I don't like to look, just in case.'

I glanced over my shoulder. The gull, possibly Roger, or possibly another large herring gull with a sense of humour and an identity crisis, had perched on the edge of the pontoon and was watching us go. 'No. He's just sort of sitting there.'

'Great.' We reached the harbour wall and climbed up to walk along it. Ropes and what I assumed were lobster pots were piled up on the edge, drying out in the sun; there were nets spread over railings and the smell of tar, hemp and what I was fairly sure was a Penhaligon's men's cologne. Several of the well-groomed men in smocks nodded to Brendon as we passed. 'Do you fancy a coffee? We can sort out details for going out to the kelp beds if you like,' he said.

'I... Er.' I had enough moral fibre to weave a poncho, but it was all straining in the face of his enthusiasm. I *wanted* to turn him down, I *ought* to turn him down, but the urge to be polite rose above all those things and I found myself saying, 'Well, I suppose we could.'

'Hey, bonza!' We walked from the harbour, into the small car park which was formed by the road down into Christmas Steepleton not wanting to fall into the sea. There we both stopped and looked around. There was, for a Dorset seaside village, a marked absence of coffee shops or cafés. A small promenade played host to a handful of small-town type shops, but none of them sold anything more promising than ice lollies. I found myself walking alongside Brendon up the narrow hill. I wasn't quite sure why, or how he was getting me to go along with his caffeine-based plans; maybe there was some sort of glamour field being thrown out by the shorts. In the old-fashioned sense of the word, obviously, there was no way those shorts were glamorous by the modern definition.

'Will you be staying in England long?' I said, still sounding like the Queen at a garden party.

'Dunno yet.' He scanned the street. 'Depends what I find, really.'

'Don't you have to get back to a job? A family?'

He gave me a quick grin. 'You chatting me up there, Leah?' Then the grin died. 'Nah. I've been in land development along the Yarra river. Fancied a change of direction. Might take up fishing. Look, there's a coffee sign up there, shall we go see?'

'But you're afraid of seagulls. How would that work?'

'All right, don't rub it in.' He led the way up the road. The heat was beginning to make the surface tacky and smell of hot tar, which was briefly overcome by the smell of sunscreen lotion as a gust of air blew off the sea and up over the beach to reach us. A family came past, walking down the hill, the man carrying blankets and inflatable toys, the woman holding the hands of two small girls. They smiled at us as they went past, and I wondered what they saw. Did we look like a youngish couple on holiday? Or the mismatched pair we really were, Brendon all salt-tan and easy, walking around in rope-soled sandals, me pallid of face and disapproving of demeanour, as though I'd been dragged on an outing by a robust colleague, away from my day job in a mortuary.

'Like I said, here to find out what happened to Great-grandad. Might even stay over for a while, it looks like a nice place,' Brendon went on, making me uncomfortable. I'd only asked out of politeness. 'How about you, Leah? How long are you here for?'

We reached the café, which did double duty as an estate agency, and went inside. Probably because of the weather and the fact that it was still early, it was empty.

'I'm just here to get these seaweed samples, and then I go back to Bristol,' I said. 'I've got papers to write.'

He acknowledged my conversation-killing statement with a sideways nod and then went up to the counter. I sat down at a little round table in the window. From my seat I could see the beach, its restless geography being even further disrupted by the activity of small children with buckets and men building outsized sandcastles in a display of competitive parenting. The sun on the glass whited out the rest of the view, so I focused on the families. Mums in bathing costumes encouraging toddlers into the gently breaking surf, men locking horns through the medium of moat-excavation. Babies on blankets or in buggies whilst their older siblings ran and shrieked and dug.

We'd never had days on the beach. There wasn't the money, Mum had always said, and she couldn't manage both of us out of the house. I would have wandered off and Dylan would have sulked and we'd have wanted ice cream and entertaining, and she'd rather have been at home, indoors, where the soap operas never let her down or fought in public. These families in front of me seemed to be managing though. Occasional bucket-wars would break out but the discovery of an interesting piece of shell or the promise of a paddle seemed to de-escalate things very quickly. I wondered what my mum had really been afraid of. Why we'd spent all our holidays indoors with the curtains drawn and the TV showing us what could have been.

'Coffee. Looks all right.' Brendon came over carrying two cups, and sat down opposite me. 'So, when do you want to go out?'

Politeness warred with will, and didn't use a plastic bucket. Will won, although politeness was still armed. 'I'm not really sure I want to "go out", I'm afraid. I'm just getting divorced

41

from a man who thought physical intimacy meant a pat on the shoulder, so I'm really not ready for—'

'On the boat. When do you want to go out on the boat? To collect your seaweed? I guess there's going to have to be a few trips.' Brendon managed to hide most of his expression behind the giant coffee cup.

I felt myself redden and pretended to choke on a mouthful of coffee in order to have a coughing fit and cover up the real reason for my blush. When I felt my face cool down a little, I said, as though I hadn't just made a social faux pas, 'How about tomorrow?'

Brendon nodded. 'OK. It'll have to be early though, get out on the tide. Around six? Do you need to dive?'

'Oh, no, I just go in with a snorkel. Scuba isn't necessary, not for the weed we are collecting. The deep sea stuff is someone else's job, thankfully.' And then, despite the fact that my entire being was telling me to pretend that my previous outburst hadn't happened, 'Sorry. About bringing up my divorce.'

'No worries. Everyone has a past.' Brendon tipped his head on one side. 'Even, it appears, grouchy seaweed scientists.' A big grin, emphasised by his tan. 'Hell, even I've made the odd romantic mistake or two.' And then he performed a peculiar movement, he half recoiled and half hid under the edge of the tablecloth. 'Holy shit! Is that thing following me?'

I looked out of the window to see a large gull strolling down the hill, pausing every so often to peck at likely bits of concrete. 'No, that's a different gull.'

Wide brown eyes looked at me over the coffee cup, which was trembling slightly. 'You can *tell*? And aren't they all just one homogenous mass with one controlling brain, like, I dunno, bees or something? So, in effect, they are *all* out to get me?'

'No.' I said, shortly. I didn't have a lot of experience with phobias. 'And the worst they can really do is steal your chips, maybe give you a bit of a peck.'

'That's bad enough.' Brendon subsided back into drinking his coffee again, but threw glances out into the bright day every so often. 'And you're only a whisker away from "they're more scared of you than you are of them", y'know.'

'I'm fairly sure that's not true.' The door opened and another couple came in, nudging one another's shoulders and laughing. A proper couple, comfortable with one another. I looked at Brendon, he was still on gull-alert, but his body was relaxed in the chair, legs stretched out in his board shorts, strong and tanned. He even managed to hold his cup in a chilled way, whilst I had mine cupped in both hands as though I was afraid someone might try to snatch it away. I uncurled my fingers and leaned back in my chair, trying to copy his easy posture. The uncomfortable sensation that I was merely playing at being human crept over me. It was not an unusual feeling.

'OK. Better go up to the house and start doing some research.' Brendon tipped his cup at an angle that indicated emptiness. 'If that will be OK with – Tass, wasn't it? You walking back up?'

The thought of having to make conversation all the way back to the house filled me with the kind of horror that, it seemed, gulls inspired in him. Being polite. Trying to remember to ask questions that weren't phrased like a job interview. 'No! No, I have to…' I searched around for any possible alternative, and my eyes alighted on the noticeboard on the café wall. 'I have to go and see about being an extra in the TV series they're filming down here.'

'Really? Wouldn't have thought that would be your thing.'

'Oh yes, huge fan. Can't wait.' I squinted a bit until I could read the printing underneath the heading of EXTRAS

WANTED: MEET AT TOP OF VILLAGE and today's date. 'They need lots of women of all ages, apparently, so I thought it might be my chance.'

'OK-aaay,' Brendon blew out slowly. 'Well. Might see you back at the house later then. And I'll see you early tomorrow anyway. To take the boat out,' he added, when I obviously must have looked blank.

'Boat. Yes.' I waited for him to go and then got my phone out. Texted Tass to tell them that I seemed to have offered use of a computer to Brendon, who was on his way. Messaged a few co-workers, just giving them a brief itinerary and notes of when to expect samples. Checked for any incoming messages, which there weren't, not surprisingly. My social circle was more of a small square these days.

Then I went into my emails. Sitting here in this scone-scented café with the remnants of a flat white in front of me, it was easier to deal with my mother. Probably because the environment was so far removed from any I might have found her in.

I could practically picture her now. It was still what she would call 'early', so she'd be in her dressing gown, curtains drawn in case the neighbours looked in. Dylan would be up in his room under the eaves, where he could only stand upright down the spine of the house. He'd probably still be asleep, all-night gaming marathons being what they were. I surprised myself with the brief pang of homesickness that came over me. But then, I wasn't homesick for actual *home*, that tiny flat above the chip shop in Devizes, or even my house in Bristol. It was more a nostalgia for a time when I'd not had to worry about more than getting to school on time and my Saturday job looking after the lizards in a pet shop. Well, yes, I'd had to worry about Mum and Dylan too, and all of us not having enough of anything, and doing the laundry and everything, but – it had been a different kind of worry. More specific. Now I just worried a generalised kind of worry.

Mum had emailed again. This time complaining that Dylan had used all the credit she'd put on the electricity key and she was down to fifty pence. Almost without thinking I found I was transferring money into her bank account, composing a short email to tell her that I'd done it, and that I'd be working over the next few days and not able to pick up her mails.

Tell her she can't lean on you. You don't have to pay her back for parenting, she's a grownup who can sort her own problems, she shouldn't be making them yours too. Claire and I had had that discussion so many times. And I'd leave her lovely, cosy kitchen with the Aga and the pine table and the flowers and head back to Mum's flat with the sticky lino floor and the sun-bleached curtains and the smelly fridge. I would mean, truly I'd *mean* to sit Mum down and tell her that she should go and get a job and kick Dylan out if he refused to pay his way and stop relying on me to support them and myself. But then I'd get there, and Mum would be crying and Dylan would be yelling and the place wouldn't have seen a hoover or daylight for days, and I'd give in. It had become like a little routine now, one that fitted neatly in with the run of daytime soap operas and the nightly gin.

There was another email in the inbox.

I've had a think. And I've come up with an idea – how does this sound? I challenge you to do a few things that scare you just a little bit. Something that you wouldn't do under your own steam. Just something that brings home to you a little bit of what you're missing by living the life that you do.

*I just want you to look outside yourself a bit, Leah. You
know the tendency you have to overthink everything until it
becomes meaningless? Well, sometimes it really is just dead
simple.*

Are you ready?'

It was only when the phone slipped out of my hand and only
a quick catch saved it from landing in the half-centimetre of
coffee left in my cup, that I realised my hands were sweating.

Who the hell was sending these?

And then that awful, creeping thought. The one that brought
blood to my cheeks and gave me the urge to run, out of the
shop, across the hills and not stop running until that burning
feeling of shame had cooled to a manageable heat.

Lewis.

Along with the name came the face. Lean, carefully bearded
with the kind of trendy beard that looked as though it had
been shaved with a set square. Collarless, linen shirts pinned
with badges that proclaimed his attachment to 'Anarchy in the
UK' and unstructured suits that looked elegant on his spare
frame.

Lewis. Even the name made me blush. And I didn't want
to think of him now, *couldn't* think of him now, with the sun
so sharp it was cutting holes in the road, the easy sound of
children playing on the sand and the gentle roll and swish
of waves against the harbour wall, audible now that I was I
standing outside the café.

I gritted my teeth, turned my face towards the sun, and
walked up the hill to where the buildings started and a bunch
of parked vehicles surrounded by a group of women corralled
by orange tape, like a restless WI outing, into which I slipped,
grateful for the chance to lose myself among others.

I didn't actually want to be an extra, of course. As excuses went it was right up there with 'washing my hair', but it did give me somewhere legitimate to be, so I paddled around on the extremities of a group of women who all seemed to know each other. They couldn't have done though. There were so many of them. There must have been a subset of holidaymakers – fans perhaps, of the programme filming – I didn't know what it was, but there seemed to be a lot of giggling going on so I presumed it was something to do with a handsome leading male actor. If they *were* all local then the village must have some sort of magnetic effect on oestrogen. I stood and watched as a couple of people came out of a van and began to marshal them – a tubby man in glasses and a woman with an iPad – with lots of pointing and waving.

It made me feel lonely, in an odd kind of way. Not as in a longing for the presence of others – I spent most of my time actively trying to avoid other people – but a yearning to just fit in. To know how to behave in a group that wasn't made up of my peers and students. That effortless ability to fit in, that so many people seemed to have, knowing the right thing to say and how to nudge shoulders and laugh or when to make the solemn face of understanding someone else's pain. Logically, I knew how to do it, but my brain sometimes seemed to skip over those niceties. It was easier to be thought of as solitary and grumpy than to try to work out how to act in any given group.

I shook my head. Brendon should be back at the house by now and I could safely take the path over the clifftop without worrying about walking into him. Leaving the woman-corral, where the tubby man was trying to shout over a lot of laughter, I ducked under the tape, circled back down the road until I could squeeze over the gate and back onto the beaten, dried-earth of the track, keeping sharp eyes open in case Brendon had loitered on his walk back.

There was no sign of him. Or of anyone, thankfully. My walk had no company but a phalanx of screaming gulls, practising formation flying overhead. Idly I wondered if one of them was Roger, and if he fitted in to the lifestyle of ordinary gulls after being raised with humans, and whether the zoologists had ever done any work on domestically reared gulls. I found myself mentally drafting research material as the birds draped across the sky and intersected the few fluffy clouds that were bubbling up, peeling off the horizon and drifting towards the land.

You're using it to stop yourself from having to think. Claire's voice came into my head again. *Distracting yourself from what's important by trying to make something else* more *important. It really isn't, you know.*

'Stop it,' I said aloud, in an attempt to drown out the internal voice.

So, what are you going to do? Is this it, then? You spend your days as a spinster scientist, overthinking really boring stuff to stop yourself from thinking about the things you really should be thinking about? Sending money home whenever you're asked?

'It's fine. It's no more than I can afford and, besides, why shouldn't I help out?'

Very good. Very 'dutiful daughter'. But what about you? What about your life? What happens when your mum dies – are you going to move in and look after Dylan? Take over her role and her downtrodden slippers?

'Shut up.' I walked faster to try to outwalk the voice. I knew it wasn't Claire, she'd always been a lot kinder in her attempts to make me face reality. This was me – the little internal whisper that hissed fear of the future and generalised resentment into my ear whenever I gave it headroom. I avoided it by keeping busy, but those emails were beginning to work a needle point through the carefully insulated fabric of my life.

* * *

'Oh great. Did you find a boat?' Tass was doing something with cables outside the house when I arrived.

'Yes, I'm going out in the morning with Brendon.' Then I lowered my voice to a whisper. 'Is he here?'

'Yep, in the kitchen. Googling, I think. I'm staying out of his way, he keeps muttering on about seagulls having it in for him; sounds like he thinks this place is only a couple of chainsaws away from being a horror movie.'

'OK. Can you bring me a laptop out here so I can get on with some work without interrupting him?'

Tass did their best 'your humble servant' bow, which annoyed me but I knew how lucky I was to have the funding for any assistant at all, let alone one I knew, with a background in our subject, so I ignored it.

I did some preliminary work ready for our sample collection, sitting out on the step of the house in the sun. Across the field the cows were back, mooching and swishing against the flies of the day, patient under the weight of the sun. It all smelled very agricultural, with a top note of salt from the wind off the sea. I kept finding myself lowering the laptop and just looking out at the view or stopping typing to feel the way the wind roamed over my exposed flesh and then away to rustle the leaves in the oak tree.

The remark in the anonymous email about overthinking had stung more than I'd acknowledged at the time and working and admiring the view was keeping me focused. I was absolutely *not* going to start thinking about Brendon or my mother. Absolutely *not…*

The absence of sound was disconcerting after a while and I realised that I was listening to the silence as though waiting for it to be disrupted by sirens or general background racket. My little house on a hill in Bristol, close to work and shops, had no double glazing and let the noise in as much as it let the heat out. But I'd got used to it. Used to the fact that passing lorries made the windows bulge and boom in their frames and used to the fact that I could discern every individual word of conversationalists on the road outside. It all formed a sort of blanket, things to stop my mind sinking too deeply into itself, whereas here…

My inbox pinged. Expecting it to be a reply to my request for a timeline for testing, I flipped it open.

> *'OK, I've been thinking. I don't want to start you with anything scary, because I'm still a little bit worried that you might just decide to delete all my mails and pretend none of this, none of any of it, ever happened. You're a bit too good at that, you know? Compartmentalising your life and only dealing with the bit in front of you at that time as though the rest doesn't matter, like none of it is interlinked. So. We'll start slowly. And remember, I will know if you don't go through with it!*
>
> *I'm not doing this to hurt you, Leah. I just want you to think about your life and about what you really want out of it. I'm not telling you who I am, not just yet, but I know you. And I know that you put up with far more than most people would, and you don't fight back. You've had all the fight knocked out of you, but that doesn't mean you have to settle for second best. I want you to be*

totally sure that the life you are living is the absolutely
right one for you.

That's enough mawkish waffle for now. So. What I'd like
you to do, today if you can, is to go and find an animal.
Can be anything, dog, cat, walrus, whatever you've got to
hand. And I want you to stroke it. I want you to feel that
connection. To know that you can feel that connection;
that there are things out there you can connect with.

You don't have to be lonely forever and not everyone
will hurt you.
X'

The letters on the screen melted and dripped and I feared, for a second, that I was having a stroke. It was only when my eyes started to sting that I realised I was crying. I looked over my shoulder quickly, but both Tass and Brendon were still in the depths of the kitchen, I could hear them; the dragging sound of chairs moving against the tiled floor, a voice raised in comment or a laugh. The sound of the kettle boiling. It all felt very distant – those people, engaged in tasks, communicating, nothing to do with me as they went about their business in the dark shade of the house.

Just in case one of them came out though, I put the laptop down on the step, got up and walked to the edge of the cliff. Far enough that, should they call me, my face would be completely composed by the time I got back to them. I stared out over the sea, where the blending shift of silver and blue looked the same whether I had tears in my eyes or not. Part of me wanted to lose myself in the emotion of the moment, just let myself cry tears of self-pity, because all the things the email accused me of were accurate. I *did* live a second-best life without resistance. But what else could I do? My mother, Dylan – they needed me to help them. I'd married Darric ten years ago because his brand of controlled affection was what I was used to. Love came with conditions – of course it did. Be nice to me and I will be pleasant in return, cross me and I will refuse to speak to you for weeks and pretend you don't exist. That was just *life*!

But a tiny little shard of me, held deep inside my heart, knew it should be different. That love should be like it was in the films, all holding hands and kisses on beaches at sunset. Gifts exchanged by a roaring fire, and soft twilight chats on a sofa in a garden. I kept that shard well buried, though. My analytical side wouldn't allow me to forget that sunset kisses and hand-holding desires dwindled in the face of bill paying and family responsibilities, and that soft twilight garden chats were usually accompanied by biting insects and other people's strimmers. And gift exchanges were fraught with the fear of giving the wrong thing and receiving something you had no interest in or use for. Darric had given me a leaf blower for our first Christmas together. It was still in a box in the house, somewhere.

Only once had I broken my mould. And that one time had been riddled with guilt and feelings so torn and tattered that they had flown like flags. I'd patched them up now, and that would never happen again.

'Leah!' It was Brendon, calling from the doorway. 'Do you want to make any plans for our sail tomorrow?'

'Six o clock, you said. And I know where the boat is, thank you,' I called back, across the field. A couple of the cows raised their heads from the grass at the sound of my voice.

'And that's all…? All right, OK, I'll see you down there tomorrow.' Brendon sounded a bit disappointed, as though he'd wanted to engage me in conversation. There was nothing to talk about though. 'I'm going down to the village now, to talk to some people about what I've found on Google.'

He left a gap, one which I knew I was supposed to use to ask what he'd found out. Convention, politeness, dictated that I ask, and I opened my mouth but couldn't frame the words.

'Come and eat with us tonight.' That was Tass. 'We've got proper food now and I'm going to do a lemon chicken. We might as well all eat together, economies of scale and all that.'

'That sounds good, yeah, thanks. I'll be there.'

This exchange had been held at a volume that reached me across the field and let me know that I was supposed to join in. But I still couldn't.

The cows raised their heads as I approached and it gave me an idea. *'I want you to feel that connection.'* I didn't know just how close the writer of those emails might be – close enough to *actually* be watching me? I furtively looked around, wondering if I'd catch sight of the sun glinting off binoculars like in a Poirot novel, but the sun gleamed off nothing except the sea and a few rooks arguing in the topmost branches of the oak. All right. But I couldn't be sure, could I? And something, maybe a kind of superstition, told me I had to go through with the suggestion. Plus, the cows were just standing there.

I walked up to the hedge that separated the cow field from the rather barren stretch of grassland that the house occupied. The Jerseys eyeballed me with their heads up and back, looking at me down their noses like the university grant board. I stood still on my side of the hedge and they jostled and snorted, crowding close with their dark faces and huge eyes. I could feel their exhalations over the top of the hawthorn separating us. There was something curiously comforting in the warmth of their breath and the sheer solidity of their sleek forms, something that made me lean closer.

Slowly I reached out a hand, intending to stroke the nearest cow on her topknot, which stuck up between her ears in a curiously comic way and made her look a little bit like Stan Laurel. As I raised my arm and leaned forward, I half-slipped, catching myself on the thorns in the hedge and toppling down onto it. The cows snorted and backed off, all rolling eyes and alarmed stamping and, as I tried to disentangle myself, they stampeded away across the field to watch me suffering impalement from a safe distance. The electric fence concealed among the wispy red shoots at the top of the hedge gave me a massive kick and I squealed, jerking back in a panicky attempt to get myself unsnagged from the branches, which made the cows snort and gallop even further away.

'Wriggle out of your shirt,' a voice came at the same time as another jolt of electricity, and I squealed again. 'You're stuck on the thorns.'

I wanted to reply that, yes, I could see that, thank you, I was well aware of what was holding me face down in this hedge with what felt like forty thousand volts booting me in the chest. But, of course, I didn't.

'Come on, quickly!' the voice urged.

'Ow!'

'Yeah, that's going to keep happening. I can't see what's powering it, so I can't disconnect…'

'Ow!'

The last jolt was enough. Dignity cast itself to the wind and I yanked myself out of the shirt I was wearing and was pulled suddenly backwards by warm hands on my shoulders, scattering buttons and a few cows who'd overcome fear to come and peer curiously at the new object in their hedge.

'Yeah. Electric fences. You want to watch those.' Brendon released me as soon as I was upright.

'Yes. I realise,' I snapped. I folded my arms over my chest. My bra was a non-frivolous build, made to contain not enhance, and it covered me as thoroughly as well-applied scaffolding. But I still felt exposed in front of Brendon, even though he kept his eyes on my face.

'OK then. Take care. See you later.' And he was gone, without so much as a question as to what the hell I was doing falling into a hedge, and without a backward glance at me and my exposed anatomy. I didn't know whether to be grateful that he was gentlemanly enough not to look or annoyed that he hadn't.

'And you lot can bugger off out of it,' I said to the cows, who were now crowding back to the hedge, snuffling at the edges of my shirt, careful not to touch the fence. Here I was, PhD and everything, and a herd of cows knew more about electric fencing than I did. All right, I bet they didn't know the Latin names of five hundred different types of sea growth, but even so I felt a bit humiliated in the face of their skittish bovine intelligence.

The shirt could stay where it was. I didn't want to risk another rush of volts up my arm with an attempt to rescue it. My body was aching from the shocks it had received already. So, keeping my arms firmly folded in case of watching binoculars, I walked back to the house.

Tass stayed in the kitchen, I could hear their fingers rattling over keyboards, so I went up the bare staircase and hid myself in my room.

The house smelled of dust and hot wood. Sun streamed through the sash window, sliced in two by the raised lower half which threw a thick shadow across my bed, into which I slumped. I knew I ought to go and find myself a different shirt to put on, get back to work, even go and offer to help Tass in the kitchen, but somehow I just couldn't. The feeling that all my muscles were slightly bruised by the electricity didn't help either.

I lay and stared at the dust rotating slowly in the sunbeams and wondered if some of the stories of fairies had been inspired by people lying, thoughtless and half-dreaming, in a dusty, sunny room. Then I wished that fairies were real and I could somehow imagine myself to be a changeling, switched at birth from another family into the one I grew up in. Then I argued with myself for a bit about whimsy and whether it served any purpose in life today. And spared a moment for wondering whether my mum was actually employable in any context at all, since she'd left school the year before exams, and so had no notable qualifications to her name, other than a certificate of some kind in history. She always said she only got *that* because she'd fancied the history teacher, but I wasn't entirely sure.

After a while I decided that none of this introspection was helping at all and was merely proving the 'overthinking' comment. So I put on a T-shirt and went back downstairs.

Chapter Three

Brendon arrived back as the late shadows began to gather round the house. I saw him come up the track from the window of the living room, where I was sitting with my laptop on my knee. He didn't come to the house, but veered off towards the shed. I found I was half waiting for the sound of him coming in, either to the kitchen or through the front door, and when that didn't happen I stood up to look outside.

I needed to stretch my legs anyway, I reasoned. Sitting for too long wasn't good, especially on this sofa which had all the hallmarks of having been well used by students for all purposes over a lot of years. One end sagged, one end was artificially elevated – and I didn't like to investigate by what, and there was the vague smell of very stale alcohol and wet socks that it gave off. It lay in the room like an old dog that nobody wants to talk about having put to sleep, and it was the only thing available to sit on, unless I wanted to stay in the kitchen with Tass. Which I didn't. They were cooking their special lemon chicken and it seemed to involve more swearing than I'd ever been aware was necessary in a domestic kitchen.

Brendon had left the shed door open. If I opened the window and stuck my head out, I could hear him making rummaging noises and occasionally expostulating in that slow drawl of an accent. Overhead, the gulls were circling and calling, in competition with the rooks. The gulls hung over the sea-end of the field and the rooks over the old oak tree, as though some kind of avian demarcation existed. I wondered if Brendon was hiding from the seagulls.

'G'day!' He popped out of the shed suddenly and saw me leaning on the sill, staring upwards at the birds. 'How's it going?'

'Oh, you know.' I shrugged.

'Did you get picked? As an extra for that TV thing? Everyone down in the village is talking about it, some kind of new detective series with some bloke that all the women seem to fancy.'

I'd forgotten I was supposed to be doing that, so I made a non-committal noise that he could take to mean anything.

'Hope there's no ill-effects from the electric fencing.' He came over to the window, bag still slung over his shoulder, so the effect was that of being approached by an erudite tramp. 'What in god's name were you doing to get stuck on that?'

'Do you know anything about tracing emails?' The question burst out of me, bypassing my brain and going straight from my heart to my vocal chords. 'Only I'm getting these messages and…' I tailed off. It was none of his business. None of it.

Brendon came in closer. 'You're getting anonymous emails?' His face had gone from the good-natured, crinkle-eyed, outdoorsy expression that was pretty much the only one I'd seen on it so far, and over to a narrowed down one, that made his eyes tight and his mouth look as though he was chewing something bitter. 'Threatening?'

'No. Well, not really, I don't think. Just – sort of strange.'

'And you've no idea who they might be from? Only I'm not much of an expert, but I know a few people who could probably… y'know, if you're really worried.'

'I…' I began, but how to phrase it? What to say? And again that image of Lewis in his crumpled grey suit with the T-shirt under his jacket floated into my mind. The way his overlong hair hung to his collar, the scent of old paper that clung to him and made him smell like the most intriguing second-hand bookshop in the world. All accompanied by the crippling stomach-churning. 'I'm just wondering if it might be someone – a man – I used to… an ex of mine?' And then, because I didn't even want to consider the possibility that Lewis might have traced me to this quiet corner of Dorset. 'No. Forget I spoke, honestly. It's just stupid stuff, probably some students of mine having a bit of a laugh.'

'By making you fall into an electric fence?' He still had that look on his face as though all his features were being pulled from the inside.

Go on. I want to see how you talk your way out of this one. Claire's voice was so distinct that it almost made me jump. *You don't half get yourself into some situations, Leah. Come on, how are you going to phrase this so that you don't sound completely bonkers? You need to say something…*

'I was going to stroke a cow.' I sounded a bit sulky.

'OK, let me get this straight. You got an anonymous email from god-only-knows where, and it told you to *stroke a cow*? Bloody hell, Leah, did you really piss off the Old MacDonald Mafia or something?'

His face had relaxed now, and gone back to the sideways look of barely repressed cheerful madness. He'd caught the sun more today and his skin had gone an even light brown. There were incipient blonde streaks in his hair too, that made him look younger and surf-ier. His type were probably ten a penny in Melbourne, but here in Dorset he looked exotic.

'Forget it,' I said, pulling my elbows off the window ledge and preparing to take my head back inside. 'It's nothing. Just stupid stuff. I don't really need someone to trace the emails, if it starts to get threatening I'll get my provider on to it. Or the police, yes, I think cyberstalking is a crime, isn't it? I'll report it. If it gets worse.'

Brendon also turned. 'If you're sure.'

The rather awkward silence – that was me attempting to pretend that I'd never even brought up the subject, and his clear dubiousness about dropping it – was broken by Tass hurtling into the room behind me and yelling 'There's no stock! I ordered a four pack of stock and it hasn't come!'

'Ah, some of Shakespeare's loveliest lines,' I said, and caught sight of Brendon starting to grin, before I turned indoors. 'I'm sure the food will be fine, Tass.'

Tass was something of a perfectionist. It was what made them such a good research assistant and such a complete pain in the backside in general life. 'It won't be right!' they wailed. 'I can't serve my lemon chicken without stock! It would be like…' there was a moment's groping for the right simile, '…like Jade, Perrie and Leigh-Anne without Jesy!'

'Unless those are recently discovered forms of sea-growth, I am failing to see why I should grasp your analogy.'

'Leah!' Tass sounded genuinely shocked. 'You actually don't know the lineup of Little Mix?'

'Draw your deduction from my expression.' I pulled my head completely back inside. After the bright blaze of the day outside, everything inside was shadows and lines.

'Oh. My. God. You really don't. What the hell do you *do* in the evenings?' Tass flopped onto the sofa, which gave an ominous creak.

'Oh, you know, spin. Lance my plague boils. Chew animal hide to make my own clothes from.'

There was a moment's silence and then Tass let out a sharp shriek of a laugh. 'Prof, you are having me on!'

'Number one – Leah. Number two – yes, I am. I spend my evenings in the same way as most researchers, trawling for funding. And three – I have no idea what Little Mix is but I appreciate your sentiment. Can you use white wine instead of stock?'

Tass sprawled dramatically for a moment. Today's jeans were a little more 'jean' and a little less 'hole', but the overall effect was still that of posing. 'You're not *that* old, though,' they said, thoughtfully. 'I mean, yeah, maybe Little Mix is a bit adolescent for you, but you've got this whole thing about you, like… unworldliness? Like you just beamed in from somewhere else and you haven't quite caught up with the rest of us yet.'

I bit my tongue. I knew enough about Tass to know that they came from a loving background; two parents who supported their gender-fluid identification and life through university. A few siblings, all of whom were making their way in the world. Add in a cheerfully anarchic personality and a refusal to care about what anyone else thought and you had someone that was as diametrically opposed to me as was possible whilst being the same species.

And of *course* I'd heard of Little Mix. I just never thought I'd have to pick them out of an identity parade.

'I'm a post-Doctoral researcher,' I said, and my tone held a note of irritation. 'I cultivate an otherworldly persona so that those I am applying to for funding don't realise my very precise grasp on the world of finance.'

'So they reckon they can cheat you into doing stuff for them?' Tass was also astute.

'There is a certain amount of fiscal argy-bargy that goes on, yes.'

'And they don't realise that you realise what's going on, because they think you're this professor type who hasn't watched TV since 1989?'

'In essence, yes. Now, I am supposing that the lemon chicken is almost ready?' There was a delicious smell of cooking wafting through the house, bringing its chilly, dark interior towards a kind of life, like watching a moribund animal raise its head toward the smell of food.

'Shit, yes!' Tass leaped up. 'You get Brendon in, I'll start serving up.'

Brendon must have been lurking close by, because almost as soon as Tass finished speaking, he was coming in through the front door, minus the rucksack but plus a bottle of wine.

'Something smells good,' he said.

'And the winner of "banal statement of the year" goes to…' I said, somewhat waspishly. I was feeling a little bit exposed because of my random blurting of the email problem. There was absolutely no reason for Brendon to know that much about me. Even him knowing my name made me feel a bit twitchy, but then I was like that with most people, feeling at a disadvantage in his presence didn't make him special.

'I know. But it's expected, isn't it? I mean, I come in saying "this place smells like it's been full of chundering students for years" – well, it's not going to do my ambition to be invited back for dinner again any good, is it?' He gave me a look, with his head half tilted, as though he wanted an answer to what, to my mind, was a purely rhetorical question.

'I suppose not.' I led the way through into the kitchen, where Tass was bringing a steaming roasting dish out of the oven. I felt as though I had the word 'grudging' printed on my forehead.

'Too much to hope that it's one of those bloody great birds that keeps trying to have my eyes out?' Brendon asked cheerfully.

'Dunno. It's from Sainsbury's, so probably not, unless their supply chain is particularly corrupt.' Tass spooned sauce.

There was a tapping sound from the kitchen door. Tass didn't seem to hear it, Brendon cocked his head. 'Visitors?'

'Probably the wind.' The noise had come from quite low down, as though a piece of plastic was being blown against the door.

The tap came again. 'Sounds like a gnome wants in,' Brendon got up and opened the door. He made a strangled sort of noise, slammed it shut and came over to sit down again, looking a bit green.

'Anyone there?' I asked.

There was a momentary flurry and a shape appeared at the window. A huge orange beak, backed by a small sallow eye, which rolled at us. The beak tapped at the glass now.

'It's mail order horror,' Brendon said, weakly. 'They've progressed from swooping down on visitors, they actually come to your door now and demand sacrifices in person.'

The gull had the giveaway black spot on its head.

'It's Roger.' I shaded my eyes and peered through the window. Roger peered back, and opened his beak in a slightly threatening manner.

'Great. Now it knows where I live.' Brendon took his plate from Tass. 'Can't you close the curtains or something?'

Since the curtains were a filmy yellow gauze, neither use nor ornament, and dirtier than anything near a food preparation area should be, I didn't think this would help.

'I'll just throw him out some leftovers,' I said. 'He might take the hint.'

I went to the door and threw out some bits of chicken skin and a few chopped carrots. Roger hopped off the window and arrived at my feet before the first bit had hit the ground.

'Those birds couldn't take a hint if it came wrapped round dynamite,' Brendon said, as I came back in. He couldn't keep his eyes from wandering to the door. 'And feeding it chicken? Isn't that, like, cannibalism?'

'Seagulls are like the zombies of the bird world,' Tass said, mouth half full. 'They attack en masse, and they eat *anything*.'

'Great. I feel so much better knowing that,' Brendon said, in a tense voice. 'And that's a tame one. *Why* would anyone do that?'

'He's not so much tame as hand reared.' I didn't know why I felt obliged to defend Roger. Maybe because he was one of the few creatures on the planet that seemed to genuinely like me. If all he asked in return was a plate of scraps every now and again, I'd take that. It was practically effusive affection where I came from.

'OK, can we make a vow now, that, if he comes back, we hole up in a local shopping centre with handguns?'

We sat around the horrible Formica table, Brendon and I opposite one another, with Tass at the head and the opened bottle of wine between us. The food was good, the conversation sporadic and mannered, a bit like a Mike Leigh film. Tass and Brendon talked about Australia – Tass had been several times to visit a sibling – and science fiction. I kept my eyes on my plate and listened, trying to get to grips with what they were talking about, and failing. It could have been anything from Harry Potter to Star Trek. They changed subject and switched around from topic to topic, their words swooping and soaring like the gulls I could see flying high outside the window. Maybe Roger had summoned his People.

They'd been talking about families, comparing numbers of brothers and sisters and chatting idly about parents in a way that had made me feel hard done by, but eventually there was a gap long enough for me to trickle myself into.

'What did you find out?' I asked.

Brendon frowned. 'About what?'

Now this was unfair. He and Tass had followed one another's changes of conversational direction without so much as a raised eyebrow. *I* asked a reasonable and related question and he was acting as though I'd suddenly started speaking Polish.

'You said you were going down to the village to talk to some people about things about your family that you found on Google?' I drank some wine, mostly so that I didn't have to look at him.

'Oh yes. I found a local history society, went to talk to someone. They know someone who might remember Great-grandad's family, they're setting me up a meeting.' He mirrored me and lifted his wine glass. 'It's pretty exciting this genealogy, y'know.' A sip. 'What about your family, Leah? Any black sheep you might feel like tracing through the generations?'

I thought of my family. Mum in her trodden-down slippers and tracksuits, Dylan and his ubiquitous camo gear, as though he really needed to be able to conceal himself from real life. 'No, not really,' I said.

Have you ever thought about finding your dad? I remembered Claire asking; we'd been sitting in her garden, eyes closed and faces turned towards the sun. The air had smelled of carnations and roses and the sound of bees hung heavy. It had been like existing in Rupert Brooke's poetry, that perfect day. I could almost feel the snaggy plastic of the deckchair behind my back and the mild tickle of the grass on my bare feet. *It might help you. Give you more of a sense of your own identity. Help you to stand up to your mum a bit. I'll help you, if you like.*

And I'd half thought it over, and concluded that she may be right, but when I'd gone back with the few bits of paper that I'd managed to find, she'd broken the news about her cancer and everything else had taken a back seat after that.

'No,' I said again, aware that I'd been quiet for too long. 'No point.'

'You don't fancy finding out where you come from?' Brendon was smiling at me over his glass.

'I know where I come from. Devizes. Shall I wash up, Tass? Is there any hot water?' I picked up my plate and took it to the sink.

'There's no rush,' Tass made a face at me. 'Plates'll keep. We might need to pump some more water up into the tank anyway, the taps made a really weird noise when I filled the kettle earlier on.'

I'd been told about this before. My urge to clear the table, start washing up, almost before people had finished eating. Darric had complained that I sometimes whipped his plate away from under his fork. I explained it away as just habit, whilst my inner eye saw the sink in the flat, dishes piled high and teetering, one mug and spoon away from an explosion of china all over the tiled floor.

I sat back down and listened to them chatting, idly now, about travel. Tried to analyse the way their conversation moved, one of them laying down a thread that the other followed, only to chop it off and start again with another, a warp and weft of talk that baffled me.

'You're very quiet, Leah.' Brendon made me start, addressing me directly. 'Are you all right?'

'I'm fine. I just don't know anything about the films of Guillermo del Toro, I'm afraid.'

'She's always like this,' Tass put in. 'Ask her anything about *Ascophyllum nodosum* and she'll be right there.' They drained their glass. 'Really clever, but no pop culture to speak of. Sad, really. Absolutely no knowledge of Hobbits, Ariane Grande or Doctor Who. I really don't know how she manages to exist.'

'Quite nicely, thank you,' I put in.

Tass stood up. 'I'm off to call some people.' They mimed holding up a mobile. 'Using a tel.E.phone, for those among you who still regard the horse and cart as the epitome of technology.'

'Shut up,' I said, without any particular emphasis.

'So I shall leave you to bring her up to speed on the twentieth and twenty-first centuries, Brendon, and tactfully inform her that the loom is no longer the pinnacle of human achievement. See you around.' And Tass was gone, closing the kitchen door behind them whilst making a kissy-faced expression, as though Brendon and I were about to fall upon one another and begin some kind of protracted snogging session as soon as they left the room.

My face went tight with horror and a prickle of embarrassment raised the hair on my spine. Was that what Tass really thought? That Brendon and I were just waiting for them to leave? It was more comfortable to assume that Tass was just winding me up, so I let the horror subside, although the uncomfortable tingle of embarrassment remained.

'So. Any reason you're not up to speed on stuff?' Brendon collected the plates and stacked them by the sink. 'Too devoted to your research to spend any time watching *Loose Women* and stuffing your face with takeaways?'

I shrugged. 'Maybe.' I didn't have a television – couldn't see the point. Rarely streamed programmes because – well, really, what *was* the point?

'I'm picturing you roaming around your house with about a million cats trailing behind you,' he leaned his back against the work surface. 'Or is that stereotyping too? What about friends? Dinner parties?'

'My best friend died,' I said, to shut him up. 'Cancer. It put a crimp in my dinner party lineup, I'm afraid.'

'Oh.' He shifted about. Was he nervous? Embarrassed? I couldn't tell. 'Sorry about that.'

'Not your fault,' I said tartly. 'Anyway. She died a year ago and I haven't… I mean, it's been… I haven't really had anyone to tell me what to watch and read since.'

I couldn't see his face. He had his back to the window and the long, late shafts of sun were slotting their way past him, blinding me and putting him in shadow.

'You need telling?' he said, quietly. 'I'd have thought someone as intelligent as you could work out for yourself how to stay up to speed with modern life.'

I bit my lip. 'I prefer to concentrate on my work,' I sounded stiff, as though our conversation was scripted and I was afraid of forgetting my lines.

'So you lead a bit of an excluded life then,' he said. 'Concentrating on your work and all that.' A pause. 'Does it make you happy?'

'I beg your pardon?' I coughed over the wine left in my glass.

'Just… ah… I dunno. You said you were divorced, and for me, being a bit of a workaholic was partly what did for my relationship. Great girl, I was stupid, but, yeah… ah… it was never going to work out, I can see that now. Just wondered if it was the same for you.'

Oooh, he cuts to the chase, doesn't he? Claire would have poured a gin at this point and sat back to enjoy herself, while I went pink and sweat ran down my back. *No, no, this is good for you,*

Leah. Making you think about things. Making you think about other people.

'No. We divorced because Darric... because he didn't understand relationships.'

Go on, imaginary-Claire goaded. *Tell him how Darric behaved. How he wouldn't ever have breakfast in bed in case it made a mess. How he couldn't ever cuddle you or hug you. How he allocated you your jobs in the house as though he was writing up a work rota.*

'He doesn't really "do" people, you see.'

He was a fucking robot! Tell him about how the sex made you feel as though you were a blow-up doll! I snorted at the thought of saying this aloud to Brendon. It was so far over the TMI line that it made the density of *Propagation and uses of Fucus in history, 1330-1950* sound like a Twitter message.

'So no. Not my workload. More his desire to never have to hold another conversation.'

Brendon flipped around suddenly. Roger was there at the window again, regarding us with an expression that was somehow both menacing and pleading, and all through the medium of no more than a beak and an eye like an osprey in reduced circumstances. 'Holy shit! It's back.'

I was relieved. Now he'd stop asking me personal questions. It would be hard to quiz me on the reasons for my divorce with his very own hell fiend staring him between the shoulder blades. I felt a momentary fondness for Roger and his mad-eyed begging.

'Do they go dormant at night? Or am I going to have to sleep on the floor in here?' Brendon kept his face turned towards the window, but I had the feeling his eyes were shut.

'Are you afraid of birds in general? Because that can be a deep-rooted phobia, maybe some therapy would help?' I felt a little bit evil asking as he'd shown no fear of any other birdlife but I felt like dealing him out the type of question that that felt as though someone was going about your psyche with dental floss would serve him right.

'Just your gigantic, genetically modified Boeings of birds.' He took half a step back, probably he'd squinted at the window again. Roger was paddling his flat orange feet on the wooden ledge. 'There's really no need for them to be so big. Or so threatening. Do you think he's armed?' Roger stropped his beak against the window catch and Brendon recoiled further into the room. 'He's trying to get in!'

I sighed, picked up a plate and went outside. Roger tipped his head on one side and flopped down to the ground. 'This is your lot.' I put the plate of scraps down. 'Eat this and go.'

I knew that feeding him would likely only make things worse, that he'd start hanging around more, but, from my perspective, anything that kept Brendon at arm's length was an advantage. If that meant keeping a hungry seagull on high alert, then so be it.

'So, I'll see you early tomorrow morning,' I said in a businesslike way to Brendon as I came back in and started putting the other plates in the sink. 'To catch the tide.'

'Er. Yes.' Brendon was peering through the little glass inset in the door as though expecting a gunman to burst in at any minute. 'And then… well, I wondered, would you come with me to this meeting?'

I gave him the sort of stern look I gave people who asked stupid questions about my research. 'They aren't going to come with seagulls on their arms you know. They aren't like falcons.'

He laughed. It was an attractive laugh, I hated to admit. 'Nah. It's just that some of them have got an accent and some of the dialect is a bit… well. I could do with a translator, put it that way. I mean, how was I to know what "dropping a clanger" meant? I could do with an extra pair of ears to filter all that out.' The laugh died away and his face was serious. 'I want to find out about Great-grandad. He just kinda vanished from the family record and my mum's a bit worried there might be some kind of scandal. Now my sisters are having kiddos, it'd be nice to put it all to bed for her. Give her some answers. And answers that are comprehensible and don't include words like "gobsmacked", whatever *that* means.'

It was unexpected, but I felt a faint burst of sympathy for him. People saying things that you were supposed to understand and then laughing, whilst you had no idea what they were laughing at, as you were too busy winnowing the sense out of their phrasing – yes, I knew how *that* felt.

'I'll come with you. Although if they break into Dorset dialect I'm afraid I will be no help at all.'

A broad grin. 'Bonza! Nah, it'll be good just having a wingman.' He looked out of the window. 'Not that I really want to think about things with wings, actually.'

I followed his gaze and looked out of the window too. The sun sank slowly towards the sea as the branches of the oak tree, sprinkled with a condiment of rooks, stood dark and stark against the sky. Roger took to the air with a flop and scoop of feathers, and was gone into the dusk.

'It's safe to go out now.' I said, turning on the tap to the kind of groaning sigh that ought to have come from a porn film. Two dribbles of water splashed sadly into the sink, the groan intensified and then stopped, as did the water. The pipes knocked in the walls. 'Bugger.' I didn't really know what else to say. Brendon's confession about his disappearing grandad had been an insight into his life and I didn't know if I was supposed to ask questions about it or not.

'Yes. I should get back, it's an early start. Meet you down at the boat, then?' With a quick check to make sure that Roger wasn't hiding round the corner, Brendon threw open the door. 'Thanks for dinner,' he said, over his shoulder and dashed across the yard to his shed.

I stood and looked at the plates in the sink. I *should* wash up. I *always* washed up, leaving dishes overnight was the beginning of the sheer slope that led you down to where my mother was, bins overflowing and a fridge that contained jars of green stuff that hadn't been green when they came home from the supermarket.

I checked the kettle, but it only contained enough water for a cup of tea. There were no bowls of water elsewhere either. It was no good, I was going to have to leave it overnight. That or go and find either Tass or Brendon to help pump. I envisaged asking them, and decided against dragging Tass from their phone call back to civilisation or making Brendon face the possibility that Roger or his ilk might be hanging around.

'Bugger,' I said again, and went off to bed, closing the kitchen door firmly behind me, as though I was afraid that the unwashed pots might follow me upstairs.

Chapter Four

The alarm on my phone went off at five, but that was all right because I'd already been awake for nearly an hour. The sun had woken me first. Then the sound of the gulls trying to shout down the rooks had kept me awake. But the thing that had really made sleep impossible was my own brain.

I'd woken with a start to the realisation that I hadn't actually managed to cuddle an animal of any description yesterday. In that hot sweat of fear you get when only half awake, I'd worried that the sender of the email would somehow know and there would be censure winging its way to me already. After a few rotations in bed I managed to console myself with the thought that it was still possible to stroke something within the twenty-four-hour time frame, and then my mind had moved on to who could be sending me the mails. And who would want to?

And then it went right back to Lewis. But – surely not? I mean, yes, he knew me well enough to know what frame of mind I would be in, and it would be just like him. His sense of humour was so offbeat as to be positively discordant; he would find it amusing to try to think up ideas to push me out of my comfort zone. But why would he? That part of my life was over, I'd made *myself* that promise, but maybe he was still harking back?

Well, that was all right, it cut both ways, I knew where to find him and I was not above shouting passive-aggressive comments through his letterbox.

I turned onto my back and kicked the cover off me. The day was already heating up nicely and, through the open window, I could already smell the cows and the sea. I could hear the cows too, a vague, gentle background presence and, although I couldn't hear the sea I could hear the effects of it on the very edge of hearing. Voices from the harbour drifted up the cliff face as superficial sailors got started early for a day of leaving the boat to go into Dorchester or Exeter for cappuccinos and designer shopping.

My mind tried to turn in introspectively again, asking me what the hell I was doing here, but I managed to derail it by leaping out of bed and getting dressed just as the alarm went off. My sample bag was already packed so I swung it onto my back and headed out of the house for the harbour.

I'd hoped that I would beat Brendon to the boat. The thought of his surprise when he realised that the outdoorsman could be beaten getting up and out in the morning by what he clearly regarded as an emotionally repressed townie spurred me to half-run down the path through the fields, over the gate, down the road and into the glistening, ringing semicircle of sea that was Christmas Steepleton harbour. Gulls, terns and some smaller less seaborne birds scooped the sky overhead and there was a newly washed feel to the air as the cool of the night built up to a proper day; grasshoppers wound up to their sunlit hum and the last edges of crepuscular dimness were burned away into caves and short shadows by the climbing sun. It was already hot.

I needn't have run. And the voices I'd heard from my bed should have given me the clue that boat people start early. A couple of the sleek-hulled boats were already on their way out, thrusting their way from between the protective walls and out into a navy sea, sails billowing like clean washing on a line.

Brendon was sitting outside the harbour master's office. She was standing in the doorway, one hand shielding her eyes from the sun as they conversed, or maybe they were trying to mitigate the effect of his shorts which, today, were a bright turquoise, like someone had cut a piece out of the sky and wrapped it round his legs.

'Hello, Leah!' He was way too cheerful for this time in the morning. I am not a natural morning person. In fact, I'm not really much of an evening person either, as Tass always says, I have a cracking half-hour somewhere round lunchtime and the rest of the day is touch and go, so his cheery greeting annoyed me. But then, it was so early that being gently caressed by some gorgeous young man bearing a cup of coffee, a bouquet of roses and promises of undying love would have been met with sarcasm and a plea for more sleep.

'Brendon.' It came out as more of a grunt than I'd intended.

'So, you ready? Looks like being a ripper day, eh, Izzie?'

'Izzie' appeared to be the moniker of the harbour master. I wondered if he'd be so friendly if he knew that she was the one responsible for Roger. 'Yes. Wind steady, glass is set fair, you should have a good trip.' She stopped speaking to watch another of the sleek, gleaming yachts wend thread its way out of the harbour mouth, riding the turquoise waves like a seal. 'If you steer clear of the hobbyists.' She sniffed. 'They seem to think tacking is – actually, what *is* tacking, other than boats zig-zagging?'

I just shrugged. I hadn't even known that boats *could* zig-zag, let alone that's what it was called.

'Right then. You two have a good trip, stay safe out there.' And Izzie went back inside the office. I had an evil moment of imagining Roger sitting in there on her desk, head cocked as he followed the conversation in the manner of a Bond villain, whilst eating his way through her lunchbox, but guessed at his actual absence from Brendon's easy manner.

He led the way out along the stone quay and the floating pontoon against which his boat was moored.

'What's her name?' I tried to distract him from noticing the way I was trying to keep my footing on the restlessly bobbing wood, which seemed to rise and fall with no reasoning.

'Izzie. You don't often see a female harbour master. Nice change. Plus she thinks all the boat-hiring Londoners are drongos, which is great, cos they are.'

'I meant the boat.'

'Oh.' Riding the motion of the sea as easily as he walked the land, Brendon jumped down onto the deck of the little craft, swinging the bag off his shoulder. 'I've called her *Southern Cross*. After the star formation, not the railway station. Be a bit bizarre calling a boat after a train stop, wouldn't it?'

Clumsily, and trying not to look as though I needed the hand he offered, I lowered myself down onto the boat, which bobbed and shied at the motion of sea below her. I was trying not to think about the condition of the wood below decks and hoping that the gentle slapping of the waves wasn't knocking holes in the planking. Above deck, things were sparkly and newly painted. Under my feet I knew it was a different matter, and hoped that all this wasn't some kind of analogy for Brendon himself. If I found myself murdered, chopped up and thrown overboard, I'd only have myself to blame after a metaphorical warning like that.

'What's in the bag?' Brendon tossed my rucksack down under one of the seats.

'Ziplock bags for packaging, GPS positioner, snorkel, depth and light meters.' I stared out towards the horizon, bracketed between the harbour walls. It was the colour of tin, broken by streaks of white where breakers rolled and smacked offshore.

'Complicated, this seaweed collecting?'

The upward inflection of his accent meant I couldn't tell if it was a question or not, but I answered it anyway. 'There's a lot to take into consideration. We need to record where it was collected, what the water conditions are like, before we even get into the nutritional content.' I took the complicated package he held out to me. 'There's a reason they're hiring a PhD to do it, rather than using student labour.'

'You're a PhD? That's terrific. Now, put your lifejacket on.'

The complicated thing had an explanation, which I was glad about, because at first glance it looked like something from Bondage 101. I shook it until it made more logistical sense, then put it over my head and tied up the straps.

'I hope this isn't an indication of your sailing prowess,' I said tartly.

'Nah, it's an indication that if you fall overboard I intend for you to stay alive long enough for me to come back for you.' His tone was jocular, but I sensed a certain degree of censure in the words. The most annoying thing was that he was right, a lifejacket was an essential piece of equipment to be wearing.

'I'm not really used to doing the boat thing. I'm more on the research side.'

We lapsed into a sort of silence. I sorted through my bag, double checking my equipment, whilst he did things with ropes and bits of boat. I had to admit that I was half watching him as he capably walked the deck, riding the motion of the waves as though it was more normal to him than walking a pavement, in his lairy shorts and with his sun-bleached hair. All casual and relaxed, life fitting around him like a suit that had been made with him in mind. 'Comfortable in his skin', I think they called it. I had a moment of envy so sharp and intense that I had to pretend to dig deep in my bag for the light meter that was already in my hand to disguise the fact that my face had gone tight.

'Right, you ready?' Brendon was standing in front of me, a coiled rope in his hands. 'Have you got an actual location in mind to head for?'

Without speaking I passed him the general coordinates of the kelp field that Tass had worked out. I kept my eyes turned down, focused on his legs, strong and braced as they absorbed the motion of the sea, and his feet in their canvas shoes. His shoes looked dirty, trodden in, as though he wore them every day for everything from walking across the hills to working on the boat. I was wearing a pair of Converse trainers I'd bought in town before I came down, and they were still rigid and rubbed my heels.

'Great! Right. You OK, Leah? You're not seasick or anything?'

I sat still, listening to the wet smacking of tide against hull, the gulls screeching their broken cries overhead. I bit back the sharp retort that I wanted to make.

'If I tended towards seasickness, I would have made Tass do the collection,' I said, as mildly as I could.

'Fair point.'

He went off to start the engine, and I watched his back view. Tried to conjure an opinion from my memory of Claire – what would she have thought of Brendon? A ribald wink over a long glass of gin was as close as I could get, a nod towards a nicely constructed backside in well-fitting shorts. An acknowledgement that he seemed a decent guy.

I dismissed memory-Claire. She was altogether too accepting, too keen for me to meet a man who treated me as though I was a 'human being and not some kind of cross between a mother and a domestic robot' as she'd always said Darric treated me. I hadn't seen it then. I'd thought that was love.

'Are you looking forward to finding out more about your great-grandfather?' I had to speak, to distract myself from the way my thoughts were going, and so it was either talk to Brendon or shout at the sky.

He half turned towards me. He was steering the little boat out of the harbour, gently guiding her between the cliff faces of the big yachts, which overhung us as we pottered towards the gap in the walls that led to the restless surface of the ocean.

'Yeah. Oh, I dunno. Looking forward to it is putting it a bit strong. I'm a bit worried there might be some awful family secret to come out, y'know? He obviously left my great-grandma with three small kids, it's not going to be a happy story now, is it?' He turned back, expertly piloting us further out to where the waves started to catch at our hull. The boat began to pitch. 'There's just no paper trail after he got married, it's like he just fell off the planet, but, ah, wartime... anything could have happened to the records, I guess. Bit worried about how Mum is going to take it all, to be honest, if I turn up some kind of scandal, like he left Great-grandma and ran off with another woman. She's mostly worried one of the grandchildren will end up marrying a cousin accidentally, I think. I mean, y'hear of it happening. Or maybe he murdered someone and went to prison? It was never talked about. That's what gets her. No stories down through the generations, nothing, and her grandma died before she was born, so she could never ask her.'

The wind was quite strong now we were out of the shelter of the harbour walls. It flapped at the legs of his shorts so they looked like very small sails, and parted my hair at the back so it flew into my mouth. I hung on to the sides of my seat, with my upper body swinging about as though I was riding a bumper car and my air of being used to this kind of thing was wearing thin.

'It's one of the reasons I asked you to come along too,' he carried on, hips absorbing the movement so that he rolled and gyrated like someone dancing whilst standing still. 'In case I need someone to help me keep a stiff upper lip. Oh, and the translation thing.' He adjusted our course a little and the waves started to hit the boat sideways on. 'And I'm still on a mission to get you to come for a drink with me.'

'Why?'

He turned round now. 'What do you mean, "why"?'

'Why is it a mission to get me to go for a drink? Maybe I don't drink. Maybe I don't go out with men I hardly know. Maybe there's nothing to be gained by it.'

Brendon pulled a face. 'Are you over-analysing this just a bit? Can we not just go for a drink and have a chat? I'd really like to know more about the work you're doing; seaweed as nutrition sounds a pretty good mission when we're running as short of food as we are.' Running counterpoint to his words, a McDonalds carton floated past us, bobbing cheerfully over each wave. 'I meant globally.'

'It's an interesting proposition, yes. Seaweed is mostly rich in minerals rather than proteins, so it could never be a complete diet, but as an addition…' I tailed off. He was smiling. 'What? Did I say something amusing?' I mentally reviewed my statement. There was nothing I could see as even vaguely worth a weak grin, unless he was finding the word 'weed' chuckleworthy.

'Nah, nothing. Just your serious face. Not that there's anything wrong with your face,' he added hastily; obviously an expression had come into my eyes that warned him he was on dangerous ground. Or sea. 'You have a most, er...' I could feel my eyes narrowing. 'Er. You've got a face,' he finished, and hurried to the other end of the boat to do something with some instruments.

I decided not to think about this too hard. Instead I looked down over the edge of the boat, into the depths of the water, which was something else I tried not to think too hard about. I could swim, but I was most comfortable where I could at least put a foot on the bottom. This black deepness, with its foamy white tips, made me hold onto my seat again a little tighter.

There was a momentary flurry. A gull had tried to snatch the burger box out of the water and been landed on by three others, all with the same idea. There was momentary tussling, then one gull wheeled away triumphant. The others sat on the surface of the waves and bobbed, trying to look as though this had been their intention all the time.

Brendon whipped around. 'Are they following us?'

'They're following the rubbish.' None of the bobbing remainers seemed to be Roger. 'They clean up the stuff we leave behind.'

Brendon stared. 'Not even your British seagulls can digest plastic, can they?' And then, with a little worried frown line between his eyes deepening, '*Can* they? Please say they can't, they already look like they dispose of bodies in their spare time.'

This made me smile, and I watched the frown line smooth out a little. 'No. But they can open packaging to get to what's inside.' I looked over at the floating threesome. 'They're a lot cleverer than people think. Not as bright as corvids, of course, but they can problem solve.'

He gave a dubious sniff. 'In Oz they just stand around looking stupid. They will steal your chips, but they're not as macho as yours about it. They more kinda *suggest* that you'd like to give them a chip. With their eyes. They're the Derren Browns of the bird world.' The boat swayed as a larger-than-usual wave hit us and he rolled with it as though he hadn't even noticed. 'You know a lot about birds for someone who does seaweed.' This puzzled me, which seemed, in turn, to puzzle him. 'You're frowning. Why are you frowning?'

'I didn't realise that knowing about seaweed precluded knowing about birds.' I looked over the side again. The water had become darker, which usually meant there was a weed growth down there. 'We must be nearly there. The plants don't grow in really deep water, they're usually fairly close to land. They need the light.' I began digging in my bag for my equipment.

'You know about a lot of things, don't you?' He hadn't moved. Was still standing there, straddling the boat, absorbing the motion with his hips, like a really good horse rider. There was an odd note in his voice and I hoped I wasn't going to have to beat him off with one of the oars that I'd noted lying in the bottom of the boat.

'Well, yes.' And here came imaginary-Claire, chiming in, her voice high with laughter. *Of course you do, darling! You do nothing but read. Read and study. And you know what they say about all work and no play…* She was right. I knew about a lot of things. But I didn't know much about men, clearly. My body had gone onto high alert simply because he was asking me personal questions and I knew that was silly. But I also knew myself. That my tendency to be polite and not make a fuss, always think the best of people, could be my worst enemy. 'Why?'

He turned away to check the instruments. 'I should have just got you to do my family research. You'd have got Great-grandad's middle name, his address and probably his shoe size without all the mucking about I'm doing.'

'You can only work with the information you have,' I said reasonably.

'Yeah, but you'd know where to go to get it.'

The sea was a little bit calmer here, so I released my hold on the seat. 'No, I wouldn't. I know nothing about genealogy. I'd just assume you'd look up census results to find past addresses, death certificates and marriage certificates, maybe check church records if they haven't been digitised.'

Brendon stared at me. 'Are you trying to make me feel stupid?'

Again I could feel myself frowning. 'Why would I do that? And wouldn't it be extraordinarily stupid of *me* to upset a man in whose boat I am currently bobbing, some several tens of feet from the bottom of the sea?'

His face suddenly crinkled into a rather attractive laugh. It made his cheeks lift and his mouth went a very appealing shape, there were even dimples. 'Yeah, sorry. I'm a bit of a drongo at times about stuff like that. Left school without much in the way of qualifications, y'see. Bit prone to getting aggro. Ignore me.'

Cute when he smiles. Sensitive about his lack of education though, keep an eye on that, Leah, some men don't like feeling that a mere woman can be cleverer than them. Claire raised the gin glass to me, toasting clever women everywhere.

'I'm sorry. I spent a lot of time in the library when I was younger, reading up on things.'

There was a momentary silence and when I looked up, away from the light and depth meters I'd got out of the bag and was switching on, Brendon was looking at me, thoughtfully.

'Why would you need to be sorry?' he said. 'Not your fault I spent more time on Aussie Rules football than studying, is it? I wanted to be a pro player, y'see, but I just didn't quite have the… well, all of it. Discipline, dedication. I'd go out on the board rather than train. So I didn't study and I didn't work out, fell down between the cracks of sport and learning.' Another quick smile. 'Told you, bit of a drongo.' The smile slowly faded. 'You don't need to apologise for being intelligent, Leah,' he added, so quietly that the words were almost washed away beneath the slop-slap of the water beneath our hull.

I blinked at him a couple of times and then pulled my wetsuit out of my bag.

* * *

The cold of the water made my breath stop for a moment, even with a swimsuit and a wetsuit on. I had that moment of wondering why the hell I was doing this again; the moment I had almost every time, when the icy waves slapped around my head and the water stretched below me. Then I remembered everything that had gone before and had led up to this, pulled my mask down over my eyes and upended myself into the depths. I had a momentary view of Brendon, suspended above me, and then I was gone, my bags and equipment knocking at my waist and my ears filling with water.

I took my readings, clipped my samples and then just swam for a few moments, enjoying the feeling of water against my face, the sound it made as it bubbled over my wetsuit and the thought of Brendon's face as I'd gone backwards into the sea. But then the cold depths began to get to me and the whole 'Cthulhu' myth didn't seem quite so mythical when there was seaweed wrapping itself around my feet and I couldn't see the bottom.

The surface broke around me as I crested a wave and bobbed up. The boat, *Southern Cross*, was curling and dipping just in front of me, but there was no sign of Brendon. I caught at the side and hauled myself back aboard, trying not to pop any of the sample bags like bubble wrap as I flopped my weight onto the deck. There was still no sign of Brendon, although a knocking noise told me that he was either below deck or there was sentient seaweed driving the boat.

'Hey!' The lightly tanned face rose suddenly in front of me, hair turning blonde at the ends and twisting into unruly shapes under the influence of the sea breeze. 'That was fast.'

'I told you it wouldn't take long.' I pulled off my mask, which was making me talk like someone who lived at the bottom of a bucket. 'I'll need to come back and collect more later. On different tides. So we can check that water quality is consistent.'

'Tea?' He shook a kettle at me. 'There's a little stove in here. I've even brought cake.'

Reasoning that the boat was probably too wet to burn, I nodded, and the head dipped back down again, to be followed by a voice raised in song. At least, it was *probably* song, I thought, there were words in it and a sort of warbled rhythm, although it could have been an expression of displeasure at the stove, or even an outburst of seasickness. I stripped off my wetsuit and put my clothes back over the top of my damp swimsuit. Despite the fact that the noises below deck were continuing, I couldn't be sure that Brendon wouldn't pop back up and catch me in the act of dressing, so I didn't dare strip off. No man had seen me naked since… well, it was a long time ago.

'Is it all right if we get back quickly? Only these need processing before they start to degrade, and Tass has to get them dispatched.' I ducked my head down into the little cabin once I considered that I was decent again and my lifejacket was securely fastened.

'Of course. You don't need to sound so shy about it, if you need to get them back fast, then we'll do that.' Brendan gave me a sideways look. 'It's your job, after all.' He passed me a mug, a greaseproof packet that contained fruitcake, and followed me back up onto the deck.

'Yes. Yes it is,' I said, trying to inject some authority into my voice. My hands were cold and I cupped them round the mug, juggling the cake slice as the boat wallowed, turning against the tide, rising and falling with each wave like a swing.

'You looked like you were enjoying yourself down there?' He was looking away, out over the rippled surface towards the harbour mouth, still plugged up with several of the yachts which looked as though they were all trying to exit at once and engaging in a posh game of shove. 'You enjoy swimming?'

'Yes, I like—' I stopped. It was none of his business that I enjoyed the touch of water against my skin, the weightless feeling like endless possibilities, even the slight, dark fear of the drop below me. 'Yes,' I said again. Then I bent, put my mug and wrapped cake down on the bench and began sorting through the bags of samples, checking for leaks, and putting them into the cool bag I'd brought for the purpose.

'Yeah, me too. Different in Oz though. Have to be careful where you swim, sharks and all.' I looked up now at the tone of his voice. It was wistful, yet held a little note of resentment.

'Not the sharks' fault,' I said, over my plastic bags. 'If someone came into your house and started jumping about, you'd get pretty irritated too, I expect.' Then, because I was concerned that I'd sounded a bit condemnatory, 'But it must be hard not to be able to just get in the sea whenever you like.'

Brendon looked at me for a moment, then twitched his head, casting crumbs of cake around him. 'Got a point there,' he said, half into his tea mug. 'Never thought of it like that before.'

'Humans tend to be arrogant. They forget it isn't their planet, other things were here first.'

'You say that as if you aren't one of us, Leah!' He started to laugh, then put the mug down and came over to where I was standing close to the rail, watching the little village on the hill come closer, listening to the engine working against the tide. 'Is that how you feel? More at home in the sea, not quite the same as all of us on the land – what are you, a mermaid or something?'

His tone was enquiring rather than annoyed and the concerned look in his eyes made mine start to prickle. I wanted so much to explain. To tell him how being clever in a family where even the easy quiz shows on TV were condemned as being 'for posh smartarses' and that having a mind that worked faster and sideways meant that I was permanently out of kilter with everyone else. Tell him that my lack of knowledge of social conventions and niceties meant that people avoided me for being 'weird' and had all left me with the feeling that this wasn't my world, wasn't my planet. That I felt I was always mentally two steps ahead and emotionally three steps behind the rest of the human race. For the first time since I'd met Darric, I wanted someone else to know what it was like to live inside my head.

I'd tried to tell Darric, of course. He hadn't listened. Hadn't cared. If it wasn't happening to him, then it wasn't happening and didn't matter.

I opened my mouth. Something about the endless acres of sea curling behind us and the tight cosiness of the little town glued to the cliffs ahead made everything feel unreal. As if I could say anything and it wouldn't count against me. I turned again to face the miles of open water so I wouldn't have to look at his face. Formed the words to tell him that he was spot on with his assumption that I didn't feel human. 'It…'

Behind me there was a sudden feeling of a weight dropping, a movement of air. Then a strangled scream and a plop, and words being shouted at me from below. 'Cut the engine! Turn her round!'

'What?'

I looked around. Brendon was in the sea, bobbing in the wake of the boat, held up by his lifejacket. Above him, circling, was a seagull. I was pretty sure it was Roger, because it was grinning around a slice of cake and two little black feathers at the back of its head waved in the wind.

'Engine... off! Turn the wheel... Bring her round...' Brendon spluttered.

I bustled over to the controls, which were fairly simple. Despite Brendon's somewhat gurgled instructions, I reasoned that I needed the engine going to turn the boat, so I swung the wheel until the boat half-curved around itself like a horse performing a dressage manoeuvre. Brendon bobbed closer. His lifejacket had a line attached to the boat, I noticed, and then wondered why mine didn't. A moment's reasoning told me that I wasn't driving and didn't need to be attached, plus I'd taken my jacket off to go in the sea. It was sensible for him to be tied on, not a personal affront to me.

Once I'd got the boat more or less alongside, I turned off the engine. There was quite a lot of bobbing, some heavy-duty swearing – some of which was uniquely Australian – and after a few minutes heavy hauling Brendon was back on board and reunited with his tea mug. He stood and dripped.

'What happened?' I asked, reasonably enough I thought. He was staring at me.

'Does that happen a lot to you? People going overboard?' he asked.

I cupped my tea and thought. 'I don't think I generally inspire people to go overboard in any way.'

'Only you handled the boat like it was a normal thing.'

I mentally ran through all the reasons that might be the case. I might be a professional boat driver, if that was a real job, for all he knew. 'It wasn't difficult to work out. And I'd seen you do it.'

He wrung out his shirt, which was stretched and baggy under the weight of water. 'I just meant, you were quick to react. For someone who doesn't really seem to like boats much. You got in close before you cut the engine, most people would try to turn the engine off first. Make sure I didn't get cut to pieces by the prop.' He raised his eyebrows at me. 'Plus I was yelling "turn the engine off", for much the same reason.'

'But how could I get the boat in close enough without the engine?' I began to panic. Despite the fact that he was, obviously, safe and not drowned or cut to pieces, had I done it wrong? *Was* there a wrong way to save someone? 'The tide is going out, wouldn't we just get pulled further away from you? And the engine is at the other end of the boat, you weren't anywhere near it.'

He carried on wringing and looking at me. 'Yeah. But that's not how most people would think.'

'So why were you yelling at me to turn it off?'

'I was confused!' He splashed his hands through his hair, droplets of water rainbowed through the air. 'Besides, if you hadn't been quick, then I really could have got caught in the prop. But you were fast, so – yeah. No worries.' Another hand swipe. 'Balance of my mind was disturbed. It came out of nowhere! One minute I'm tucking in to a big slab of deliciousness, next minute – whoosh.' His hands performed the action of a high-diver.

'What came out of nowhere?' I asked, to make him change the subject. I didn't like the expression on his face, as though he was analysing me. I hadn't even thought of the propeller.

Hadn't considered that I could have been putting him in danger by keeping the engine running. I was only concerned about getting the boat close enough to pick him up. And again I felt that gaping hole between me and other people, heard my mother's shouting 'Why haven't you got any *common sense*!' as clearly as if she'd been floating alongside us. I found my fingers clenching around my equipment bag, as if I was preparing to throw it at the mental image, and forced my hand to uncurl. I didn't want to risk losing my samples, and besides, even had my mother been bobbing alongside us on some form of floatation device, I couldn't really have interrupted a tirade from her with a packet of wet plastic bags full of weed. You couldn't interrupt my mother with a thermonuclear device.

Brendon raised his eyebrows and seemed to give himself a mental shake. 'That… that… *creature*!' He looked up in the sky and ducked his head. 'That bloody bird! It hit me full in the face!' There was no sign of Roger now or any other gulls, except those swooping on the horizon. 'D'you think it's following me?'

'Following the cake, probably.' When I checked where I'd put mine, on the bench beside my mug, it was also gone. So was the wrapping. I counted myself lucky he'd left the tea. And the boat.

Brendon slumped down to the deck as though his legs had been shocked from underneath him. 'I thought England would be easier than this,' he sighed. 'On the map it's just this tiny little blob, y'know? The wildlife is all small and cute, you can drive around it in a day, and the sun doesn't try to boil your blood if you go out without a hat.' He looked up at me, his blonde-ended surfer hair stuck down as though he'd been immersed in glue. 'They never warned me about the birds,' he added sadly.

'To be fair, it's really only Roger. Oh, and the other gulls.'

'That's bad enough!' He sat and dripped dejectedly.

'Most of our other birds are little and cute,' I said kindly. 'Well, not buzzards and kestrels and things, but the others are. And they sing.'

'I thought, take a holiday, get away from all the crappo, find Great-grandad and go home, conquering hero sorta thing. Tell Mum about her family, buy myself a little place out in the bush, take up… I dunno. Cattle ranching or something.' He pushed his hair back. 'And I'm living in a shed, trying to avoid a bird that wants me dead.'

The boat twisted in the water, yawing above the waves which rolled deeply under us. 'To be fair, he just wanted your fruitcake,' I said, trying to bring the conversation back to somewhere I understood. 'Your death would be incidental.'

'That makes me feel so much better.' He looked down sadly at his dripping clothes. 'I'm going to have to change. I can't go to this meeting looking like *The Beast from Forty Thousand Fathoms*. Oh,' he added, turning now to go back to the controls of the boat, 'and thanks for not asking what crappo I'm running away from back in Oz.'

There. There it was again, that disconnect between what I *thought* I was meant to say and what I was *actually saying*. 'Should I have?' I was confused. People didn't usually pick me up on my conversational discrepancies. They usually just talked about them after I'd gone, apparently.

A bit of a grin over his shoulder. 'Nah. You're not interested. That's cool, y'know? I've had an overdose of women trying to drill into my life choices.' The engine caught and he concentrated on checking where we were, squinting at the instruments and then back to the little harbour neatly stacked on the horizon.

I looked at his back view. Square shouldered, with his hair just touching the neck of his T-shirt, filling the shorts nicely and with his long, strong, lightly-tanned legs planted firmly on the boat's decking. *Ah, go on,* imaginary-Claire chuckled at me over her gin and tonic. I could almost smell the mint in the garden, the sliced lemon on the plate in front of us. *He's not bad. You could do worse.* A sip of the gin and another giggle. *I'd give him a go. You're a long time dead, Leah, and I should know.*

'It's not that I'm not interested,' I said carefully. And then, chickening out and back pedalling desperately, 'I mean, I've always thought I'd like to visit Australia. It sounds like an amazing place.'

Another look over his shoulder at me. Another grin. 'Yeah, she's beaut. Very different to here. Where I'm from, we don't do hills much. But go up the Eureka on a clear day and you can practically see the nineteenth century.' And then, when I frowned. 'Tallest building in Melbourne, second tallest in Oz, you can go up to the Skydeck and look out. Bloody amazing.' There was a fleeting expression in his eyes, as though he was mentally gazing out over the city, and a sort of frowning smile on his face. He missed the place, but wasn't sure he was welcome there any more, I thought. Something had happened, something that had sent him half way around the world; the quest to find his great-grandfather was simply a handle to hang the reasons on.

Should I say something? I opened my mouth, but closed it when I realised I didn't know whether he'd want me to acknowledge his expression or whether it would be an intrusion. Or did he *want* me to speak – was this one of those occasions where someone said something that they needed you to pick the subtext out of? The 'saying without saying' that was so prevalent when I'd been growing up, when everyone got indignant when I acted on the words rather than the intent, because I'd been concentrating so hard on listening?

Just go with it. Claire's advice. *Don't worry so much about what people think of you, just do what you feel.* But then, she hadn't had to live with the stares and the headshakes and the avoidances, had she? No. I'd keep quiet. I could pretend I hadn't seen his expression, after all, most of it was obscured by his hanging, dripping hair anyway.

The water beneath us grew bluer, losing the steel-dark colour of depth as we headed nearer to shore, then picked it up again in the channel leading in to the harbour. I kept my eyes on it, focusing on the jump and rock of the boat against the waves and the smack and splash of the hull. There were no sounds of splintering, and no chunks of wood floated past us, so structural integrity seemed to be being maintained, for which I was grateful.

'You don't think it's waiting for us, do you?' Brendon said, guiding the nose of the boat between the guarding walls. 'The gull?'

'It's an opportunist thief, not a serial killer.'

'I've got some more fruitcake. It's in the bag.' He held up a small carrier. 'Do you think they know?' A nervous glance upwards. There were gulls, just a few pottering on the edge of the harbour wall and the rest circling overhead, heads tilted down to keep an eye on the comings and goings of likely comestibles.

The question didn't seem to need an answer, so I just held on to the side of the boat as he steered it in to its mooring and then leaped over on to the pontoon to secure it. No gulls zoomed in, so I presumed he was reassured.

'Had an accident, eh?' A man in a blue smock called over, jocularly from a nearby deck. 'Tricky things, boats!' He inclined his head towards Brendon, who was still dripping slightly. 'Need to learn how to handle them, old boy. Like a woman, y'see. Firm hand on the tiller and all.'

We both ignored him. 'He's wearing pink trousers,' I whispered, as I climbed down onto the pontoon beside Brendon.

'Occupational hazard,' he replied.

'Pink trousers?'

'People telling you how to sail. I've been handling boats since I was four.'

We walked along the pontoon towards where Mr Pink Trousers was standing, on board his huge yacht, all shiny brass and clean ropes. I strongly suspected Staff.

'Here,' I said, on impulse, taking the greaseproof paper bag from Brendon. 'It's a fruitcake, we didn't have time to eat more than a slice.'

'Oh I say, that's very kind of you.'

I held the bag up as I handed it over, and we started a fast walk along the slippery bobbing surface towards the harbour. We'd made it almost to the wall before we heard the scream. 'Don't look back,' I advised. 'Keep walking.'

Brendon was trying not to laugh. 'That was…'

'Unkind? Mean?'

'I was going to say quick thinking.' A glance over his shoulder. 'Yep. They're mobbing him. But he's doing well, he's kept hold of the bag. Oh, now he's running, that's bad.'

But now I'd started to worry. *Had* I been unnecessarily unkind? 'Maybe I should go back and apologise.' I started to turn, my Converse squealing on the wet wood.

Brendon startled me by throwing out an arm to stop me. 'Nah. It was his own fault for hanging around. Everyone knows if you've got food in harbour you need to keep it below decks.'

'Everyone including you?'

He looked slightly ashamed. 'Yes, I guess I was a bit of a drongo, waving a slice of cake around. Maybe it wasn't *all* that bloody bird's fault, me falling overboard.'

We'd reached the harbour wall now and climbed the narrow steps that took us up onto the cobbled walkway, dotted with crab pots and nets in a way that I suspected as being more for the photographers than for the fishermen. The little car park was full of lorries and there were crowds of people hanging over tape barriers near the beach, as though a terrible accident had taken place.

'What's all this about?' Brendon asked a woman who was standing nearby holding an iPad in one hand and with a small scruffy dog sitting on her feet. 'Has something happened?'

'We're filming for a TV series. *Spindrift*. At least, we are if we can get everyone pointing in the same direction – it's like pushing clouds through a sieve trying to get this lot organised.' She gave us a rueful grin, then looked up and started to run across the road. 'Larch! *Larch!* You've got quinoa on your costume!' Brendon and I looked at one another, united for a second in lack of comprehension. The dog joined in.

I bent down and untangled a piece of dried seaweed that had got wound into the messy fur. It didn't, noticeably, improve his appearance. I was usually wary around dogs, they had more unpredictability issues than a student with an all-night revision schedule and a twelve pack of energy drinks, but this one had an air of general downtrodden weariness that made sudden attack look unlikely. He looked at me and, against all probability, shrugged. I ruffled his fur, then wiped my hand down my leg.

'He's sticky.'

'Yeah, looks like he's part floor mop. Well, I'm heading back, the meeting starts at ten and I need to change and you've got samples to offload.' Brendon started walking up the hill. The dog headed off in the direction of the woman and the iPad without a backward glance at me.

I stared at Brendon, who had stopped to wait for me, then at the sample bags in my hand. Then back at Brendon. 'Yes,' I said, slightly feebly. 'Samples. Yes.'

'What's the matter?' He was leaning against the rail that ran down the centre of the road and provided something to hang on to during the precipitous clamber towards the sea. 'You look like you've just had some kind of epiphany.'

In my head, Claire was wiggling her eyebrows at me over her gin. *He remembered your samples. He remembered that you have to get them back sharpish.*

'You remembered my samples,' I said, and my voice was still feeble.

'Well, yeah! You've been going on about them pretty much since I met you, figured they might just feature quite largely in the whole "what am I doing here" scenario, and you don't want to waste the whole of this morning's little expo having them get all brown and shrivelled, do you?' Then he looked at my face, and squinted. 'Why?'

'I've never... I mean, nobody's ever cared about... it's just...' I trailed off. How could I explain? It had always been me, on my own. Thinking about *my* work. Nobody else ever did that – except occasionally in a professional context. No one had ever casually reminded me of something, or talked as though what I was doing mattered. It had shaken me, as had the realisation of it all.

Was my life *really* that isolated?

'But you said you were married?' Brendon started to walk again as I caught up with him, but steadily, matching his pace to mine.

'Yes. I was.' I kept my eyes focused up the hill.

'Did you not, y'know, talk about your research? Have conversations?' He sounded slightly affronted and I wondered why. It had been *me* married to Darric, after all, I wasn't about to propose that *they* got together.

I opened my mouth to explain that conversations weren't what you had with Darric. You said something, and he replied, but his reply usually referenced himself, his own work or whatever was on his mind at the time. 'We didn't so much converse, as have parallel tangents,' I said carefully. 'Darric was... *is*... not a bad man. He didn't treat me badly.'

He just didn't treat you at all, ghost-Claire said inside my head, but they weren't words I could say. They were words I thought, but I couldn't really put into shapes in my mouth, because so much of the way Darric and I had been was just normal for me. I hadn't known, until Claire had sat me down and explained things, that there was any other way to be.

And then there had been that brief experiment in being otherwise. And Lewis.

Memories of what had been didn't sit well against the view from the top of the road, where we climbed into the field and headed on the track towards the house. Those memories had an iron tinge of cold about them, they came frosted at the edges. Here the heat was already building and shimmering against the horizon as though the world felt faint.

'So, what are you doing after this?' Brendon broke the silence that we'd walked in.

'Well, there's your meeting, helping Tass get the sample information logged, emails to answer,' I said, and he grinned.

'I meant long term. After this gig is over. What's the next job?'

Oh, I remembered this. Questions about my future intent, I'd had those at board interviews before. 'I'm looking at writing some papers on the nutritional content of this seaweed,' I said, trying to sound professional although I was puffing a bit after the steep hill, and most interviews hadn't been conducted whilst wearing a wet swimsuit under my clothes. The chafing was distracting.

'And personally?' Brendon wasn't even slightly out of breath. It annoyed me for reasons I couldn't fathom.

'Er. That *is* personally. They won't let you do it by remote control.'

He flicked a quick look at me that I saw out of the corner of my eye, but he didn't say anything else. We walked the rest of the way in silence over the clifftop, but it was a friendly sort of silence. I'd heard of those before – read of 'comfortable silences' between people – but I'd never really had one before. Darric had used any silent time to inwardly plan the next step in his research and couldn't cope with being interrupted, so I'd had to wait for a cue that he was ready to start talking again. That didn't make for comfortable silence, it made for time that felt like an extended sulk.

Somewhere deep inside me, in the part of me that knew there was more to life than the way I'd lived it, I wondered about Brendon. About how he spoke to me as though I was a perfectly normal woman. Maybe even a woman he found it pleasant to be with? And, despite everything, I had a brief moment of daydream, in which Brendon walked through my little house on the hill in Bristol; cooked scrambled egg in my tiny kitchen, and where a tanned leg stuck out from under the duvet in my cool bedroom, and I felt reassuringly normal for a moment.

The driveway to the house came into view, and with it, Tass, who was standing sentry-like on the doorstep. An unfamiliar car was parked at the front, and Tass was scanning the scenery with the slightly desperate air of a farmer whose animals have escaped. My daydream broke as the weight of reality piled onto it.

'Oh thank god you're back!' Tass erupted at me as soon as we were close enough to be erupted at in a tone less than a yell. 'People are here!'

I immediately thought of the research board who were paying for this whole thing, and inwardly started to justify all my expenses, but before I got far along this path, an all-too-familiar figure appeared behind Tass, shuffling from the darkness of the house and pausing when the daylight hit them.

'Ah, there you are, was wondering when you'd be back. You'd better pay the taxi, Lee, he's been waiting for ages.'

It was my mother.

Chapter Five

We sat in the kitchen, in silence. Tass had gone to start sorting the samples and putting them into the tubes to send away to the lab. Brendon had vanished out to his shed, presumably to change. My damp swimsuit was now chafing unmistakeably and one shoulder was beginning to itch.

'So, who's looking after Dylan?' I asked. There was no point asking how she'd found me; my mother had a spy network equal to GCHQ when it came to my comings and goings, which was why it was so surprising she hadn't found out about my impending divorce yet.

'Oh, he's upstairs. Brought his Xbox and he's got it plugged in. He's happy.'

'You brought *Dylan*? *Here*?' I didn't think my brother had seen daylight since 2003, he was probably lying blind and traumatised on the bathroom floor.

'Thought we needed a holiday. Saw you was here, by the sea, thought we'd come and visit. What? You not want your poor mum and brother to have a little holiday, when you've got all this place to yourself?' Mum sniffed and pushed back her velour sleeve. She must have boiled in the taxi here, she was dressed like a cross between an arctic explorer and a three piece suite. 'You wasn't answering my emails.'

'I'm working.' It seemed to cover all bases.

'Well, we won't be no trouble. You got any ice cream? Dylan was saying how he'd like an ice cream, being his summer holiday and all.'

'I think we've got some in here.' I went to the freezer and investigated Tass's delivery. 'There's cones or some of that block ice cream?'

'Just stick some of that in a bowl, love. You can take it up to him shortly.'

I was scooping ice cream into a dish when a commotion at the back door made me look up. Brendon was there, wearing black jeans and a very white shirt.

'Our meeting,' he said. 'You ready?'

I looked from him, capable and smart, to my mother, slouched over the kitchen table. 'I ought…' I said, and I didn't know which one of them I was saying it to.

'Only it starts soon and we might have to hurry.' Brendon was looking at me with one eyebrow raised.

'She's just sorting her brother out with some snacks,' my mother said, complacently. 'Then she can put the kettle on.'

I think it was the complacency that did it. That Brendon was asking me and she was assuming that I would do as she said. And Brendon seemed to listen to me and he wanted my help. She never listened and just took my help for granted.

'I need to go,' I said, and tried to keep the note of apology out of my voice. 'I'm helping Brendon with research. He's looking for his great-grandfather. Brendon, this is my mother, Jackie.'

'But what about Dylan's ice cream?'

Brendon gave her a smile that glittered off his teeth, like a cartoon villain. 'Well, you're here now, aren't you? We've got to run, great-grandad Gabriel Gass waits for nobody. Nice to meet you.' And he half-hustled me out of the dark of the house and into the brilliance of the sunshine.

Again, we didn't speak as we crossed the fields. As we reached the gate that opened onto the road, I said cautiously, 'Are you angry?'

Brendon stopped so suddenly that I was several metres past him before I realised. 'Leah,' he said, and then shook his head. 'Look,' he began again more gently, 'I'm not exactly an expert in family relationships and everything but surely…' he shook his head again. 'No, of course not,' and he seemed to be talking to himself now. 'It's your normal, after all.'

I hadn't a clue what he was talking about, but it made me wary.

Brendon consulted a piece of paper and we went into a small square building half way down the street. It was a single-roomed old school, and seemed to stretch back inside, as though it was tunnelled into the cliff itself. There were posters and pictures on cork boards all over the walls which marked out its change of use to a village hall, but it still had the smell of stale dinners and plimsolls that all schools seem to hang on to.

Three people were sitting on plastic chairs. Two men with faces as slumped and sea-torn as the cliffs and a lady who had reached the 'parchment skin' stage of elderliness. Her chin pointed at us as we came in.

'This the one looking for his granda?' Her voice was gruff and low as though she'd spent her entire life smoking unfiltered roll-ups and inhaling storm-force winds.

'Great-grandfather, yes.' Brendon said, then shook hands with one of the old men, calling him 'Wilfred' – I assumed him to be the member of the local history society that Brendon had been emailing – who introduced him to

'Silas Cooper' and 'Eliza Marsh', the other two in the room. Eliza carried on watching him down the length of her chin. Cataracts, I thought, or obfuscated sight of some kind, and maybe growths in her throat giving her voice that husky tone.

'Ma's family knew yours, back along,' Silas said. He was the older of the two men, a kerchief tied around his neck maybe disguising a recent lack of shaving ability, his cheeks bore little nicks and cuts.

Brendon and Eliza began discussing family. She'd apparently been born in 1931, so was nearly ten years younger than Brendon's great-grandad, but had been born in the village and knew the family.

'Gass, weren't it?' She coughed, heavily. 'They had one o' they cottages that fell into the sea back along.'

'Yes, that was my grandmother's maiden name. My great-grandad was Gabriel Gass.'

'Oh, ah.' Eliza nodded. 'Course, we didn't know him as Gabriel, mind.' She started a wheezy kind of laugh that sounded like perforated bellows being called into action.

Brendon had gone very still. 'But… that's who I've been looking for. Gabriel Gass.'

Eliza was still nodding, and the two old men had started up too now. 'He were christened Gabriel for his granda, but there was a sinking. 'Tis bad luck to have a babby named after someone lost in a sinking when you're a fishin' family. So lad was always known as Henry, after his da.' Nod nod went everyone.

Brendon carried on the conversation while I walked around the hall reading the posters and occasionally interpreting. Eliza had moved to Devon upon her own marriage and, caught up with her own family ('lost two to polio, nasty time'), she'd not been back and had fallen out of contact, so she couldn't tell us much about the Gass family post 1949. It was only because one of her sons (the ineptly bearded Silas) had a daughter who lived nearby and who knew Wilfred through the local history society, that she'd been brought in. 'Not many of us locals left here now,' Eliza said, folding her hands comfortably on her walking stick. 'People only comes here to stay now, not many as comes here to *live*.'

'If anyone does any more quotes that sound like they've been lifted from a horror movie, I'm out of here,' Brendon said quietly to me, as the three old people began discussing how life had been in the village during the war, and my circling the hall had brought me back beside him.

'So, do you have any idea what happened to make my great-grandma move out to Australia?' He gave me a look that said 'apart from the desire to escape Edgar Allen Poe and his hunt for locations'.

There was a moment of quiet. I wondered if the old lady had paused for a drama-building effect, as we listened to the sounds from outside filtering through the open window, children chattering on their way down to the beach, and a snatch of music. Inside the hall it was bleak and dark, the posters on the walls seemed mostly to be about filming of the TV series. Photographs of impossibly attractive people gazing out to sea under the heading EXTRAS WANTED, where it looked like the only extras they needed was, maybe, a good sturdy outdoor coat and, possibly, a shave.

'Who can say?' Eliza muttered eventually. 'There were a lot of comings and goings after the war, what with people lookin' for work all over. Like I said, I lost touch with Steepleton after I married, and my mum died in fifty-one, so if it hadn't been for my son, Silas, here and his girl, Lillian getting' in touch with

Wilfred on that there computer thing, I wouldn't even have known you was looking.'

Brendon slumped beside me and I realised how important this search was to him. Not *just* a reason to come to England – away from whatever it was that made him feel that the whole continent of Australia had become unviable – but a real thing.

'Just thought you'd like to meet someone who knew your family,' Silas grunted. 'Sorry we can't be more help.'

Brendon pulled himself together with a visible effort. 'No, you're good,' he said. 'It'd be great to hear more about them, course it would. I guess I was just hoping that it would all have some happy ending and I could message Mum back in Melbourne and say "Yeah, found your grandad, family tree's all sorted".'

He sounded firmly upbeat, but then, Brendon didn't have the accent for depressed. The upward inflection that made almost everything sound like a question also made his words sound as though they were moving towards a kind of desperate cheerfulness, the accent like bubbles in champagne.

Everyone chatted for a while longer. Eliza told Brendon about her youth, about her memories of his great-grandfather. She told him how they'd all been to school in this little building and spent the time they weren't being educated either fishing with their fathers or keeping the little fishermen's cottages where they lived ('all gone into the sea now, they have') spotlessly clean as their badge of respectability.

''Tis much better now,' Eliza concluded. 'Runnin' water in all the houses and you don't have to take the carpets out for a beating every week.'

I had a sudden flash of Claire, trying to make me feel better about where I'd been brought up. 'At least you had indoor taps, hot water and all that,' she'd said, cutting up oranges for marmalade. 'Could have been worse.'

I'd agreed that, yes, it could have been worse, and hadn't reminded her that we only switched the immersion tank on for half an hour every night and morning because the electricity was too expensive. One hot bath and you were washing plates in cold water until evening. But listening to Eliza made me feel that Claire had had a point. I'd been so busy dwelling on what we didn't have that I'd forgotten that we'd actually not had it quite so badly, compared to previous generations. I just had to learn to compare myself with people a hundred years ago, that was all. And, given that I sometimes felt like a Jane Austen wallflower, that was not that hard.

Brendon was uncharacteristically quiet as we left the hall and walked back to the track across the fields. The road was reflecting the heat from the sun, hanging bronze and unrelenting overhead, but he didn't seem to feel it, even though it was burning through my Converse, the soles of which were slightly tacky against the surface.

'Are you all right?' It seemed like the right question to ask.

'I just…' He stopped and scratched his chin, gazing out over the steep drop that was the village climbing slowly down into the sea like a reluctant paddler. 'I dunno. I feel like I never prepared for this properly. I could have found out that Great-grandad lived under a different name if I'd not gone off like a bucket of petrol on a barbie. Ah, just another example of me not thinking stuff through, I guess. I kind of hoped that she'd have answers for me, y'know? Instead it was like an episode of *When the Boat Comes In*, only with weirder accents.'

'Did you get *When the Boat Comes In* in Australia?' The uncharacteristic lack of a smile and his confusion made me uneasy.

'Netflix,' he said, as though his mind was elsewhere still. 'I mean, I guess I thought… England is like this little tiny country. I'm from Victoria and it's twice the size of Britain, just that one state. So I got this impression that… I mean, Eliza's moved from here to Sidmouth, it's like, what, twenty, thirty kilometres? But she lost all contact with everyone here like it's a different country! You could *walk* across to visit.' He dropped his head forward and floppy hair fell over his face. 'I just wanted…' he tailed off. He sounded defeated.

'There will be other people though, other ways of finding out,' I said, in a voice that sounded so unnaturally cheery that I reminded myself of Claire a little bit.

'Maybe I'll just have to accept that we'll never know,' Brendon was still bent forwards. 'Might just be one of those things. Records get lost, people disappear, all that. Might just go back and tell 'em no dice. Nothing to see here. Great-grandfather just ceased to be. Or, at least, Gabriel did, never even thought we might be looking with the wrong name.'

I felt a snatch of pain in my stomach and had to stop and analyse it. Not hunger, but similar. An incipient emptiness as though I was pre-empting lunch, a hollow feeling. Brendon sighed and then it hit me. *I'd miss him.* I jumped away as though he'd announced typhus.

'Ought to get back,' I said hastily. 'Help Tass with recording. And my mother will need me.'

Brendon's head swung up and towards me. 'What?'

'Well, she's not good at being away from home, in fact I'm amazed that she's actually *here*, I mean, she doesn't leave the flat very often, and she's even brought Dylan which means she's wanting to stay at least a few days. She won't leave him on his own for more than a weekend, like when she sometimes goes to stay with Auntie Jo.' I gabbled.

Brendon's eyebrows made a whole sentence-worth of expressions. Then his mouth joined in and his face ended up looking as though a very high wind had passed, very quickly. 'Dylan? Is that your brother?' he asked, eventually, once his features had settled down a bit.

'Yes. Mum might need a hand with him.'

'Oh.' He seemed to reach a conclusion. 'So he's… yeah, OK, I see.'

'What do you "*see*"?' There had been a tone in his voice, as though a whole load of conclusions had been reached.

'Why your mum needs you there. I mean, yeah, one of my sisters is married to a guy with MS, he needs a fair bit of help sometimes, so, I'm understanding a bit more now, why you are like you are.'

His conclusions were so wrongly drawn that they were practically a caricature, but it was none of his business. And his use of 'why you are like you are' made me want to hit him with a shovel.

'Well, I am very sorry if my personality causes you any difficulties,' I said, stiffly, and with the feeling that I would miss him if he vanished back to Australia developing into the feeling that Australia probably wasn't far enough, and that shooting him into the sun might be a better solution. 'Rest assured that it won't trouble you any further.'

And with my back so rigid and my head held so high that it was surprising that I couldn't see France, I stalked off down the trackway through the fields, back to the house.

* * *

Tass was sitting in the kitchen, stirring something on the stove with one hand and inputting data onto the spreadsheet with the other. Their face had a somewhat fixed expression and the rigid set of someone who's spent time with my mother.

'Sorry,' I panted and sat down at the table. 'Anything I can do?'

Tass looked over their shoulder at me, away from the screen, and a blob of fluorescent something dripped from the stirring spoon. 'Get me earplugs and a new job?'

'Is my mother being—'

'Leah? That you? Oh, thank god, Dylan wants to know how you work the telly in this place. Says there's no signal or summat. And I need you to go down the shop, get me forty Richmond Blue, my nerves is shot to hell with all that travelling.'

My mother wandered in from the front of the house and I looked at her properly. She was still wearing the velour trousers but had taken the top off to reveal a T-shirt with a slogan that had been washed until it peeled off. I felt a pang in my chest. She looked thinner, but not in a good way, more in a 'smokes rather than eats' way, and her hair was receding at the temples. 'Sorry, Mum, I don't know anything about the TV here.'

She shook the kettle. 'What the hell do you lot *do* in the evenings then?'

'Eat dinner, walk, you know.'

The taps made an ominous groaning sound as she turned them on. 'Hope you're not expecting me and Dyl to go walking. You know he has trouble with his feet.'

'Actually, I wasn't expecting you and Dylan at all, Mum,' I said, as mildly and unconfrontationally as I could. 'I'm doing a research project so I haven't got time to show you around or anything.'

My mother sniffed. 'Well, there's this young man, he can take us about, can't he?'

Tass stiffened and another blob of foodstuff fell. To prevent anyone taking offence, I jumped in. 'We're working, Mum, and you shouldn't really be here at all.'

Another sniff. 'Well, if your work is so *important* then...'

I closed my eyes in a long blink. *Don't jump in. Don't justify yourself. You have every right to be annoyed that she's turned up, you don't need to make everything all right.* I tried. I really did, Claire, but she'd got that look, the one that says 'you ungrateful brat, all I ask is a little bit of help from you, now and again'. That look she wouldn't give voice to, because someone else was in the room, but the words were there, hanging like the gulls over the cliff. 'Maybe you can stay and just enjoy the scenery. For a few days.'

I wished I could bite my own lips off, but it was too late now. Too late, and the slow smile that spread over her face told me that she'd known I'd back down. I *always* backed down.

'I'll go and tell Dyl he can unpack then.' She shuffled off, her plastic flip flops clacking against the tiled floor, and Tass let out a long breath.

'You never told me you were descended from House Lannister,' they said, twitching away the stirring spoon. 'She's got me heating this stuff up, and I don't even know what it is! It might not even be legal.'

I looked at the pan. 'It's tomato soup. Dylan's favourite.'

'Are you sure? It looks like house paint.'

'Dylan and a discerning palate are not natural bedfellows,' I said, peering at the spreadsheet. 'Samples all packed up?'

'And picked up. Cute courier on a bike.' Tass turned right around to look at me properly. 'Leah, what are you going to do about your mother? I presume your brother is here too, only I've not seen him yet, just heard thumping about upstairs; it's either

Dylan or she's brought the family poltergeist on holiday. Only, I don't think that we're allowed guests. Or ghosts. Ancestral spirits we can just about accommodate.'

I thought about confronting my mother again. About calling a taxi and piling her and Dyl into it, back to Devizes. Back to the little flat with the debris and the unwashed sheets. 'We'll just give them a couple of days,' I said. 'They won't do any harm.'

A heavy thump from above our heads gave the lie to my words. 'Give us a hand pumping some more water then,' Tass said. 'She's emptied the tank already. They've both had showers.'

'OK. But I need to change first.' My swimsuit had scissored the skin away at the tops of my legs and chafed both shoulders.

Tass hesitated. 'Um. Your stuff is at the top of the stairs. She's taken your room. It had "a decent bathroom", apparently.'

I felt my face drop and that awful duplicity of emotion in my chest. She *couldn't* do that. She couldn't take over my room. But then, on the other hand, she *could* and she *had* and arguing with her just wasn't on the cards so…

I picked up my bags of stuff and moved them to the tiny room at the end of the landing. It was a long way from the house bathroom and had only a pair of single beds, but – well – the place was big enough for all of us, wasn't it? And Mum was right, she hadn't had a holiday for ages. And the weather was far too glorious to spend in a town. And she and Dylan could do with some sea air and…

…and I wished I could stand up to her. Wished I didn't want her to approve of my life choices so badly. Wished she could see that I wasn't some 'jumped-up little tart, too big for my breeches' but was making the best use of the brain that I'd been given by her and whichever random stranger was my father.

And then I hated myself for thinking that, because I knew she hadn't had an easy time of life.

My inner eye could see Claire's rueful grin, and the grin reminded me of Lewis, and *that* reminded me that I hadn't checked my emails today.

'Oh, you're back.' Tass had given up the stirring and was using both hands on the keyboard, filling in little squares on the spreadsheet meticulously. 'Thought you might have been out of the window and away. Look, I know she's your mother, but…' they tailed off and performed a mime that indicated either they thought my mother was a witch or that they had run into a glue wall.

'Just a few days,' I repeated myself.

'Well, OK, but any longer and we might enter a "her or me" situation.'

I looked at Tass as I opened my laptop. They'd always been so relaxed in situations that had made my stomach close up, so laid back that they'd been only two degrees off horizontal. The thought that the appearance of my mother and brother could have unsettled them to that degree was horrifying.

'You, every time,' I said, and opened my mail.

Yes. There it was. That mail from the unknown address, with the heading WELL DONE. And I wondered, what had I done? I remembered the last email and the abortive attempt at cow cuddling which had left one of my best shirts draped over the neighbour's hawthorn.

'Hey, Leah.
Well done. I mean, I know you won't think you tried, but you did, you really did. You thought about what I said last time. You actually achieved something.

I know it's hard for you. Harder than for most people, and that's not your fault. But I know you are capable of so much more than you let yourself be; baby steps and you can become so much more of the person you are meant to be. So here's another challenge for you. I want you to tell someone a secret. Something they don't know, obviously. It'll be hard for you, but sometimes just getting things out into the open can be a good thing.
X'

It was, as ever unsigned.

'But… but I *didn't*…' I flipped back to the previous mail. '…*find an animal… And I want you to stroke it.*' Then I stared at my hand, as if it was personally responsible for my lack of animal finding, and a gradual image came to mind of a small, grubby little dog with slightly sticky fur that I'd ruffled and then regretted. I *had*. I only bloody had, and somehow the sender of the email knew it.

I leaped up and ran to the window, staring suspiciously up and down over the bare field and then narrowing my eyes accusingly at the Jersey cows, grazing blamelessly over the hedge.

'Nope,' Tass said. 'Even the peeping Toms don't hang around here for long. This place is like a cross between the Bates Motel and the Overlook.' Then, and more slowly, '*Psycho* and *The Shining*, Ms "still thinks *Blue Peter* and *The Young Ones* are current TV schedule favourites".'

My brain was being battered by my internal monologue. Lewis? He was the only person who would do anything like this! He was the only person who might care enough about my getting over Claire's death, but that would mean… no. Surely that was the point, he *wouldn't* care enough. What had passed between me and him was nothing. Just a thin thing, a slice out of real time when things were so bad that it felt as though the air was too thick to breath.

'You OK?' Tass asked, carefully. 'I didn't mean it, y'know. I'd not leave you here on your own, even if your mother takes up permanent residence. I might blow the place up, mind you, but I'd watch the ruins smoulder with you.'

'Er, thanks,' I said vaguely. 'No, I'm fine, I'm just… thinking.' *All this would imply that Lewis was here. Somewhere. Watching. He'd seen me with the dog. Here. Watching.* The skin on the back of my neck prickled.

There was a noise at the door which made me look up. A long, lean shape arrived in the doorway and stood cautiously just outside the kitchen.

'I can't make the telly work,' a plaintive voice said.

'I told Mum, I've got no idea how it works, or if it does at all,' I replied, half distracted by my screen and the implications it contained.

'Well, this is a bit of a dump then, isn't it?' The shape came into the room.

'Bloody effing hell,' Tass leaped off their chair.

'Oh, yes, Tass, this is Dylan. Dylan, this is Tass, my research assistant.'

I always forgot. Every time, I forgot about Dylan. He was just my brother. Just the noise in the attic, the catalyst for the procession of similarly pale blokes who occasionally came by to raid the fridge, make incomprehensible gaming jokes or hold all-night gaming marathons scattered around the tiny flat. The dropper of dirty plates and socks. Just Dylan.

'*You're* Dylan?' Tass's voice sounded a bit shaky. 'But I thought…' the sentence ended there.

Dylan shrugged. 'I guess,' he said.

Dylan. Six feet of – so people who met him said – physical perfection. I couldn't see it, of course. All I saw was a bloke. Claire, after fanning herself, told me he was gorgeous. *Big brown eyes, floppy hair, a chest like Brad Pitt and an arse like… you're his sister it would be very very wrong for me to tell you what your brother's arse reminds me of. Just take it from me, Leah, your brother ought to be on the covers of those books your mum reads and hides under the sofa cushions. Ripped shirt, low waistband… don't suppose you could persuade him to get a tattoo, could you?*

I sometimes forgot he was a real person too. Presumably as affected by our upbringing as I was, but we never spoke about it. We hadn't really talked much at all since I went off to university, almost as though Mum had annexed him like a foreign country she didn't quite trust.

'What's that?' Dylan had slouched his way over to Tass, peering over their shoulder at the spreadsheet.

'I'm inputting the data from Leah's sampling trip,' Tass said, somewhat faintly. In a couple of seconds they would be fanning themselves like the eighteenth-century heroine I sometimes imagined myself to be.

Dylan jerked his head. 'Right.' His long hair fell over his shoulder and I wondered when he'd last had a haircut. When I'd taken him, I suspected. 'You missed off a zero.'

'What?' Tass's voice was still faint, struggling to escape from Dylan's gorgeousness-aura probably.

A nail tapped the screen. 'There. Zero missing. Unless you've got a tenfold increase in just that area.' Into the stunned silence, Dylan grinned. 'Gamer. You don't play Dead By Daylight to professional level unless you can do attention to detail.'

And suddenly my brother – my younger brother who I'd used to force to come to the park with me so he wouldn't get rickets, the boy who'd been the source of the annoying noise, series of smells and dirty clothing since he'd stopped being the cute baby I could read to – was a man. An actual person that I didn't know at all.

'Um, Dyl…' I'd been about to warn him off, Tass didn't like being interrupted when they were working. And I needed that data sent off as soon as possible, it needed to be with the samples as soon as they were tested. But Tass wasn't showing the usual signs of irritation; rather, they were moving aside to let Dylan have a better look at the spreadsheet, and explaining what we were doing. Dylan showed every sign of being interested too, which made my brain hurt. Dylan hadn't been interested in anything to do with me since I'd won the Achievement Prize at school and his mates had tied him to a tree with their PE shirts. I *think* it had been done in an affectionate way, but with our school you could never really be sure. It was the only place I'd ever been where setting someone's hair alight was a fun way of making friends. Apparently.

At least going over the spreadsheet had distracted Dylan from his plaintive questioning about the TV. I left him and Tass and went outside.

Where I found Brendon being held at bay by Roger.

'Can you, I dunno, lure it away, or something?' he said, his voice a hoarse whisper. 'Throw it a sardine. Or a small car.' He kept his eyes fixed on Roger, who had him cornered against the wall of the little outbuilding, webbed feet paddling against the cobbles and a focused yellow stare firmly on Brendon's shins. 'Or some dynamite.'

'Just flap your arms at him,' I suggested. At the sound of my voice, Roger turned round.

'I don't want him to think I'm making fun of him,' Brendon said, weakly. 'Or trying to fly away.'

Suddenly it was suddenly all too much. Something in Brendon's apologetic tone dug through me and released a load of feelings about my mother and Dylan, the emails, even imaginary Claire. My eyes began to prickle and my throat became a hollow tube that seemed to stretch all the way to my heart.

'Leah?' Brendon took a tentative step forward, trying to sidle round Roger. 'Are you all right?'

'It's just…' I covered my face with my hands. 'No.'

This didn't happen to me. I kept my emotions for those moments when I was alone. No use letting them out in front of my mother, who'd just ask me what the hell I thought I had to cry about. I didn't have her life, *my* life was charmed and all parties and glitz and money. Crying in front of Darric had been pointless, he'd just leave the room 'until I felt better'. Nobody had ever tried to comfort me. I'd not cried in front of Claire. I'd been trained out of it by the time I met her – trained into crying silent tears into the pillow in the spare room while I'd been married, and the occasional burst of tears alone in my house. No point in crying. No point.

'Hey.' A warm hand on my shoulder. 'Hey. Is there something you need to talk about?'

I uncovered my face. Brendon was standing in front of me, looking concerned in a surfer way. Next to him, only lower down, Roger had his head on one side and had stopped paddling. Brendon had clearly suspended his terror and Roger had moved his focus of attention. They were united in a little duo of pity.

'I can't,' I said, sniffing.

'Look, let's go in here.' Brendon opened the padlock to the outhouse. 'Mainly to sit more comfortably but also to get away from the seagull. Actually, *mostly* to get away from the gull. To be honest, if he turns round too quickly I might shriek like a girlie.'

I gave a snotty, tear-ridden kind of chuckle.

We went into the shed, and Brendon leaned against the wall. 'OK,' he said. 'You can tell me as much as you like. Edited highlights or the whole bloody lot, I'm good either way. What's bothering you so much?'

Another snotty laugh. I wiped my eyes against my wrists. 'How long have you got?' I asked, a bit shakily.

'Given that this is the first real sign of human emotion I've seen from you and I was beginning to wonder if you were some kind of really realistic robot, I'm gonna say, you've got as long as you need.' He leaned back more comfortably and folded his arms, then unfolded them and put his hands in his pockets.

'You don't need to worry about body language,' I said, delighted to have something else to centre my thoughts on, somewhere else to send them.

'You got that, huh?' He jerked his head. 'Then you should be able to tell that I'm a sympathetic ear, and it kinda looks as though that's what's missing. That,' he carried on as an afterthought, 'and some indication that you're actually *not* a realistic robot with added tear-function.'

I took a deep breath. Outside in the yard, Roger took off, I saw him swing up past the tiny window, wings beating furiously as though he bore the air some personal grudge

'Sorry,' Brendon went on. 'About the robot thing. I know you're not. Obviously you're not.'

I let the breath out again. The tears had stopped now, only the fact that my nose was running kept my hands over my face, that and wanting to keep my expression hidden as much as I could.

'No,' I said, my voice strained through my fingers. 'I'm not on the spectrum, I am, to all intents and purposes, neurotypical, is that what you wanted me to say?' No need for him to know about the tests I'd put myself through as a confused adult. The 'inconclusive' results.

Brendon took a step away from the wall and a gentle hand encased my wrist. He tugged one hand until it came a few centimetres away and he could see my eyes. 'No,' he said. 'I mean, it's nothing to be ashamed of, either way. What I want you to say is what made you cry.'

Inside my head vast lists clicked into place. *So many reasons. So many. But most of them emotional, nothing he can do anything about. So, the practical reasons: My mother turning up and taking my room as though she was owed it, the strange emails, my best shirt being stuck on a hedge...*

'My shoulders are sore. My swimsuit rubbed.' I said. No point in telling him anything else. My emotions were mine, carefully guarded. Not his to poke around in.

Brendon let go of my wrist and my hand swung down. 'Will it help if I ask direct questions?'

I shrugged.

'How do you feel about your mother?'

And that was all I needed. As though he'd managed to lever open a little crack that let the side of me I refused to acknowledge burst out; I started to talk. About my upbringing, how we'd had so little that my mother and I had slept in our living room while Dylan had the crawl space in the roof. How I'd not fitted in at school – unable to keep my cleverness hidden, always accused of 'showing off'. How I'd married Darric because his brand of aloof control had been the form of affection I was used to and how Claire... how Claire had gradually shown me that I processed things differently to most people. And then Lewis...

'Lewis?' Brendon handed me another tissue. We were sitting on the floor by now, cushioned from the bare earth by some straw and his sleeping bag.

'He – he was the first man who...' I tailed off. 'He made me laugh,' I said at last. 'He showed me that I really liked to be hugged, that I was allowed to talk about myself without someone telling me to shut up. He made me feel...' I rubbed my hands up my arms. It was cold in here, and the sun had dipped away from the windows. 'He made me feel normal.'

My heart was beating really fast now. Was it the thought of Lewis, his long, lean body and the way it made me feel when I realised what sex – what *love* was really meant to be like? The memory of his soft voice, his ribald laugh, his clever jokes? Or the thought of what came next?

'So, you and Lewis,' Brendon was talking slowly now. As though, I thought, he was picking each word carefully out of his vocabulary and hand-crafting it to fit the situation. 'You broke up because...?'

My heart went faster. Adrenaline was making my mouth dry and the tips of my fingers so cold that I had to warm them against my neck. 'We didn't break up, he dumped me. We'd got together for the wrong reasons, you see. He was right, we would never have worked.' I finally looked Brendon in the eye properly, hoping it would help me gauge his reaction. 'Lewis was just a big mistake. Darric was a big mistake. I don't trust myself in relationships, they make me feel stupid.'

And I walked out of that shed with my head held high. Well, not very high, in case Roger was about and might aim for my scalp. But fairly high.

Chapter Six

I spent the rest of the week avoiding everyone.

It wasn't hard to do. I'd had a lifetime of learning how to avoid people after all, from hiding up the apple tree in the little orchard at school to leaving university halls as soon as lectures were finished rather than hanging round in the coffee bar like everyone else. As a child I'd learned that the library was the place I was least likely to be found, so almost every school holiday had been spent in there, avoiding my mother, or at the park with Dylan, avoiding everyone else.

Here in Dorset, the place to go seemed to be inland. The beach drew everyone to it like it drew the sunshine, a bright band around the coast. Walk just a couple of miles in the opposite direction, and there were valleys where the night seemed to outstay its welcome in thick shadow. I knew Brendon looked for me – Tass told me that he hung about the house or took *Southern Cross* up and down the coastline trying to find me. But Tass had known me a long time, knew my occasional need for complete solitude, and never asked questions. I'd got my phone, if I needed anyone I would call, and Tass knew that, eventually, I would have walked off my emotional overload and I'd be back, 'sorting us all out'.

Inland, Dorset was like a different world. Wide chalk hills, deep sudden valleys. Old villages where the Domesday Book felt like it was written yesterday and thatched cottages with low roofs sat like whitewashed tortoises under the heat of the sun. I walked and walked, ordered my thoughts. Not thinking about Lewis was a lot easier than thinking about him, so I thought about my samples, about the potential for seaweed as nutrition; about the repairs to the roof of my house in Bristol. About good, solid, practical things that had definite answers and didn't fall under the nebulous heading of 'emotions'.

Lewis had taught me to offload. That a problem shared truly was a problem that wasn't really halved, but was certainly reduced to some form of fractions that were manageable. With someone else's input, problems felt less like climbing a steep, rocky slope and more like humping a load up a small hill. And now there was nobody to offload to again, and so I drove it all inwards and climbed those mountains alone.

Grasshoppers sang in the long grass as I stood beside a river, staring into its depths.

'I hope you're not going to jump in there.' The voice came from behind me and made me do the kind of jump that tries to look as though it's known the other person was there all the time and is just a little startled that they've chosen now to speak.

And, of course, the accent told me who it was, so I responded in a light tone, 'No, I'm wondering if the varying light levels are affecting the quality of the weed and thereby the type of fish in here.'

'Working. Well, of course, that's beaut.' His tone went a bit flat. 'I was worried about you. I've been trying to catch you about the place but you've been up and out before even the seagulls are up.' There was a pause, into which I knew I was supposed to speak, but since everything he'd said was true there was nothing to say. 'I was worried,' he said again.

The grasshoppers buzzed. The river glooped as a fish jumped for the low-hanging mayflies. Nobody had ever said they were worried about me before and I had no idea how I was supposed to react. 'I'm sorry,' I said. 'I need to process things.'

'No. I get that.' More silence. His shadow was alongside me now, he must be standing just behind my right shoulder. 'Your brother has been helping Tass out with some data inputting y'know. He's a fast learner.'

The surprise made me turn round suddenly, the little cloud of midges that had been accompanying me on my walk and which I'd come to think of as really annoying and itchy friends, were temporarily left behind. '*Dylan?*'

'Unless you've got a load of other brothers stashed away somewhere, I think that's a logical assumption.'

Brendon was wearing a bright red T-shirt and turquoise shorts and, in consequence, looking like an overdramatic sunset. His hair was even more streaked with blonde and he'd got David Beckham brand stubble. In this oddly liminal place he seemed very solid. More real than most people. And the accent lent him an added groundedness, almost as though it was impossible to be ethereal and Australian.

I stared at him, but wasn't really staring at *him*, I was staring at my inner vision of my brother doing anything useful for anyone else at all. 'But *Dylan*... I mean, how?'

'Dunno. But something about those games he plays has given him an eye for the kind of input detail that Tass needs. And the pair of them sit around talking about—' he waved an arm '—what I can only assume comes under the heading of "pop culture". No idea, it's all streaming bits of music and laughing, far as I can tell. Guess I'm about ten years too old to crack that code.'

My mind was boggling so hard it had practically driven me into the river. Dylan. Who'd basically shown no interest in anything else since he'd discovered YouTube, apart from games and his pale, stretched friends. And now he was showing an aptitude for data and detail? Where the hell had *that* been during GCSE year?

'And your mother has discovered how to work the TV, so we've sat her down in front of *Loose Women*, which seems to be on a near-perpetual loop, so there's that.' His words were flat, held no trace of anything, but I immediately jumped to justify his non-existent accusation.

'I should have talked to her – she can't stay, getting in the way and annoying everyone. Has she been sending you all out for cigarettes? I told her she can't smoke in the house. They ought to go back to Devizes.'

Brendon raised his eyebrows. They too were bleached from the sun but showed against his tanned skin and brown eyes. 'You're not responsible for her, Leah.'

'She… she can't always cope,' I said, slightly feebly.

'She's doing a pretty fair job, I'd say. I've talked to her, a bit. She's been asking about me looking for Great-grandad, but she's also got some pretty stringent views on kaftans and *Guardian* headlines; OK, maybe I went in a bit soon after a *Loose Women* curveball. And we talked about you.'

I had an odd feeling, a mixture of protectiveness and irritation towards my mother. 'And what did she say?' My eyes wandered off him and his tanned Australianness, back onto the trees that dipped their branches in the water with every wind shiver that passed.

'Your mother has some very – err… strange ideas.' Brendon sounded as though he was picking his way through a minefield of epithets. 'A few headline acts were gender roles, class, the ineptitude of men, conspiracy theories and a general overarching dislike of the world. Was she always like this?'

'I didn't know her when she was young,' I pointed out reasonably.

Brendon sighed. It was something I'd got used to, people sighing when I was logical. 'I just meant…'

Something about the peaceful tranquillity of the location, with its buzzing grasshoppers, fairy-folk flight of midges, the smell of damp ground and cool water made me irrationally angry.

'Of course I know what you meant,' I snapped. 'I'm already three conversational steps ahead! Do you have any idea what it's like being me? Like my brain is dragging my body through life while everyone else is living properly? Like I never *quite* get the chance to stop and catch up and find out the things other people already know, because my mind has to go at a million miles an hour and it *won't shut up*!'

I turned my back on him and my eyes towards the thin silver line that was the little brook edging its way down the steep chalk hill to join the clattering river at my feet. Sharp, bright water joining slower, darker water, merging and seamlessly becoming one single flow. Why wasn't my life more like that? Why couldn't I merge with the world like that?

He was suddenly a lot closer behind me. A hand came slowly forward, into my line of vision, flat, palm up, as though he was approaching a nervous horse. 'Boiled sweet?'

'What?' I was completely derailed.

'Would you like one of these boiled sweetie things? Never seen 'em before. Bought them in the little shop down in the village. Thought they looked bonza.' He moved around so that he was in front of me, hand still outstretched. A small wrapped sweet was carefully centred on it.

Never had the wind been so successfully taken from my sails. Usually I did the defusing. Any rising of my temper had to be bitten back or people got confused. Lewis had said— no. Never mind what Lewis had said. Not relevant.

'Thank you.' I took the sweet.

'Yeah, you have a great selection of sweets over here. Much better than Oz,' Brendon continued, pulling the paper further down from the tube to help himself. 'We don't do so well in the confectionary line. Seafood? Now, *that* we've got by the bucket load.'

A shadow fell over us. A sudden, onrushing shadow, like a missile approaching, a violent sweep of wings, a gleam of yellow eye and beak and then Brendon was yelling and clutching his hand. 'That bloody bird! It took my sweeties! Leah, that bird took my sweeties!'

I turned my face upward to see Roger, beak propped open with the packet of sweets, flapping away. If a bird with webbed feet could ever have been said to be holding up two fingers, then that's what he was doing.

'Is it following me?' Brendon was flapping his hands over his head now. 'It must be following me! How else could it have known? I mean, what do they do, sit on top of a cliff somewhere with binoculars?'

'I think he might be following *me* actually.' As I said it I wondered if it sounded boastful, as if I was showing off, and rushed in with, 'I've been feeding him back at the house, whenever I see him about, and he's been finishing off my sandwiches while I've been…' I didn't know how to finish that sentence. 'So I think he sees me and expects food.'

'Aw, great. So if I want to be anywhere near you, I have to expect the B-52 of birds to be hanging around as well? Cos that's just not fair!'

'Do you?' I asked, rather indistinctly, around the sweet.

'Do I what?'

'Want to be anywhere near me.' I shifted the sweet to the other cheek. It was bigger than it had looked and made talking difficult.

'Yeah, I do, actually.' He flicked a quick look at my face and then I saw his eyes go wandering off to follow the tiny insects which fluttered just above the grass. 'I do, Leah. I'd really like the chance to get to know you better. Properly, I mean. I guess I already know quite a lot about you after you – well, after the other day, but I'd like to, I dunno… Walk, talk, the kind of stuff people do when they hang out together.'

'But I—'

'Yeah, I heard what you said. Bad relationship choices in the past, bad breakup, all that kinda stuff. But I reckon, well, that's not just *you*. That's life. Those people who made great choices first off the bat, well, they're all paired up now and cosy – and good on 'em. The rest of us, well, we're all still wandering around out here on the loose and all. Doesn't mean we can't find someone next go around, does it? It's not like, screw up once or twice and that's it, you're out of the dating pool forever.' He was still staring at the insects, or maybe just trying not to look at me. 'We're allowed more goes, Leah. Until we get it right.'

'But what if we're so rubbish at making choices we won't ever get it right?' I was pretending to watch the insects too, but in reality I was watching him out of the corner of my eye.

'I dunno. Guess if it's self-destructive then we have to learn from our mistakes.' A sudden beaming smile and his eyes positively flashed mischief. 'So what d'you reckon? See how it goes? If it's a mistake, well – part ways, no hard feelings.'

I shifted the sweet again. 'But why?'

He shrugged. 'You're clever, you're funny, you're pretty – not that being pretty matters a damn, but it's just another pointer. You seem to make a good friend. I…' a touch of vulnerability crept into his voice and his eyes stayed very firmly fixed on a bunch of dandelions which had flowered and were now exploding into seeds across the field. 'Yeah, guess I could do with a friend,' he finished.

I had that 'out of the loop' feeling again. I had been so focused on wondering why he could possibly want anything to do with me, making it so much about me that I hadn't considered him. That he was a man a long way from home, from a support network of friends and family, trying to get information about his relative. That maybe it actually *was* more about him than me. *Why* did it take me so long to realise these things?

'Well, you're not so bad yourself, I suppose,' I said. 'Plus, you have to keep me onside because of Roger.'

'Roger?' Brendon frowned.

'The seagull.'

'Oh, yeah, cos you do such a great job of controlling him, don't you?' But Brendon was smiling. A proper smile, which meant he didn't really mind too much that Roger seemed to follow me around. Probably.

Stop trying to second guess people, Leah. Take what they say at face value if you think you should. There's no mystery to it, no magic formula. Easy for Claire to say from behind her fruit-loaded Pimms, sitting all relaxed in her kitchen. Telling me how to be, when reading people's intentions came naturally to her. To me, it did feel like a kind of magic, a spell that most people were given in childhood; one I'd never learned but had to pretend to be able to cast.

'I don't mean to be—' How could I sum it up? How could I explain that I didn't mean to be offhand, that I would love to have a relationship. That my diffidence in the face of his confession that he liked me as a woman wasn't me being disinterested, but not knowing what to say. 'People sometimes think I'm a bit odd.'

Brendon opened his mouth, closed it, then opened it again. I thought he was thinking deeply, until I heard the crunch and realised he was just chewing up his sweet. 'Nah,' he said at last, 'you're good. Although, if I had to say anything – and I'd be reaching a bit either way – I'd say… your hair is a funny colour.'

It's a joke. Yes, Claire, I know it's a joke. I can read that much from him. I didn't laugh.

'Mmm.' Brendon had swallowed his sweet. 'OK. First principles, you're intelligent, you'll have gone through the basics already.'

I sat down hard on the grass. 'I've done tests and assessments. I'm an introvert, but I don't appear to be on the autistic spectrum, from what they can gather. I've a lot in common with very high-functioning subjects, but I don't fit all the profiles.' I put my head down onto my drawn up knees. 'So why don't I feel as if I belong on this planet? *Why* can't I…?' I let that one trail off. He'd already heard about my disastrous experience with Lewis, I didn't want him to think I was completely dysfunctional.

To my surprise, Brendon sat next to me. The grass sent up a little puff of pollen and the smell of crushed wildflowers as he landed. 'OK, let's unpack this. You clearly aren't wacko.'

I gave a mirthless grin. '"Wacko" is a prejudicial term.'

'Nah. It's an Aussie term. Covers everything from rocking in a locked ward to running outside without your sunnies on.' He reached out a hand towards me as though he was going to put his arm around my shoulder, then I saw his face wrinkle in thought and the hand withdrew. 'Have you thought that you might have been damaged?'

'Dropped on my head when I was a baby, you mean?'

He pulled a stem of grass and put it between his teeth. 'I've met your mum. Sorry for saying this, but I think dropping on your head would have been the least of your worries.'

There was a sudden flash of colour from the river, a slice into the refracting surface, as though the day was collapsing, a piece at a time, into the water. 'Kingfisher,' I said. 'Look.'

Brendon didn't turn away from me. 'So you *have* thought about it,' he said. 'Ah yes, course you would, you're bright.'

That feeling in my chest again. Obligation, guilt, duty, love… *was it love*? Or just habituation? But then, what did I know about love, really? Maybe this was what it always felt like, as though I'd swallowed something far too hot and it had got as far as the top of my chest before the burning registered. Fear. Fear of doing the wrong thing, of being chastised for something that I didn't understand. And always that overarching sensation that this was my family and all I really had.

Claire had raised it too. *Your mum never took you out when you were little? What, never? No playgroups or outings or days to the park?*

'My mum had me when she was fifteen,' I said, as calmly as I could. 'She'd been in care since she was seven, in and out of foster homes and her parents never stayed in touch with her. She ran away from a children's home when she found out she was pregnant, managed to get a flat. How, I don't know but I can guess. A tiny, tiny place, with one room that was kitchen and living room, we had a bathroom in one corner, highly illegal. She didn't know what the hell she was doing – stuck in there with a baby she didn't know how to look after. But she did it. She fed me and clothed me and – well, here I am.'

He removed the grass stem from his mouth and looked at its shredded end. 'That must have been hard,' he said, his voice so neutral that it practically faded into the background.

'For her. I didn't know any different. Then Dyl came along.'

'The way you talked about him, I thought he was about fourteen!'

'He's thirty-two. Two years younger than me. Mum was seventeen. I remember when he was a baby and she seemed…'

I didn't want the memories. Not on this bright day that smelled of warm grass, with the song of the river in the background and the strobing dart of the kingfisher. The memories were dark and smelled of old nappies and sticky, sullen air behind closed curtains. The hot, damp weight of a baby in my arms as I tried to feed him mushed up bread as leaking wetness trickled down my leg.

'I think she was depressed, probably post-natal depression with a little bit of reactive depression mixed in – because of the circumstances. Reading between the lines – and those lines are as widely spaced as a Spot the Dog learn-to-read book – I don't think she ever knew how to look after herself, let alone children. I think she fell between the cracks and Dylan and I are the casualties.'

He blew a long breath. 'Well, none of that is going to be got over with fluffy blankets and a hug.'

'No. In fact, six years of therapy has taught me it's never going to be got over. All I can do is try to limit the damage.'

Silence. The sun's heat was like a physical weight, pushing down on us, on the grass, the insects. The only thing that seemed unaffected was the gravity-defying flight of that little blue bird, slicing the air between the river bank and the water.

'It also means,' I said, very, very quietly, 'that I will never have children. I will never trust myself to know how to love them. So, my mother… she took that away from me too.'

That was the crux of it. The real heart of what I held against her, the little kernel that lay beneath my conflicted feelings for my upbringing – the hatred of the fact that it all meant that I would never know how to parent my own child. A decision I'd made long, long ago. I would not let this drag down another generation.

Brendon stood up so suddenly that I found myself staring upwards, expecting Roger to have come wheeling back through the air for another go at whatever food we might have. 'Come on.'

Various possibilities flashed through my mind, but I couldn't pick out which one he might be going for. Did he plan to confront my mother? Rescue Dylan? Neither of these would work, couldn't he see? My mother knew no different and neither did Dyl. Taking them away from their world, the world they knew and understood, would be catastrophic. 'We can't.'

'What? There's a café just over the hill there. I think you need a good cup of coffee but, as Melbourne is a really long flight away we'll just have to settle for a cup of what you Brits think of as coffee. All right?'

'I suppose…'

'Look. I'm doing the deciding for a minute, OK? Just switch to motor functions only and let me take you for a coffee.' A sudden beaming grin made his eyes wrinkle up and gave him dimples. 'One way or another I'm going to get you to have a drink with me. I'll settle for coffee, if that's as good as it gets.' A hand came out. 'Come on, I'll give you a tug.'

This time I didn't interrogate his word choices. I let him pull me up and then walked at his side to the coffee shop.

Chapter Seven

There was another email in the inbox. I could see its heading there, bold and inviting me to open it. 'Hello again, Leah!' With its exclamation mark all unnecessary and making me think of Lewis with its upright pointiness and overemphasis.

It had to be Lewis. I had the uncomfortable realisation that, at first, I'd hoped it was him, and now I hoped it wasn't. *You know what you are, Leah?* Memory-Claire had her feet up on the table, and her chair tipped back. *You're fickle. Is it fickle I mean? Or is fickle that thing you put in burgers? No, that's pickles, course it is…* The chemo had, she'd said, given her a memory like an empty book and a brain that felt as though it had gone solid. And I'd tried to be there for her as much as she'd let me, but she had gone into a little bit of a huddle after her diagnosis. Natural, really, she wanted the comfort of her family and they had had to come to terms with the idea of losing her. So she'd become a bit distant and I'd tried not to mind. Got on with life, with my projects. Thought about getting a cat to have some company around the house, but reasoned it wouldn't be sensible so close to a main road. I had cleaned and polished, and then gone over to my mum's place and cleaned and polished there too. Fairly pointlessly, of course, the carpets were so worn that they had shiny patches and Dylan wouldn't let me up into his room from where a disturbingly earthy smell was coming. He was either smoking illicit substances or keeping a ferret – I wasn't sure which I'd prefer. But I did my best.

No, not fickle. What do I mean? The other thing… Imaginary-Claire waved a hand and screwed up her eyes. She'd done that a lot towards the end, when it became increasingly apparent that the treatments weren't working. The doctors kept trying – all credit to them – but we'd known… and she'd felt the failings, both bodily and mentally. Sometimes it seemed to frustrate her, and at other times we'd laugh until we cried at her 'brain farts'. *Staid. That's the one. Set in your ways. Older than you really are. I mean, come on, Leah, I've got nearly twenty years on you plus this bastard disease, and I'm still getting out there more than you! Live a little! In fact, no… live a lot!* And then that dreadful, steady calm would come over her, and her voice would go very quiet. *It can all change so quickly, and then it's gone.*

So what Lewis and I had done had made sense, really. And now, here he was.

'So, you're doing well. Well for you, anyway. You're starting to realise that animals aren't all out to get you, and that you can talk to other people – tell them things. Doesn't have to be your deepest secrets, does it?'

With a sudden heat that seemed to simultaneously flood up from my ankles and down from my forehead I remembered my earlier talk with Brendon. How his eyes had darkened with concern when I'd told him the real truth about my upbringing. About how my mother's lack of parenting meant my decision had been easier. That was pretty much as big a secret as they came. *But how did the email writer know?*

'So, anyway. You're taking those tiny steps towards recovering. Reaching outside yourself a bit more, being a bit less insular.'

I had a horrible, ominous feeling that if I scrolled down a bit further I was going to find that this email was asking me to strip in public, or cover myself in sequins and head to Rio. I had a tiny flash of myself wearing a leotard and a carnival mask, dancing in a crowd, and had to breath very carefully for a while until the vision faded. Was this Lewis's way of working up to proposing something? Deciding that now he wanted me, that we could be together?

And then I thought of the uncomplicated way Brendon had told me he liked me and wanted to get to know me better, and shook my head. OK, maybe Lewis was doing this for my own good. I could pretend to believe that, until I worked out how I *really* felt about him.

'So, you've pushed it a bit. Petted an animal when you've never really liked them. You've told someone a secret and the world hasn't ended. Now I want you to go that step further. Put yourself out there on the edge of adrenaline. Really feel life, like, grab it with both hands, feel what it could be like to lose it.

I want you to do something dangerous. Not life-threatening dangerous. That would be stupid, and, besides, I think that would be the point at which you'd slam shut your laptop and have done with my stupidity, so no free-climbing, no bareback riding. Just – well... I leave it up to you. But I want you to feel what it's like to have that freedom that comes from thinking "Yeah, it could all have gone horribly wrong, but it didn't and I have achieved something". And no, diving for seaweed doesn't count as dangerous. It's tricky, but, sharks or really bad-tempered crabs excepted, it's not life threatening.

Go. Do. There's a lot of life out there, Leah. And you're a long time dead.'

I slammed the laptop shut anyway, but carefully because I didn't want to crack the screen. I didn't somehow think that was what the email meant by 'do something dangerous' and besides, the university had provided me with the equipment.

Lewis. It had to be. He'd always said that our seeing one another was 'a little bit dangerous'. So was this his way of telling me he was coming looking for me again? That he'd rethought the awful way he'd told me we could never be a couple?

I leaned my elbows on the closed case, put my chin in my hands, and closed my eyes. If I listened hard I could hear the sounds of life going on in the house, where Tass was sitting out my latest emotional moment by streaming YouTube videos and cooking increasingly advanced meals. Brendon had gone back down into the town to poke about in some old school records for any mention of his great-grandad and my mother and brother were... actually, I wasn't quite sure what they were doing. Dylan had recently been sighted taking some photos of the cows, so he might have gone down the cliff. For some reason, being out of doors had brought out the artist in him, which was better than his inner vampire coming out and turning to dust, so I was humouring his desire to fill his phone or the Cloud with very close-up pictures of aspects of Dorset. Besides, it kept him away from our mother, who was stomping – inasmuch as one could stomp in either slippers or trainers – slightly sulkily around indoors, with no one paying her much attention. It was a little like having a visible poltergeist.

'Dinner's ready!' Tass appeared at the back door with a tea towel wrapped around their waist, doing their best Nigella impersonation. 'Leah?'

I took a last look out across the field. The cows had wandered off in a crowd to the far end of the field, where I could now see they were staring at Dylan. He had his phone out and was leaning over the hedge to frame what looked like artsy shots.

'I'm coming.' It crossed my mind to shout out to Dyl about the electric fence, but then I thought about Brendon's words and the wisdom behind them. He was right, of course he was. Dylan was no longer my baby brother, he was a grown man. All six foot of him. He wasn't the five-year-old that I perpetually saw when I looked at him, grubby knees, begging me to play with him, read to him, take him to the park, as though I was the mother and our mother was a dust shadow.

I had an uncomfortable feeling in my middle now, watching Dyl lean closer to the velvet-faced cows. Grownup Dylan didn't need me. He might *want* me around, much like our mother did – someone who knew how to programme the washing machine so everything didn't come out grey and who washed up straight after meals rather than six weeks later. But that wasn't *me*. It wasn't Leah that he wanted, it was anyone who could read an instruction booklet and didn't want botulism. Whereas Brendon… well…

'Ow! Bloody hell!' Dylan leapt away from the hedge and the cows leapt away the other side. They all eyed each other, from a slightly suspicious distance. Dylan made his way over to the house, rubbing his chest ruefully.

'What the hell was that?' he asked.

'Electric fence.' I couldn't help a small grin. First-person shooter games clearly were not much of a preparation for agricultural attacks.

'Should be bloody illegal,' Dylan muttered. 'It's like having your nipple pierced by some backstreet bloke— Er. I assume,' he added, folding his arms over his chest in the face of my piercing-level stare.

'Dinner's ready,' I said, echoing words I'd been saying to him for nearly thirty years, although given Tass's desire to be more Nigella than Nigella, it was doubtful that tonight's dinner would be a boiled egg and broccoli, which had, for a long time, been all I could cook.

'Yeah,' Tass said and flicked the tea towel. I didn't miss their whisper of '*Have* you got any piercings?' as Dylan went past them into the kitchen either, but I carefully made a lot of noise packing up my laptop to cover the reply.

Chapter Eight

A few days passed under the beaten bronze sun. Apart from the occasional coffee in the house I didn't see much of Brendon; instead his absence was made up for by my mother's thumping from distant rooms and Dylan and Tass whispering in corners. I found myself hanging out of windows, trying to catch a glimpse of him, almost as though I was trying to reassure myself that he still existed. My brain had just about got around the idea of a man who might be interested in me enough to express said interest, and I wanted to see how this panned out. But he was a bit elusive. I often caught a view of his back, bag hoisted high on his shoulders, as he hiked off towards, presumably, the village and his boat.

I'd also kept half an eye out for Lewis. There was no sign of him, for which I was thankful.

Today the empty sample bottles sat on the table in quiet reproach. Tass sat beside them, a lot noisier. 'We need another collection of weed.'

'Sssh. I'm sure most of Steepleton already thinks we're running a drugs operation up here,' I gave the pump one last jiggle. 'OK, Dyl, I think that'll do for today, tank seems to be full.'

'Be a great place for it though,' Dylan stepped back from the pump. 'You could cook meth up here and no one would ever notice.'

'And you'd know, how?' I gave him my best 'older sister' scowl.

'Nah. Just teasin'.' But he turned away so I couldn't see his face. 'You learn a lot from gaming,' he said, unconvincingly.

'Apparently so.' I sounded exactly like our mother now. In tone, if not word choice.

'I asked Brendon if he'd take you out collecting this morning,' Tass said. There was a slight grin on their face, and I wondered whether that was in response to my interaction with Dylan or to the thought of matchmaking Brendon and I. If it turned out to be the latter, words would be had.

There was a tap at the window and we all turned round.

'Your bird is back,' Tass said laconically.

Dylan looked, and then smiled a smile I didn't think I'd ever seen on his face before. A soft, besotted sort of smile, the kind of expression that I'd expect from someone looking at a basket of sleeping kittens, or a puppy with its head cocked appealingly. It was not an expression that sat comfortably on the face of a man with three days' growth of beard and hair like a lead guitarist. 'That bird likes me,' he said. 'Give him a sandwich.'

'Of course he likes you if you give him sandwiches,' I said, but I opened the window and passed out some toast crusts. Roger cocked his head and looked at me with one eye, so I gave him some bits of ham that had been in the fridge. When he gulped those down and eyeballed me again, I got stern. 'Don't milk it. You're a seagull, not a lost poodle.'

Roger 'meeped' and climbed into the air with a down-thrust of wing and a moment later Brendon appeared at the back door, hands protectively folded over his head. 'That bloody bird.'

'He likes me,' Dylan repeated.

'He likes the fact that you feed him. Got any coffee? Tass said you'd be wanting to go out on the boat today, are you ready to go, Leah?'

I'd been standing back, half in the pantry, as he came in. I wasn't totally sure how to approach him, feeling suddenly quite shy. After all, he'd said he wanted to get to know me better and had then ignored me for almost a week, which even I thought was odd.

'I wasn't sure…' I tailed off. Brendon was looking at me with an expression I couldn't read, but that wasn't surprising really. There was a directness in his eyes that showed the businessman that lived inside the surfer-dude exterior. It was almost a calculating look. I wasn't sure how to take it. Again, that wasn't surprising. 'Er, yes. I'll be ready in a couple of minutes.'

I went upstairs to my tiny room, put my swimsuit on under my clothes, picked up my bag of equipment and was about to head downstairs, when my mother poked her head from around the door to my previous, much larger and en-suite, bedroom.

'You going out, Lee?'

Irritation rose up. It was an unaccustomed feeling, at least, not a totally unknown one but one which I usually filtered through a mesh of 'It's how she is'.

'Yes, Mum, I have to work.'

More of her became visible. She was still wearing the track suit she'd been in yesterday. Maybe she'd slept in it. 'Ah, so you're going down the village then.' No mention of me working. She'd not mentioned my degree since I graduated. When I'd invited her to the graduation ceremony she'd looked at me as though I'd invited her to dance around the bonfire naked with my other witch friends.

'Well, yes.'

'That's great, only I need some more fags. You knows what I have.' And the door closed firmly as she went back to whatever she did in there. Sleeping mostly, I thought. The puff of stale air that hit me in the face as the door shut, told me that, whatever she was doing, she had all the windows firmly closed. It must be like a sweat lodge in there. But then, she didn't like fresh air much, she always said she was agoraphobic, although I suspected she had originally thought that meant 'afraid of farmers'. It hadn't stopped her getting here, had it?

I walked downstairs slowly, to a different world. Tass and Dylan were half joking about the seagull with a kind of camaraderie that gave me another weird jolt. Dylan could do what I couldn't. He could step between those worlds with the ease of a seasoned traveller. He'd always been able to do it. At school he had fitted in with a bunch of rebellious like-minded boys. After school there had been the gamers; those who found their clique in bedrooms and basements everywhere. They'd met and bonded and played and coalesced. I'd never had that. Too clever to fit in with the girls around make up and TV, not clever enough to hide it, I'd mixed mainly with the teachers. Spent my days in solitary classrooms, reading and studying and then coming home to sort out the chaos and try to soothe my mother through another day. Dylan hadn't been expected to lift a finger in the house. He was a boy, after all.

I stopped for a second in the hallway, wondering again about my mother's upbringing. What had led her to believe that the life we'd lived had been the best way to go about things? What had *her* upbringing been like? Foster homes, children's homes, I knew that much, but nothing about before that. She'd been taken from her parents at seven and either didn't remember, or couldn't talk about that life. Things must have been bad, and stayed so bad that getting pregnant at fourteen was a step up and out. Another little burst of something went off in my heart. I couldn't understand, I'd *never* understand, but I could appreciate that the ill-equipped teenager that she'd been had done her best. It was a poor, undereducated best, where asking for help was like admitting defeat in a 'them against us' situation. But she'd tried.

'Hey, you ready?' Brendon was loitering on the step, sun spilling in past him as though it came from another world.

'Yes.' I picked up the sample kit from the table.

Tass broke off from talking to Dylan and looked at my face. 'You all right? You look a bit weird. Probably shouldn't go on a boat if you feel a bit weird.'

'We'll take it steady. Got to go now to catch the tide.' Brendon held the door open for me. There was something about him today. Something – *something* – had changed between us, an almost static charge of expectation loaded the molecules of the air. I swung my bag up onto my back, trying for casual, but our eyes met and he knew I knew. It disarmed me so much that my bag swung round and hit me in the jaw.

'Keep an eye on Mum,' I said to Dylan.

He raised his eyebrows. It gave him a *Pirates of the Caribbean* Johnny Depp kind of look. 'Why, has something happened?'

How did I explain the new insights? That now I was beginning to realise just how fragile our mother was. I couldn't. Dylan couldn't see what I could. He'd had a different experience of growing up, even though our upbringing had superficially been the same.

I shook my head. 'She's run out of cigarettes. Things might get a bit tetchy.'

'Oh, 'kay.' And, showing no signs of intellectual curiosity at all, he turned back to Tass and they began discussing the relative merits of various computer systems. At least, I think that's what they were talking about, they might have been quoting alpha numeric passwords for all the sense it made to me.

Brendon was still holding the door. The light was still coming in from outside and I congratulated it silently for being such a good metaphor, although I went off it a bit when I stepped into the yard and the heat and blinding brilliance hit me. It was as though Dorset was a massively overexposed photograph today, with the sun bleaching all details and blurring all the shadows.

The cows were in their field, but they seemed restless. There was a lot of low-key mooing and some stamping going on, a bit of headbutting and generally more movement and fidgeting that I was used to from my milk.

'Wind is getting up,' Brendon said, 'it's making them a bit drongo. Probably the flies getting antsy.'

I looked up at the blazing blue sky. 'Really?'

'Yeah. Air's changing. Can't you feel it?'

Maybe that was it. Maybe it wasn't something between Brendon and me that was different. Maybe it was just a static charge, a lowering of pressure and a storm front. I felt… yes, cheated. And then the realisation hit me that I'd *wanted* change. I'd *wanted* something different. I wanted the fact that I'd told him about my past, about the way my life had swung on that loose hinge like a badly made gate, to have altered the relationship such as it was. *I wanted us to talk.* And that was a rarity. Darric hadn't done discussion. His personality had just kind of sucked me in to his way of doing things – no chat. No cooperation, no collaboration. He was the 'me' in 'team' and I'd just been the crosspole that fronted things. The 'ta', if you will. He did him, and allowed other people to stand by and watch. I wanted Brendon to be different.

'No, I can't feel anything,' I said, and I could hear the note of sulk in my voice.

We walked the track and then down through the field at the top of the cliff. Today the gulls were screaming, making Brendon look nervously around as we walked.

'Where's that nutter bird friend of yours?'

I looked into the mass of birds wheeling just off the cliff. 'I can't see him. Those are just ordinary gulls.'

'That's like saying they're just ordinary psychopaths.' Brendon hunched himself further under his rucksack. 'They'll only kill you a little bit.'

'You haven't got any food, you're safe.' I almost smiled, but bit it back. Nothing had changed.

'There's a picnic in my bag. Thought we'd take the boat round to this little cove,' he pointed. 'Over that way. Have some lunch after your dive. And I think they know.' Another glance upward. 'They can read my mind. Or the shop names on the bags.'

'Now you're paranoid,' I did smile now. He was obviously trying to make me laugh, it wouldn't hurt to let him see I was falling for it.

'Or, maybe they really *are* out to get me.'

The gulls broke formation, a couple scooped the air over us and craned their necks to look. Little yellow eyes strafed us, and then the birds dived back down over the cliff edge, clearly satisfied that we weren't about to break out the pasties.

'It's only food that they attack for. And, apparently, when they're nesting.'

Brendon gave another nervous glance skywards, as though anticipating a vengeful god. 'And when's nesting season?'

'I think it's over. Probably.'

He increased his pace and we crossed the clifftop at speed, the sun-baked grass crunchy under our rushing feet. The sun was making everything sharp. Plants were abrupt, pointed, brown

147

stalks. The straps of my bag dug into me and even our shadows had delineated edges. The only soft thing was the tarmac of the road, which was bubbling and erupting as we got out onto the hill, sticky streams of it like chewing gum under my feet.

Happy people were heading down to the beach, families laughing, children running with their sandals making a sucking sound against the melting surface. Family days out. Holidays in the sun. As children, we were kept in, curtains closed against the daylight that reflected off the TV screen. I read, Dylan played games, she watched the TV – we all fell into worlds we felt more comfortable with.

'You OK? You just, sort of, stopped.' Brendon touched my arm and again, that feel of flesh against my bare shoulder made me jump, as though my skin had become oversensitised.

'I was just thinking. Remembering.' I looked around at the children, all tanned limbs and messy hair. There was suddenly a pressure behind my eyes as I thought about the childhood I'd been cheated out of.

'Life, eh?'

When I had fought back the urge for tears and looked up, Brendon was watching me.

'It's like Facebook,' he said. 'Other people, only showing their best bits.' A wry smile. 'But there's all the rest of it to look forward to. Come on, we don't want to miss the tide!'

We half ran down to the harbour and along the pontoon to the *Southern Cross* which was bumping and swinging at anchor like a nervous horse too tightly tied. I clambered aboard and we were off, chugging out between the walls and into the choppy blue of the sea beyond. I watched the comforting arm of the harbour wall recede, felt the boat start to move above the waves, and wondered if life was going to continue to throw these rather obvious metaphors at me until I got tired of noticing them.

The sun on the sea was like metal as I slipped over the rail and into the water. The first few centimetres were warm, then the chill of the Channel began to bite and I hurried my collection of weed and water samples. I took my light readings, bagged up the fronds, noticing with annoyance the metaphorical way that they stopped their free dance and became lifeless and slimy as soon as they were cut. Brendon helped me back on board and poured me tea from a flask as I pulled my wetsuit off and dressed over my damp swimsuit.

'That's the cove I told you about.' He pointed to a dimple in the coast. 'Picnic?'

And yes, I wanted to prolong being with him. Brendon made me feel… something. He didn't treat me like a business partner or a vague annoyance, he behaved as though I was a sentient being with a secret inner life, and I now realised that was what had been so entrancing about Lewis. That acknowledgement of me as having ideas, thoughts and beliefs that he wanted to get to know and understand. Maybe Lewis wasn't really so different. Maybe this was how relationships were supposed to be?

But thinking of the word 'relationship' in the same frame as Brendon made me shiver. He was a carefree Australian and I was neither of those things. From here, looking at the way the wind was ruffling his hair and his confident hand steering the boat, it felt ridiculously flimsy as a premise for romance.

The boat swung into the waves and we bobbed along the coast for a while. The cliffs that slithered towards the sea were green and overgrown, bays of stretched sand separating them into headlands and backdrops against which people were lying, playing and walking. We sailed past the next bay, a tiny beach with only a few people, then the next, which was a long sandy expanse with a little beach hut café serving outdoor tables teeming with customers. Then on, along further, rounding a kind of promontory, and into the shelter of an almost circular cove, the entrance so narrow that it blocked out the sunlight and made the water look black.

The sand was a tiny sun-streaked smear between the water and the high face of the cliff, and Brendon brought the boat in to within a few metres, then gave me a grin. 'We have to swim for the shore.'

'With a picnic? Won't the sandwiches get all soggy?' I frowned down into the dark depths beneath the hull.

'You, Leah, are way too practical. I, on the other hand, have romance in my soul and Tupperware in my bag. Come on.' And he plunged over the side, setting out towards the beach with a workmanlike crawl stroke that stirred the water into blue life.

I sighed, took the clothes off that I'd put on over my swimsuit, and followed. The water was chilly and deep, but a short swim took me out onto the sunbaked beach, where I found Brendon flopped on the sand and opening his back pack to reveal tiny, sealed, plastic boxes of food.

Without another word he peeled back the lids, spreading the dishes on the sea-flattened sand in front of him, and then stretching out his legs luxuriously and tipping back his head. 'Help yourself. There's olives and nuts and… not sure what those things are, but they look good, and I've got some wine and orange juice somewhere.'

I looked at him. His hair was dripping down the back of his T-shirt, and he was coated in sand, like a breadcrumbed fish. There was something in his relaxed attitude, his not-caring about getting sand over everything, that made me smile.

As though he felt my smile, he opened one eye and something happened deep inside me. I tried to analyse it, some kind of hormonal surge or other endocrinological activity, maybe something to do with being plunged into cold water after the heat of the day? It made my fingers tingle. My skin puckered and drew into points and a wide heaviness slithered in my belly and along my thighs. When I found myself looking at his T-shirted chest, I recognised the sensations and felt a little bit embarrassed. But I also had a moment of feeling proud of myself and I heard that echo of Claire's voice again. It threw me back to another sunny afternoon; another time, another place. *You're an attractive woman, Leah. Love, sex, it's not meant to be like it is with Darric, you know. It's not meant to be quick and practical and 'Let's not make a mess and we have to jump straight out of bed afterwards'. It's meant to be close and warm, it's meant to make you feel wanted and loved. There's supposed to be cuddling and laughing...* and the way she'd looked across the garden at her husband, working at his desk in the summerhouse—

No. I wouldn't think of that now.

'Leah?' He got up and came to stand beside me. 'Hey? Anything wrong?'

The little cove was a silent bowl. The waves barely moved in its shelter, just a very gentle swish against the bright sand, like the cows' tails flicking away the flies.

'No.' I said. 'Nothing.' This was on me. Not to be said.

'Well. Let's eat then. I've packed enough for an army.' A gentle hand on my shoulder, warm and sandy like the rest of him. 'And you should eat.'

'I've just realised I didn't love Lewis,' I blurted the words to the rock face behind us. 'That he... lovebombed me until I thought I loved him and then he... but that wasn't him trying really hard, or being in love with me, it was the basic minimum for an ordinary relationship! I don't think I was the only woman he'd done it to, he was too... well, too *practised* if you see what I mean. But I was an easy target.' I spun round, caught Brendon staring at me. 'He didn't exactly pull out any stops for me, I'm realising that now. Does that make me stupid, Brendon?'

He was clearly caught unawares. He must have seen the look on my face when I'd started to feel the tingle of arousal and thought... what had he thought? That I was about to fling myself on him? *Why can't I read people? Why am I so inept that I can't even get a glimpse inside their thoughts?* I thought. If only I could tell whether he was expecting me to strip or to sob.

'Er,' he said, sinking down, grabbing a Tupperware box and slowly pulling the lid free. 'I think it makes you human, Leah.' He held out the olives. 'But we all make mistakes. We all do stupid things. You've kind of plotted your life carefully, a bit like a robot now I come to think of it and maybe I shouldn't have said it but, yeah. You've tried to be like a robot.'

'Because that's how I *feel!*' I took an olive, but I didn't put it in my mouth. Instead, I squeezed it between my finger and thumb. 'I don't know how it's all supposed to go, all that messy love business. I've read about it and, god knows, it comes up on every other TV programme, even the ones you think will be interesting and about algebraic integers or space exploration. It's all numbers and science and then – WHAM – there's a couple snogging and groping one another in corners!'

Brendon looked at me over the olive tub. 'Well, that's one way of describing "falling in love",' he said dryly. 'They put romance in these things because people can relate to it.'

'Well, *I* can't.' Squishsquish went the olive.

'I don't think they make the programmes just for you.'

I bristled at his assumption of my solipsism, but then he grinned and I realised he was teasing me. Teasing. Me. Only people who really liked me teased me. Like Claire. Another piece of the jigsaw of how I felt about him slotted into place. 'I'm stuck like this, Brendon. This is *me*. I don't want to be like this, so… so literal and clueless, but it's who I am.'

Brendan stood up. He reached out, very gently, and took the mutilated olive from between my fingers.

'Leah. There is nothing wrong with who you are.' And then, to forestall my incipient words, 'I mean, yes, obviously, your upbringing has broken something in you, some connection, something that the rest of us have been trained to recognise from birth, so your interpersonal skills are a bit… well, *off*, but that's not *you*.' He stepped in a little closer. 'It's not who you are in *here*, is it?' He lightly tapped my forehead. 'It's just the way the world sees you.' Another half-step. 'It's the you that you really are, underneath, that I like. And, just in case you haven't read the cues, I'd like to kiss you right now but if you don't want to, that's perfectly OK.'

I looked into his tanned face. His hair was trailing across the dark blonde stubble that ran over his cheeks like extra-large grains of the sand that ornamented the rest of him. Eyes that were, now I came to look properly, the colour of the deepest dark of the sea. Lips that were… that were…

I stepped in, surprising myself. Held myself aloof, just for that first second, while my brain caught up with the heat that ran through my body, and then let the whole thing, mind and body, fuse into one long, silver wire that ran through the core of me as his kiss set off little reactions all the way down to the pit of my stomach.

He tasted of olives. Of the sea. And there was a gentle firmness in his lips that told me he meant this to be more than a simple kiss. When he stepped away, I was panting.

'Leah,' he said, and his voice was a little bit broken. 'Leah.'

'But you're Australian!' What I *meant* to say was 'But you will want to go back thousands of miles away, how can I form an attachment to someone whose life is so different from mine?'

'What?' Brendon looked puzzled.

'Aren't we too different? Won't you… want to go home to your normal life?'

'Even us Aussies can have deep emotions, y'know. And Oz is great, best country in the world and all that, but…' an inclination of the head. 'I've done everything I set out to do at home. There's other places. And you're here, so…' He held out a hand. I wasn't sure if he was indicating something or if he wanted me to take it, so I just stared at it, until he gave a wave that took in this little bay, and I was glad I hadn't embarrassed myself. 'I know you think you're too damaged to be in a relationship, and what happened with Lewis broke you just a little bit more. But I really, really like you, I'd like to help you – and I'm not saying that in an "I want to baby you through a relationship", I really do want to see you… well, blossom, I suppose. Although, for the record, the person you are right now is just fine for me.'

The sun was burning my shoulders. I could feel its sting. Something that was so necessary for life, so beautiful, that appeared so benign, and it could hurt so badly.

'The world is being metaphorical for me, again,' I said, in lieu of any kind of answer for him.

'Does "the world" have anything to say on the subject of you and me?'

I gazed out at the relentless glare, at the little white-tipped waves running in, carelessly, up onto the sand. 'No,' I said sadly. 'I wish it did. Not even a clue. A clue would be nice.'

'You and Lewis,' Brendon said, carefully. 'You managed fine with that relationship.'

'No, I didn't. I thought it was love. I thought we were *both* in love. I didn't realise he was just using me.'

'Maybe he wasn't. Maybe he really liked you and – oh, I dunno. Maybe he changed, maybe he—' he caught a glimpse of my face. 'Or was there more to it than that?'

Could I do it? Could I *really* say it aloud? But I had to, didn't I?

I whispered an apology to memory-Claire. 'He was my best friend's husband, Brendon. Lewis was married to Claire, and we didn't even have the decency to wait until she was dead.'

I could hear how ragged the words were, as though my breath was catching on them as they came out. The boat spun in a little whirlpool, its bows dipping and rolling. I kept my eyes on it as it spun around its rope, out there, hanging over the deep silence.

'Oh,' Brendon said.

I had to tell him now. 'When she was ill, she sort of shut me out for a while. She and Lewis went on holidays and kind of went into a little domestic huddle. And I felt…'

I stopped. Brendon was looking at me now with an expression that I couldn't even begin to fathom. His eyes were different – narrow – and the hand on the Tupperware bowl looked blueish about the knuckles. 'What did you feel, Leah?' His voice had gone different too, a bit lower, as though it was fighting its way up his throat past an obstruction.

'I felt … *lonely*. Claire was pretty much all I had. She made me feel— oh, never mind. She behaved more like my mum than my mum did, she told me I could be whatever I wanted, that what I felt and how I behaved wasn't *wrong*, it was just who I was and that the right people would see me for who I really was and…' I tailed off. 'Anyway. When she went into the hospice, Lewis…' Now I really did stop talking.

'He moved in on you.' Brendon was practically growling now.

'Look, it wasn't all on him, all right? I knew he was married, I *knew*...' my voice broke. How could I ever sum it up? 'I know I don't read people well, and I know it can leave me open to – well, being taken advantage of. But Lewis... It was the first time I really felt that I could be *emotional*. A lot of the emotion was related to Claire, to both of us facing up to losing her, rather than to *us* though. We didn't really talk about us, we just...' I felt a slow heat rise in my cheeks. 'I was jealous. I just wanted a little tiny bit of what she and he had. What everyone else seems to have.'

'OK, OK.' Brendon rubbed his hand over his face. 'I get it. You were both trying to cram in as much life as possible, coming to terms with the fact that it could be gone so easily.'

'And it gave me something else to feel guilty about. I mean, I'd already got the guilt of leaving home, running off to university instead of staying to help my mum.' Despite the heat, goosepimples bunched the skin on my forearms.

'Yeah, most people leave home, Leah. Otherwise, by now, the whole human race would be living in one really, really huge house. Like an episode of *Big Brother*. It's natural to grow up and leave.'

'That's not what she said. She told me that I should stay at home to help with Dylan.'

Brendon sighed deeply. 'Oh Leah. Your life has been a real shitshow, hasn't it? Help with Dylan doing what, exactly? He seems to be functioning just fine. Better than you, in a lot of ways. So why did she want to keep you from going to university, do you think? I mean, honestly.'

I thought back. Back to my late teens, to my mother's dismissal of my excellent results, of the envelopes of university offers plopping onto the mat. Her shrugs if I asked which I should choose. The way she took to her bed and told me that it was making her ill, trying to think how she would manage if I went away to university. How would she manage Dylan? Who would make his lunches and his dinner and give him money for the games he played with his coterie of similarly etiolated friends? How would she pay the bills without the income from my part-time job? Oh, it all made her feel sick, I had to stop talking about it…

'Leah?' Brendon's voice was gentle. He flopped down onto the sand.

'She was – is – jealous that I escaped. I think she would have been delighted if I'd got pregnant at nineteen and had to come home to raise my baby as part of her household.' I thought of my mother being a grandmother, and shivered. 'She's afraid of life. She wanted me to stay at home, to prove that there *is* something to be scared of.' I sat down beside him.

Brendon was eating the olives. Something about the way he was chewing luxuriously made me hungry and, almost without thinking, I dipped my hand into the tub.

'There's crisps too,' he said, and nudged another tub towards me. A momentary cloud obscured the sun, soothed the sting from my shoulders and I was grateful.

'Are you angry?' I asked at last.

He gave a laugh that was odd in its lack of humour. 'No Leah,' he said. 'I'm not. Well, I kinda am, but not with you. I'm angry at your life, at how much you've been taken advantage of, just because you can't see what people are doing to you and you're too bloody nice to tell them all to fuck off.'

I gave a small smile. 'Those words are not totally alien to my vocabulary.'

'But you never used them on the people you should have, though, did you? OK, I can see it would be hard for you with your mum, she's brought you up to be her little maid. But Lewis? I thought he was some kind of – I dunno – great love. A missed opportunity. Now I find that he was just some bloke taking an easy opportunity for a shag. The bastard,' he added, almost as an afterthought.

'Like I said. I knew what I was doing. I knew he was Claire's husband, it wasn't all his fault.'

'But he knew *you*! Knew you'd have no defence against that type of lechy creep! You were desperate for affection, for someone to talk to and he walked right in and… if I weren't a committed pacifist I'd punch him on the nose.'

'And are you? A committed pacifist, I mean, not a lechy creep, I know you aren't one of those. Unless you keep your creepy tendencies very well hidden, which is rather ruled out by those shorts you are wearing and – oh god, I'm going to have to stop talking now.' Something about the relief of having come clean about Lewis and me was making me talk too much, which was having the effect of bringing my sheer social awkwardness to the fore.

'Well, yes. I am a pacifist. Which kinda puts me a bit at odds with the common view of your regular Aussie bloke, doesn't it?' There was a note in his voice when he said this. Just an undertone of something. I knew I should be able to tell what it was, but I couldn't, and it felt wrong somehow to have to ask. As though I was prying. 'Tell me,' Brendon said. 'I can see you thinking, but I'd like you to tell me what's going through your head.'

I crunched a crisp and tried not to laugh salt and vinegar crumbs into his eagerness. 'I'm trying to get my head around the idea of someone liking me enough to want any kind of relationship. I'm wondering about how I can ever overcome my upbringing enough to have a normal life. I'm worrying about Dylan and my mother. I'm a little bit worried about my samples making it back with their integrity intact. I'm wondering what flavour these crisps are meant to be and quietly having nightmares about what the funding people are going to say if we don't come up with the right results from these samples.'

Brendon widened his eyes. 'All that? Right now?'

'Yes. I told you, my brain doesn't function like most people's. I'm a bit multitrack.'

He started to laugh and the sound echoed around the little cove. At the far reaches it degraded until it sounded like a seal barking, and that thought made me laugh a little too. 'There is nothing wrong with you, Leah,' he said, shaking his head so that his wet hair scattered drops of seawater onto his shoulders. 'Maybe there are things wrong with the way the world sees you, but – you? You are damn near perfect.'

The look he gave me made me oddly hungry and also a bit hot, which was strange because the sun had gone in behind cloud now. I looked up into the sky.

'I think we might have another metaphor coming our way,' I said. 'Look.'

A bank of dark cloud had gathered on the horizon and was chasing towards us on a breeze that made the anchored *Southern Cross* dip and bow. The waves reaching the beach were still small, but out of the mouth of the bay I could see the rising tips of white horses breaking and curling.

'Yeah,' Brendon said lazily. 'It's just some wind coming up. They reckoned we might get a bit of a blow. It's a way off yet though, but we'd better head back.'

'Yes, I have to get the samples back,' I said. That tight rein of duty was pulling in my chest. 'And fetch my mum her cigarettes.'

'Samples have kept this far,' Brendon began gathering up the food and putting it back into his bag.

'But they're degrading all the time and—'

His hand reached out and touched my wrist. 'Leah. There isn't exactly a shortage of weed in the sea. If those samples are too bad to use, well, we go back and get more.' A quick grin flashed over his face. 'Can't we?' The grin faded. 'You don't need to catastrophise.'

'Is that what I'm doing?'

'More like constantly firefighting your way through life. Dylan and your mum, they're adults. Not your responsibility.'

I gave him quite a hard stare. 'You don't just overcome your entire upbringing because someone talks sense to you, you know.'

A sigh. 'Yeah. I got that one. And I've really got no right to talk, I grew up with three sisters in the kind of Oz idyll that you see on the TV. We were practically an advert for immigration. But I screwed up my education because of it, y'know; if everything comes easy, you kind of *expect* everything to come easy. I'm a bit like your exact oppo on the wheel of life.'

We swam back out to the boat through small breakers that shifted the surface of the sea and made it hard to climb back up on board. Brendon clambered up first and then held a hand out to help me up and I wavered for a moment, wanting to be self-sufficient but also wanting just a little bit to let myself be helped. I took his hand.

The deck of the boat moved restlessly underneath us. The waves were building in an offshore wind.

'What happened?' I asked, as the boat rocked dramatically. 'To make you leave Australia?'

'Ah, usual crap. Bombed out of school, had to pull myself up by the bootstraps, so I started a construction company. We put up some of the new conurbations west of Melbourne, and it all seemed to be fine. Then the housing market started to drop off, we had some tragic bushfires that took a lot of land, my girlfriend wanted… well. And I woke up one morning and thought "I don't want this any more". Came to England to find Great-grandad as a bit of a distraction.' He scratched his chin, stubble rasped under his nails. 'I dunno. I made money, but that's not what it's about any more.'

Then, as though he was embarrassed about saying so much, he went back to busily steering the boat as it ducked and wove through the rising swell. I looked up at the passing cliffs, rising to tall craggy faces in parts, and in others slumping dejectedly into the sea.

'And then I met you.' His voice surprised me. 'And it made me realise heaps of stuff.'

I tore my eyes from the passing scenery.

'What sort of stuff?' I never thought I had the sort of personality to make anyone realise anything, apart from the fact that most seaweed is edible. And that was more of a result of years of study than anything intrinsically *fucus* related in me. I didn't inspire men to run down the street after me with flowers, or, given my past relationships, any kind of passion at all. Except, as I said, for seaweed. And no woman really wants a man to look at her and immediately conjure images of bladderwrack.

'You fishing for compliments?' But he sounded amused.

I sighed. 'All I fish for is *Laminaria digitata*. I wouldn't know what to do with anything else.'

There was a pause as he steered the little boat, ducking and diving like a professional footballer, along the stretch of coastline. I could see the welcoming arms of Steepleton harbour ahead, the beach now less crowded as people gave up trying to sunbathe in the face of the rising wind, but the water was filling up with surfboards and shiny-headed adventure seekers in the breakers. In fact, he was so quiet for so long that I thought he'd forgotten that I'd said anything. His expression didn't give anything away. His stare focused on the narrow harbour mouth where the breakwater calmed the incoming tide to a gentle smush and wash and the yachts moored in a block, looked like a cut-price Cannes.

'I'm realising that maybe I've finally grown up,' Brendon said, quietly, into the wind.

I didn't know what to do with that information. Didn't even know if he'd wanted me to hear it, so I busied myself with the practicalities of mooring the boat.

Chapter Nine

'Tass, have you got the last lot of figures for this one?'

I was woken from quite a deep sleep by Dylan yelling through the house. My sleep had been so deep that I actually thought I might have dreamed what had happened with Brendon for a moment. I'd gone to bed almost as soon as we'd got back, pleading a sun-induced headache but really so I could rake back over his words. Imaginary-Claire – the inner voice that usually went very, very quiet on the subject of Lewis – whispered '*He likes you. He knows about you at your worst and he still likes you.*' Up until now I hadn't been able to give headspace to the memory of Claire at the same time as the memory of Lewis, it had made me feel ill. But now… no, it still made me feel ill to think of what we'd done. How we'd leaned in to one another, leaned *on* one another, whilst she'd been dying in the hospice. That wasn't the behaviour of a friend. It wasn't even the behaviour of an enemy. It was what I would expect from someone with no emotional attachments at all.

What the hell was *wrong* with me?

I got out of bed and went to the window. This small room looked out over the field of cows, who were just beginning their mooch back across the field after milking, dark heads swinging and tails flicking as the fly action picked up under the heat of the sun. Beyond the bevelled edge of the cliff, the sea was winking and twinkling, ornamented with white flicks of surf. I hated to think it, but I was getting a bit tired of this relentless sunshine. The wind had blown itself out and the sky bore only a veil of the thinnest cloud, dragged along the horizon. It didn't look as though it was going to rain any time soon.

'Leah!' My mother had joined the raised voice brigade. 'I need some stuff from the shop!'

I sighed and pulled some clothes on. This room was so small that I kept banging my elbows when I got dressed or undressed. It was more of a storage space than a bedroom and I pined briefly for the en-suite room across the landing, which now contained my mother and her huge assortment of leisure suits.

Once dressed – and I was getting a bit tired of the T-shirt and jeans thing too, wanting an excuse to wear something a bit more substantial – I made my way out onto the landing and paused at the top of the stairs. From the sounds coming from downstairs, it seemed that everyone was up and active in the kitchen, I could hear the sounds of pumping which meant that Tass and A N Other – probably Dylan with whom they'd formed a friendship that reminded me of Torville and Dean – were filling the tank. I knew my mother was there too as I'd heard her gentle scream.

Then there came another voice, one with the unmistakeable long vowels. 'Hey Jackie, why don't you come down to the shop with me? I need to go into the village for some stuff for the boat.'

A long hesitation. Even the pumping stopped. Then, 'Leah knows what I have,' said almost sulkily.

'Ah, come on! We could go for a coffee, there's a cute little place half way up the main street. Make a morning of it!'

Don't, Brendon, I silently pleaded. I'd learned a long time ago that you couldn't 'jolly' my mother into doing anything she'd decided she wasn't going to. I sat on the bare wooden treads of the staircase, my head in my hands.

'Nah. I'll just wait for Leah. Or maybe I'll go and get her, she should be up by now.' The shuffling sound of trainers came across the stone floor closer to the open doorway through which the voices were coming.

'Let her sleep.' Brendon's voice was quietly powerful. It made the skin along my spine tingle, not with fear but with something else, something I couldn't even begin to describe. The Brendon in my head slid into two personas, the earthily attractive, tanned and blonde Australian visitor and the version I didn't know, the one he must be when he was on his home turf. Certain and assured. 'She's had a rough week.'

Was he thinking about my outburst yesterday? Or the confessions that had driven me to avoid everything for a week, wandering around Dorset like the Ancient Mariner, deprived of a ship and with an albatross downgraded to a hit-and-run seagull?

'She's fine. Given to a sulk, that one.' But the shuffling retreated and I heard a chair pulled out.

'Mum…' Dylan. Doing what he always did, trying to defend me without actually going against anything that Mum said. But he went on, and my eyebrows almost fell off my face with surprise. 'Leah's working, remember? Just cos we're on holiday don't mean that she can just go to the shop all the time for you.'

This was as astonishing as if David Attenborough had walked in with a couple of endangered species and proceeded to batter them to death against the kitchen table. Dylan had actually spoken against our mother! In fact, Dylan talking much at all was a rarity, he usually grunted from the attic in random syllables. When he'd been fourteen I'd begun to wonder if he was suffering from some kind of mental regression, he'd apparently lost the ability to say more than 'no' and 'gimme'.

'Don't you back chat to me, my lad,' my mother said, but it was with the weary resignation of tone that she always used to Dylan. As though he'd been out of her control since the day he was born and she was merely paying lip service to bringing him up properly.

The rest of the kitchen was silent. I could imagine Tass and Brendon exchanging looks, but there was no sound from either of them. Then there was a throat clearing from Tass, and they said, 'Right, Dylan, let's start getting these samples packaged up then. The jiffy bags are in the cupboard.'

'I'll get them.' Again, this keenness was alien from my brother. The only time I'd seen him enthusiastic was during gaming marathons.

Slowly, taking each step as though it might melt beneath me, I made my way down and along the stone-flagged hall to the kitchen. My mother was sitting at the table picking varnish off her nails with a dedication that told me she felt out of her depth. Tass was sorting seaweed out of the little sample bags and into the tubes of preservative that we used to dispatch them to the lab. Brendon was standing facing the window.

'That bird is out there again. It's watching me. With its beak,' he said, to the room at large.

'I think he likes me,' Dylan's voice was muffled by the cupboard and still breathless from pumping. Twenty-odd years behind a handset was no preparation for physical work. 'He followed me around the yard yesterday when I gave him a sandwich, and he came and sat on the grass with me. I like him. He's like a budgie only really, really big.'

'I usually give him the breakfast leftovers,' I said and everyone jumped.

'Oh, it's you, Miss "lie in bed 'til lunchtime".' My mother sulkily swept the picked off varnish onto the floor. 'Thought you was supposed to be working?' There was a plaintive note in her voice, like a child kept waiting for a treat.

'Sorry, Mum,' I said, reflexively.

By the window, Brendon winced, but didn't say anything. Tass was concentrating much harder than necessary on bottling up the samples, head down so that their face wasn't visible.

'You going up the shop now, then?' my mother continued. It was as if nobody had ever questioned her demand for me to go and buy her cigarettes – as if Dylan's objection hadn't happened. And I saw, in a moment of clarity that, for her, it hadn't. That nothing that broke her world view could ever register. And for the oddest moment I felt a moment of affinity with her. Her single-mindedness had passed down to me – sideways and translated somewhat – but it was part of what made me what I was. OK, so mine took the form of holding onto an idea and researching the hell out of it until it squeaked in protest, and hers was more focused on getting what she wanted, but still… a moment of communion. Unexpected.

'Only I'm right out of fags. And Dylan wants some sweeties.'

In my mother's head I was sure Dylan was still the cute six-year-old he'd once been. And, with another moment of shock I saw how he'd become so stuck in life. How could he progress when his mother still treated him like a wilful primary school child? These thoughts were all new and needed processing.

'I'll walk down there,' I said. I needed to be out. To be away. So that I could think all this over. And also to get away from my mother's leisure suit, which was so full of static that it was making the computer screen strobe.

'I'll come with you.'

As soon as Brendon spoke, Tass and Dylan looked at one another. A form of silent communion, this one was a lot less 'wine and wafer' and more 'raised eyebrow and conspiratorial wink'. They had clearly discussed our burgeoning relationship in more detail than I was comfortable with.

'I want to drop in and see Eliza's son, Silas,' Brendon went on. 'He's texted me to say he's found some stuff that might give me some more information about Great-grandad.'

We walked out into the sunlight and Brendon glanced up. 'Is that that bird again?' Overhead a flock of seagulls were performing Red Arrows-esque movements, only fortunately without the coloured smoke.

'He's probably one of them,' I checked. 'He doesn't really seem to fly with others much though. He's a bit of a loner.'

'Is that why you identify with him and give him your sandwiches?'

I smiled. Smiles always felt slightly odd on me, as though I was wearing someone else's clothes, but it was the only appropriate response that I could come up with, and from Brendon's answering grin it was the right one. 'You should smile more often.'

'That is the sort of thing that men say to women. Never the other way around,' I said, trying to be stern and #MeToo and everything, although I wasn't sure why I was feeling defensive.

'Well, you *are* a woman.' Brendon looked relaxed today, hands in his shorts pockets; he was tanning almost before my eyes like a chicken on a rotisserie grill. 'And I want you to know that I appreciate that.'

Wow. I'd take that. How many times did Darric ever acknowledge that you were *female? He wasn't exactly heavy-handed with the compliment, was he? Or the chivalry?* Claire's voice was suddenly strong inside my head.

I'd never encouraged Darric to think of me as a woman though. I'd been so keen to maintain my independence and not let any chink of weakness show that I'd never let him so much as offer to carry a heavy shopping bag. Weakness wasn't allowed when I was growing up. Weakness was what got you taken into care. My mother had only said it once, but the words had stayed with me.

'Err,' I said, temporarily thrown, not just by his words but by my realisations. 'Thank you. I think.'

'Best make it forty!' my mother's voice drifted out towards us on a mild breeze. 'Don't want you to have to go back again today!'

Brendon let out a small breath and patted my arm. It seemed like an unconsidered gesture, which made it all the more appreciated, because people usually approached touching me as one would approach stroking something that was capable of disembowelment.

We set off down the track towards the clifftop. Brendon turned his face up towards the sun. 'Maybe we could go for dinner,' he said, and the angle of his face told me that he was trying to avoid looking at me. Maybe he didn't want to gauge my reaction? *Stop second guessing!*

'Is that dinner as in an evening meal or as in midday?' I asked carefully.

He snorted and his hair sort of flopped. It made something inside me move sideways, an odd sort of feeling, as though I

169

was expanding my heart. Which was anatomically impossible, obviously.

'That is a question that only you could ask,' he said. 'Shall we just agree that we'll have a meal of some sort? At some point when we are hungry?'

'You sound like Darric. All this specification.'

'I'm trying not to give you any excuse to get out of it,' he said, cheerfully, and held the gate open for me.

* * *

The village was busy today. There were vans and lorries parked on the main street, cables like overweight pythons coiled and ran along gutters and down onto the sandy little beach, part of which had been partitioned off with orange crush barriers, as though there was about to be a tiny little music concert. The sea flopped, languid and unconcerned onto the sand, while small groups of people with headsets clustered around and stared at it, and the crowd contained very politely behind the inadequate barrier licked ice creams and stared at the lack of action.

'What's going on?' Brendon asked and a woman in a T-shirt with the inexplicable slogan 'I love Davin' turned around, brandishing a Mr Whippy.

'They're doing a bit of filming for Davin's new programme,' she said, broad Dorset accent stretching the vowels nearly as much as Brendon.

I stared out to where nobody was filming anything and lots of people were watching the sea as though trying to catch it out.

'Are they?'

'Oh it takes 'em ages. Hours.' The woman licked thoughtfully at her dripping ice cream. 'I'm waiting to see Davin O'Riordan.

He's the star. He sometimes comes and talks to us when we're watching, like.' Lick, lick. 'He's gorge.' She nodded her head up the beach. 'Lives over in one of they houses up there, but we don't see much of him. He's away a lot, they says. Got a girlfriend, but she's a nice one, we sees her about a lot, her and that dog.'

Since I had no interest in who or what Davin O'Riordan might be, I couldn't do much more than smile a kind of vague 'nice to have been standing in front of your words' smile.

As Brendon and I walked along the little parade of shops towards my mother's forty Richmond Blues, a little ripple of excitement broke out among the crowd. We turned to see a man walking along the sand, a blue whippet at his heels and another rough-coated dog running along in front. The women in the crowd were communally jutting their chests in a way that told me this must be the much-desired Davin, and I hoped that the ice creams weren't going to get in the way of their admiration or things might get messy.

'Can I borrow you two?'

The voice came right beside me and made me jump. A chunky man in big glasses had popped up alongside Brendon and I; it looked as though he had just come out of the shop, and the large bar of chocolate in his hand reinforced my belief.

'Sorry?' I said.

'We just need a couple to walk along the sand for a tracking shot. We'll follow you and then Davin walks into shot and we follow him. It'll only take a few minutes.' The man bounced on the balls of his feet, as though he was as anxious to be off as the whippet which was currently sprinting along the sand. 'I mean, you are a couple and not, like, two people married to other people having an illicit weekend away or something?' he went on, his voice becoming more loaded with concern as he carried on. 'That would be just my luck, but then I guess if you were on a jolly you'd not be hanging around the village stores, you'd be holed up in a love nest somewhere, you lucky buggers.' He broke a piece off the chocolate and put it in his mouth without looking at it, almost like a nervous reaction.

'Er,' I said. 'No. We're not illicit anything.'

'And a couple. We're a couple,' Brendon said, and then gave me that toothy smile again.

'No, we're not.'

'Well, we sort of are.'

'Can we leave the dictionary definitions for another time?' The little man bounced again. 'Only this shot is a bit desperate. All we need you to do is…'

* * *

'Three hours,' Brendon whispered in my ear, as we walked along the rapidly diminishing beach yet again. His arm was over my shoulders and we were walking in a peculiar crab-wise way because we were supposed to be staring into one another's eyes lovingly. We were actually mostly falling over ruts in the sand and each other's feet, but it was the look that counted. Apparently. 'We've been doing this for three hours.'

'*You* were the one who said we were a couple,' I tried to relax again. The feeling of Brendon's arm around me was making me a feel a mixture of things that I wasn't being given time to process. The weight of his arm, pulling me against his side was unnerving, but there was an odd kind of comfort in it too, even though he'd been told to do it. I was half enjoying the closeness and half being made sweaty by the warmth of his body added to the heat of the day, making me alternately lean in and lean away, so we were oscillating down the beach like a sine wave.

'Well what would you say we were?' Brendon was smiling as he said it, but his mouth was tight. I wanted to go with his words, but his expression and the tension in the muscles of his arm let me know that I shouldn't be that simplistic.

'Er.' I wasn't good at these definitions. 'Couple'? Did that imply sex? That we were sleeping together? 'Partners' made us sound like a business transaction.

'Friends?' I suggested tentatively.

The arm muscles slackened a trifle and his mouth smiled a more believable smile.

'Well, that's progress,' he said. 'I suspect you've got the rest of humanity filed under "people I want to kill and people I'm not allowed to want to kill" haven't you?'

That actually made me laugh, for reasons I didn't want to think about and, as I laughed, the long-coated figure of Davin O'Riordan walked past us for the millionth time, eyes focused on a distant horizon and the wind catching his hair in a picturesque way. He walked on a few strides and then, to everyone's collective relief, we heard the voice of the director – who I now knew to be called Keenan – shout 'OK, I think that's the one! Let's call it a day.'

Davin turned around and walked back through his own footsteps in the sand. Brendon and I evaporated into the crowd and kept walking, heading up along the main street until we were clear of the mass of people. It took until we reached the steep slope up to the top of the cliff before I realised he still had his arm around me.

At the top, we turned and looked back down the street. Beyond the tape that marked off the square of beach where filming was taking place, normal family activities were carrying on. Children played, splashed and paddled. A group of teenagers were ostentatiously throwing a ball to one another, with maximum jumping and showing off, in the shallow surf. Families were breaking out picnics, feeding babies, reclining in the sunshine. It all made me feel even more separate than usual, and the gentle, warm weight of Brendon's arm felt like some kind of film prop.

I stepped sideways, until he was forced to drop his arm or dislocate his shoulder.

'Leah,' he said, 'it's OK.'

'What is?'

'I get it, you're scared. But, look, I'm happy with being friends. You aren't ready for anything else, it's cool, I'm just going to hang around here and wait until you decide that you'd like to get a bit closer; I'm not going to do anything scary, I'm not that much of a bogan.' He'd turned to face me and the brown eyes that were normally crinkled with sun and laughter were very serious. 'I really like you, Leah.'

My mind flickered, processing. 'You're going to hang around and wait for me to decide to want to date you? What if it takes years?'

'I said I'd be your friend, not your stalker. I'm not creeper material, I don't have the stamina.'

'So I've got a deadline? What? Do we put it on a calendar now?'

He laughed now and the way his eyes scrunched up made me feel better. This was his usual face. He wasn't angry.

'I think you're further along the road than you think. You told me about Lewis. And I know he was the first guy to show you affection, but, like you said, he was pretty much hitting base standard. People in a relationship *should* kiss, they *should* have affection and they *should* talk. You're using your husband—'

'Ex-husband.'

'Yeah, that, you're using him as your normal. But, from what you said, he was so far from normal. Leah, having sex when he had a free evening and having to shower before and after – you know that's not normal, right? You know that most couples cook together, eat together, watch films together, don't you? I mean, you've seen TV.'

The sun glinted off the sea. The little houses along the bay looked like a postcard. Soft waves rolled gently against the shore, gulls called along the cliffs. I wished there could have been thunder and lightning, storm force winds. Wished the weather could be as jagged and tumultuous as my brain right now, because it was hard to remember the bad stuff when everything outside was as benign and smooth as a Cornetto.

'I've never really believed stuff I've seen on TV. I mean, how many people's houses are that tidy in real life? Also the murders, lots of murders and I've never had one.' I spoke quickly.

Brendon scratched his chin. 'You could have a point there.'

'And…' I stopped. Talking about Darric was hard. It gave me a feeling that I'd been stupid, somehow. 'He taught me that was the way it was done. I had nothing else to compare it to,' I said, while the inside of my head rioted and screamed. *Of course you knew. You'd seen all those lovey-dovey couples walking along hand in hand. You'd watched* Notting Hill. *You cried, silently, in your room every Valentine's Day, and tried not to watch the adverts telling you all the things you should be doing, because nobody wanted any more from you than regular clean laundry. You knew…*

I didn't even pretend to myself that it was Claire inside my head now. Claire, who'd tried to tell me what I already knew. What I'd been telling myself all this time.

But I wasn't ready. Not to talk to Brendon about it, not yet. Even with his scrunchy eyes and his lurid shorts and his wanting to be 'more than friends but let's take our time'. Not yet. Maybe not ever. Being on my own wasn't so bad, after all, not even if all it gave me would be a lifetime of cat ownership to look forward to.

'You were brought up without love, I get it,' Brendon was continuing. If he carried on much longer he was going to make my 'people I politely want to kill' list. 'Not really anyone's fault. Your mum didn't know how to change and there was nobody around to help you out, so you kind of arrived at your own definition of love and it was, I have to say, pretty basic. And that's why Lewis—'

'I pretend Claire is still talking to me,' I said quickly. 'I talk to myself, you know, inside my head. And I pretend that it's Claire giving me her opinion. I mean, I know it isn't, I know it's just me, but there's something about pretending it's advice from someone else that makes it feel more… acceptable, somehow.'

That surprised him.

'I feel things but I don't know if I feel the *right* things or that if I'm feeling the things I feel in the right way, because I've made horrible mistakes and – well.' I stopped.

He still looked surprised. 'Well. I still want to be your friend. Even if it does come with all that baggage. And a terrifying seagull. And your mother.'

'I think I'm trying to say that I'm not sure how good a friend I will be.' I averted my eyes.

'I got that.' There was a moment of silence. Well, not silence exactly, there were the shouts of children on the beach, applause from the crowd watching the filming taking place, the yelps and skirls of the gulls on the cliffs, all the normal day-to-day noises of a seaside town. I did my best to ignore them and the way they made me feel even more excluded from the world.

'Well. I'm going to go and see Silas, if you fancy coming.' It seemed like an olive branch.

'I ought to get back. I've already been away too long. There's work to do.'

'Right.'

Neither of us moved. It almost felt as though a kind of force field had enveloped us, I had the strangest feeling that, even if I had tried to walk away, I'd be unable to get more than a few metres. There was a phantom weight on the back of my neck where his arm had rested adding to the illusion that I was existing in a dual universe – the ghostly sensation of his body against mine. He was touching me, yet not touching me.

'Are you overthinking something?' Brendon eventually said.

'I might be, yes.'

'Well don't. Let's just go along, go with the flow. See how things pan out, yeah? I'm off to meet Silas, and I'll catch you later, back at the house, all right?'

His normality shook me out of my introspection. 'Good idea. Yes. Er, good luck, I hope Silas tells you something to your advantage.' *Well, that could have been phrased better, you sound like something out of a Poirot mystery now. David Suchet, not the other one. And definitely not John Malkovich, that's much too postmodern. All right, shut up now.*

I didn't give him chance to comment, but swung myself round and headed off towards the track across the fields.

* * *

When I got back, Tass was alone in the kitchen.

'All right, where've you buried him?'

'If you mean Brendon, he's gone to meet up with someone who might know something about his great-grandad.'

'You haven't done him in and thrown him over the edge of the cliff then?'

I sighed. 'No.'

Tass closed down a computer screen and went over towards the kettle. The kitchen was dark and cool after the relentless brightness of the day, and suspiciously quiet.

'Where's my mum?'

Tass looked at their watch. 'At a guess… *Judge Rinder*. Or it could be *This Morning* re-runs, I'm not sure. My all-encompassing knowledge of modern pop culture doesn't really include daytime television.' A rattle of the kettle. 'Did you get her ciggies?'

A horrible sensation that my stomach had had its moorings cut and was descending towards bowel basement.

'No! I forgot! We got distracted with all that walking up and down the beach. Hell, I'll have to go back!'

Tass looked at me from under a fringe and eyelashes that made them look slightly like a badly clipped alpaca. 'No. Don't.'

'But she'll be unbearable.'

'And in what way is she not currently unbearable? Sorry, Leah, I know they're your family and all, and Dylan is an absolute dish and amazing and all, but your mother – look, I know we all reckon you're odd, but having met her I'd say you are nowhere near odd *enough*. Where the hell did she learn her interpersonal skills? Stasi 101? Watching her talking to you, it's like a cross between the Wehrmacht and Jeremy Paxman.'

I could feel it. The old familiar feelings rising up inside me. Feelings that I had never learned to let out but had just forced back down again to keep on fermenting. I had the sensation in my stomach that I had recently swallowed a cup of live worms. 'She's… she's had a hard time.'

The look Tass gave me now was almost… what was it? *Pity*? Some kind of emotion that teetered on the edge of sarcasm but never made it over.

'Unless she was raised by wolves, I'd say—'

'Did you get my fags?'

The voice was raised, coming through from the living room, underscored by the dramatic music that heralded some show or other that involved people telling their sad stories to the masses. Part of me wondered if my mother watched shows like this to feel better about herself, to reassure herself that there was a whole subset of humanity that she could look down on. Maybe she just watched to congratulate herself that at least she'd never got botched plastic surgery that left her unable to close her lips around a cigarette, or whatever the latest celebrity tabloid disaster story might be. Maybe she *needed* to feel superior to someone.

'Sorry, Mum, I forgot,' I called back. I opened my mouth to suggest that I'd go back, but Tass made extreme 'throat cutting' gestures, so I stopped talking.

'You what?' The volume went down on the TV and I felt a moment of acute and complicated emotions. She'd heard. Of course she had. But she'd turned down her programme to make me repeat my failing more conspicuously. To exaggerate my failure, make me overcompensate, to make me… what? Feel small.

I didn't answer. This also wasn't usual for me. I normally straddled the line of least resistance so hard that I could feel it cutting into my flesh. But today… somehow things were different.

'You forgot my fags?' My mother appeared in the doorway. I wondered why she shuffled. She wasn't old, not by today's standards. Fifteen years older than me only made her forty-nine. Maybe the lack of vitamins and sunlight were affecting her skeleton. She certainly had the dipped back and stoop of someone much older, someone with fewer options. 'Are you going back out, then?'

It doesn't have to be like this.

'You can go yourself, if you really want them,' I said, my heart whirring in my chest. 'It's a short walk over the fields and the fresh air will do you good.'

I had to turn away then. What I saw blazing in her eyes was an emotion I shouldn't have had to see on anyone's face – betrayal mixed with a kind of fear – the expression I'd imagine someone would wear if a beloved family pet had attacked them.

From over by the kettle, Tass gave me a speedy thumbs up. And while I appreciated their support, I still had to go outside and take some deep breaths. I forced myself to walk out across the little meadow to the cliff edge to prevent myself from breaking down into apologies and attempts to make it all right again by walking to the shop and coming back laden with all her favourite snacks.

Above my head, the gull with the telltale marking wheeled in and landed close to my feet.

'Hello, Roger,' I said, to further distract myself. 'I haven't got any food, I'm afraid.'

Roger didn't seem to take it personally that I wasn't armed with cake. He pecked the iron-hard ground a few times, as though experimenting, then turned his head sideways to look up at me out of one mad, yellow eye.

'All right,' I said, because I was slightly afraid that he might start on my legs. 'I'll go and see if there's anything in the house.'

When I went back into the kitchen, it was empty, although the machines were still whirring busily. I'd opened the pantry door to search through for any scraps of bread that even Dylan wouldn't eat to throw out for Roger, when I heard the voices. Cautiously I peered out around the kitchen door into the hallway, to see Tass standing just outside the living room, with my mother visible through the gap, inside the room. I instantly pulled my head back into the kitchen, and froze, half holding my breath and clutching the pantry door as though it was keeping me upright.

My mother was shouting at Tass. 'She was a good girl before she came out here and started mixing with your lot! I knew I should never have let her do this kind of thing!'

Tass sighed. 'Look. Your relationship with Leah is nothing to do with me, but if you asked me – which you won't because you have clearly made up your mind with no real evidence – I'd say that she's just started to see you as a person rather than a mother. Leah is finally growing up.'

'Well she's got no business doing that,' my mother retorted. 'She's getting too big for her boots if you ask me. I needs her to run the odd errand, to help me.'

'Why?' Tass sounded almost bored. I risked another peek around the door but they were in the same place and I couldn't make out their expressions.

'Because I'm old! I can't be expected to do all this shopping and stuff, and looking after Dylan. She's young and she's got money, it's her job to help out her family and show a bit of gratitude!'

I heard Tass's exhaled 'Oh boy', and didn't know if I would make things worse or better by appearing in person. Would they both start appealing to me to see their side of things? And should I, as the person being technically fought over, be expected to take sides? I couldn't fool myself. Recent happenings with Brendon put me firmly in Tass's camp, but an entire life of expectation and duty meant that I couldn't ignore my mother's point of view, however hard I tried.

'It's nobody's job but yours to support yourself.' Tass's voice was quiet and even. 'You are perfectly capable. I've got friends – people like me. People whose parents have disowned them for being like me. People who have had to literally make themselves into the people they want to be. With no help, no support, nothing. And here's you, leaning on someone, trying to make *her* into the person you want her to be… it's just wrong. Everyone deserves to be their own best person.'

Unaccustomed tears were in my eyes. I'd been hardly aware of their arrival, I was so caught up in Tass's defence of me. But they were *right* and saying all the things that I'd wanted to say myself but hadn't been able to negotiate my mind around.

A hand on my shoulder made me leap into the air, but it was Brendon, tousled from the climb up the road and beaten to a sort of bronze form by the sun.

'What's going on?' he whispered. I gestured to the doorway and he glanced through into the hall, then back at me. 'Whew,' he blew. 'It's like the OK Corral without guns. Or hats.'

'You don't understand any of it,' my mother went on. 'She's *my* daughter. I raised her and I now I needs her help.'

Tass 'tch'ed. 'She's your daughter, but she's her own person,' they said. 'And I think you should stop leaning on her. Stop keeping Dylan in some kind of suspended animation at fourteen and all get on with your lives.' A deep breath. 'There is so much more to life, Jackie,' they said, more quietly. 'Being kind. Being useful. You should try it sometime.'

Brendon was nodding beside me.

I couldn't stand it any more. There was a weird ripping sensation inside me. I understood what Tass was saying. Academically I knew they were right – that my mother's peculiar and terrified form of child-rearing had stunted Dyl and I so badly that we had trouble functioning in society, but, still, she was my mother. She'd done what she could and I couldn't stand by and let her be abused like this. I took a step towards the doorway but found, to my surprise, that Brendon had hold of my arm and was sort of hustling me out of the back door, across the yard and away from the house.

'Let them talk,' he said, and there was a note in his voice that made me look up into that brown, surfer face.

It was still Brendon, still the guy in the shorts, looking like an extra in a Katy Perry music video. But with an extra set to his shoulders, a more rooted look to him. There was something direct in his eyes, as though there was a business transaction going down that I'd got in the way of. *He was a businessman in Australia,* the voice that I'd always tried to give to inner-Claire said. The voice that I knew was me – my subconscious trying to break through – but that I'd managed to hive off and associate with Claire's sunny outspokenness. *He's not just a beach bum, even though that's how he wants you to see him.*

'She'll start shouting in a minute,' I said, and I sounded as though I was still fourteen myself. Kind of defensive and kind of sulky.

'Let her shout. Tass isn't you, she can't get to them. She's got no ammunition for that.' He pulled me a few more strides away until I couldn't hear the voices any more. 'Your mother needs a few home truths and I think Tass might just be the person to give them. Has anyone ever told her that stuff?'

I shook my head. 'I don't know. I— we— Dyl and I, we had nothing to compare our childhoods to, so it was normal for us. It was only when Claire— when my marriage was breaking up and I had to talk to someone and she pointed out that I'd just swapped my mother for a male version when I married Darric, and that it wasn't how love was supposed to be.'

'And now you struggle without rigid control?'

That's what Lewis said. That you are looking for someone to take control over your life. Suddenly I wasn't looking at Brendon in his crumpled T-shirt and lairy shorts, it was Lewis standing in front of me. Wearing that grey suit that hung off his spare frame and twiddling his glasses by the arm, telling me that it was over. We couldn't be together, it had been a mistake. That he'd never really intended a relationship, it had only been 'a bit of fun'.

A bit of fun while his wife was dying.

Those were the words he'd used, but what he'd really meant was that my dependency bored him. He wanted bright, young things to help him to hold on to his rapidly fading youth.

'I thought I'd got it right with Lewis,' I said, my voice a little stung thing in my throat. 'I mean, it wasn't ideal but… I really thought he cared.'

Silence. Even the cows in the next field were quiet. Maybe the sun had incinerated that last little bit of grass, because when I let my eyes travel in that direction they were all standing in the shrunken patch of shade near the hedge, heads down, tails flicking. No sound from the house either, maybe Tass and my mother had suffocated each other under the weight of accusations.

A sudden sense of shadow and Brendon was right beside me, blocking out the sun. 'You've been playing a role all your life, haven't you?' he said, very quietly. 'And now I want to know the *real* Leah.'

Grasshoppers chirped. At the bottom of the cliff, the sea swirled and splashed lazily, like a languorous person in the bath. Outside the back door, Roger waited patiently for someone to throw food.

'I'm not sure I know who the real Leah is,' I whispered. 'I'm my mother's daughter, and it's all I know how to be.'

Brendon gave a sudden shout of laughter, which made Roger hop a few feet sideways.

'You do! I've seen you at work, you know what you're doing there, with the seaweed and all that!'

'Yes, well, I've trained myself to compartmentalise. That's work, that's important, so I focus on it.'

'Then turn it round,' Brendon put both hands on my shoulders and shook me slightly. 'Compartmentalise who you are for your mother and let the rest of you take over. Focus on *that* for a change! Nobody is saying cut your mother off completely – although I don't think one single person would blame you if you did, but you're not that sort – but give her a little corner of your life and let the real Leah have the rest.'

Oh. *Oh.* I felt the same way as I did when someone showed me a new organisational method, or a new computer program that performed analyses that I'd previously had to do on paper and with a calculator. As though something that had been hugely complicated had suddenly become simplified. *Can you do that?*

I turned away from the sea. Its endlessness and restlessness made me uneasy now. I looked out in the opposite direction, towards the chalk heathlands of the countryside. The high cliffs that gave way to deep valleys rolling like rows of sleepers under thin green blankets. A filmy grey cloud hung in the sky further inland and gave me hope that there might be rain at some point. The wind exhaled against my cheek.

Brendon looked up at the cloud and frowned. 'C'mon, let's get back in there and put the kettle on for the last one standing,' he said, and when I hesitated he guided me gently with an arm across my shoulders.

'How come you're so good at this stuff?' I asked.

'Ah. A dad that knew a thing or two about life. If it wasn't for him, I'd still be playing third-rate footie and falling off my surfboard. He didn't so much tell me what to do, as show me and then let me find my own way. It's one reason why I— well.'

We went back in through the kitchen door to find that Tass, looking a bit wild about the eyes, had beaten us to the kettle.

'Where's Dylan?' Tass asked, as soon as we got inside. 'Is he back yet?'

'Why?' My mother trailed down the hallway and stopped in the doorway. 'Where's he gone? Dylan don't go out, he don't like the outdoors. Says it's got too much stuff in it.'

'He was going to go out up onto the hills and take some pictures.' Tass's words were short and bitten off. 'Of the whole bay. To go with our report.'

'He don't go out.' My mother repeated herself, as though she could make it true. Brendon and I looked at one another, but my mother and Tass ignored us. They were carrying on their own private vendetta, we were purely incidental.

'Well, he has. And he's not back yet by the look of it.' Tass sounded triumphant. 'He wants to be a photographer, Jackie. He wants to train, to learn, to have a profession. To *be* somebody.'

'He *is* somebody.' Her voice was getting lower. 'He's my Dylan. And don't you go giving him no ideas.'

Dylan was doing it. Breaking free. Setting his sights on the life he wanted, the life he could see now that he'd got out of the dingy flat and seen those broad horizons. He was hurtling into a new life, propelled entirely by hope. Could *I* do that too?

Claire had told me I could. Over and over. *You're over thirty, it's time to be your own person. I know you feel guilty, but that's only because she's brought you up to feel that you belong to her. Yes, she has problems, but it's up to her to recognise that and get help, you don't have to live your life trying to minimise the damage!*

Wow. I wasn't responsible. OK, I didn't have to cut her loose. And I'd been going about things in the right way by leaving home and keeping my visits short, but I didn't *have* to manage her life.

Brendon was frowning again.

'What?' I asked. A momentary worry – *did he think he was wrong?* – but I ignored it. I chose to ignore it.

'Tass, you said Dylan's gone up on the hill?' He was craning his neck, peering out of the window as though he was trying to look behind the house. From here we could only see the closest range of hills. There was a kind of grey film over the inland horizon now, as though very localised drizzle was falling. 'Up over there?'

'That's the easiest way to get up onto the heath,' Tass reacted to the tone in Brendon's voice, and frowned. 'What is it?'

'Only, I dunno…' He screwed up his eyes as though it could help him to see further. 'But it looks like… do you have bushfires in England?'

I felt my face fall in horror. 'Yes. When it's been hot for a long time and the ground is dry. Up in Yorkshire they lose moorland every year. When I was an undergrad we did some work on the regeneration of heather... Do you think...?'

As if in answer, a distant siren wailed briefly.

'But a lot smaller than in Oz, yes? I mean, people don't die, it's just a little bit of grassland, yes?' He sounded a little bit desperate.

'Well, sometimes...' But he'd started moving before I could finish.

'Tass! Where exactly did Dylan go?'

'*Someone's* got to go for my fags!' my mother wailed, but it was almost as though the spell she'd had me under was broken. The wicked witch had lost her power. No, that wasn't fair, she wasn't wicked. She was stuck. She'd not managed to grow up past that scared teenage girl with two small children and no prospects in an inadequate and too-small flat. I could almost – *almost* – understand her now. Inasmuch as I could understand anybody.

'He went up onto the top of the hills,' Tass pointed, behind us, in the direction of the ominous grey cloud. 'He wanted to see more of the scenery and to take some pictures. You don't think—?'

Brendon cut them off. 'Can you check the local news? I think there might be a fire up there.'

Tass shook their head. 'Up on the hill? There's nothing to burn.'

'There's grass,' Brendon almost snapped. 'Trust me, I went through the Black Saturday bushfires in 2009. People died, people lost their houses. Check the local news.'

Tass turned to the computer, tapped a few keys.

'I only wanted twenty Richmond Blue!' My mother was almost crying now. 'Was that too much to ask? You're my daughter...' She turned her face to me. I'd never realised how pale and gaunt she looked, like someone who really – *really* – needed to get out more.

A curious mixture of pity and exasperation tore at my chest.

'Let's find Dyl, shall we?' I asked, and my voice sounded more gentle than I'd meant it to. *But then, there's no good getting angry with her. She doesn't know. She doesn't understand that something's shifted.*

'You're right.' Tass turned the laptop so we could all see the screen. They read out the story. 'Local fire brigade called to heath fires above Christmas Steepleton. Two large fires have broken out on Steepleton Common… blah blah… eighty hectares at risk… people warned to stay clear of the area.' Big dark eyes blinked. 'That's where he went. Steepleton Common. I didn't even know that's what it was called.' An emotional choke in the voice now.

The air in the kitchen was suddenly loaded with big, dark weights. My mother went really still and her stream of words stopped.

'Dylan?' she said, faintly. 'But he wouldn't…'

Brendon was moving, reading the screen, gathering things together. 'Who's got a car?'

'Me.' Tass grabbed the keys. 'Let's go. He's probably walking back along the road, come to think of it, trying to get away. I mean, the fire engines are up there…' they tailed off.

I looked around at everyone. *Mum doesn't really understand that he might be in danger. Tass – well, I think Tass might be fonder of Dylan than they're letting on, I hope they're not going to be disappointed… although, come to think of it, Dyl's never really had a girlfriend. Or a boyfriend. Brendon is organising. Funny, I never really saw that side of him up until now, but he seems to have a handle on what needs to be done. Why am I watching? Why am*

I not doing? *Force of habit, maybe. Analyse first, see what's most important…*

'Leah, does Dylan have a phone?' Brendon was sort of sweeping me out of the room, as though he knew that my inner monologue was occupying all but my motor functions.

'He's a thirty-two-year-old bloke. Of course he does.' I fumbled in my pocket, found my phone. Tried Dyl's number but it went to voicemail.

'The signal out here is rubbish,' Tass closed the back door behind us. 'I'd have thought it would be better up on the hill, but maybe not.'

'And he's definitely got his phone on him?' I quite liked this take-charge Brendon, even if it was at odds with the surfer hair and the shorts.

'He was using it to take the pictures.'

'Right, Leah, keep trying. Chances are he's away from the high land and making his way down.'

Organising is your job… 'Maybe we should tell somebody, the fire brigade or something. Let them know that there might be someone up there?' I felt as though I was in a brief tussle for control of the situation, but Brendon gave me a sudden grin.

'Honestly, Leah, you're a pearler and all, but just this once, give it up to a bloke whose entire working life has been sorted around fire breaks and understanding fire risk. My entire state is a bloody fire risk!' He leaned in close for a second. 'Trust me.' He practically breathed it.

Outside it felt as though the air had been taking lessons from fire. Even the cows could feel it, they were crowded in as close as they could be to the shade of the hedge. Which – the sun being almost directly overhead – wasn't that much, just a thin strip of dark like someone had outlined the field in black marker pen.

190

There was a feeling in the air of something being wrong, like an electrical charge.

We squeezed into Tass's car – Tass driving, Brendon in the front. I sat in the back next to my mother, who looked as though she would rather have stayed behind but was being carried along on the wave of impetus. Her expression was a mixture of bafflement mixed with indignation, as if she didn't believe there was any real danger to Dylan but was going along with our charade, occasionally wailing about the fact that she'd run out of fags and pulling at the neck of her leisure suit, trying to hide deeper inside its velour.

The roads were quiet on the way up the hill. Everyone was down in the village, untroubled. We could still hear the high-pitched shouts and squeals of the children on the beach and the confusion and shouting from the film crew. Almost as if there was no other life than that going on in Steepleton, as though the rest of Dorset was lying inert under the weight of this heat and had driven all occupants to the sea.

The little car growled up the steep incline, Tass going down through the gears with increasing desperation. As we climbed, the plume of grey smoke grew larger and higher flashes of yellow fire and floating orange sparks creeping up beneath it, as it floated over the smooth curve of the hills.

'He'll have seen the fire and gone the other way,' Tass said, but their tone was more hopeful than reassuring.

A car passed us, heading down the hill. It pulled up level and the driver wound down his window.

'They're closing the road up there,' he jerked a thumb back the way he'd come. 'Fire on the common. You're better off turning round and waiting it out.' Then he and his car load of teenagers were gone, continuing their journey towards sea and ice cream. Tass looked around at us silently, and we continued on up the hill.

We reached a junction, where a signpost pointed the way to a school. We were practically at the top of the hill now, the smoke was visible in the air around us as little swirls and particles, but the fire was still beyond our vision, over the crest.

'OK, I'm going to park here.' Tass pulled the car into the turn off. 'Dyl won't have gone much further than this, he wanted a picture of Steepleton Bay, any further and he'd be over the brow of the hill and he'd lose the view.'

We got out of the car. At least, Brendon, Tass and I did, my mother stayed where she was, looking up at the sky as though it might suddenly crash down onto her head.

'Well, he's not on his way down the road, maybe he headed down over the fields?' I looked at the irregular arrangement of hawthorn hedge that marked boundaries that had probably been set out in the Bronze Age.

'Why would he? Road's quicker.' Brendon climbed up onto a gate and was looking in the direction of the smoke. 'Two things. He might be on the edge of the fire and thinking he's safe, or he's in the middle of it and trying to get out.'

'Or he could be in a café in town drinking coffee and wondering what the sirens are for,' I said, reasonably.

'There's a phone signal in the village though. He'd have picked up.' Tass joined Brendon on the gate. They were looking over a field of rough grassland that stretched, boundaryless, further up to the very top of the hill, where it gave way to bracken and undergrowth. Small, spindly trees stuck up, looking rather feeble and newly established, tapering towards a small copse on the high horizon. There was no sign of actual fire, just the billows of smoke puffing our way, a faint glow and some travelling sparks, all just over the brow of the hill.

'What are you all doing up there?' my mother wound down her window just far enough to poke her face out.

'We're looking for Dylan.' I didn't even glance down at her. I knew the expression she'd be wearing – one of pursed-mouth irritation.

'Oh. Is he out here?' She looked from side to side, as though my brother was about to pop up beside the car and leer in the window at her.

Brendon met my eye. He didn't need to say anything, I knew what he was thinking, but this was my mother all over. It was almost as if she couldn't comprehend anything that didn't have her at the dead centre.

'He might be caught in the middle of a brush fire,' I said, and my tone was harsher than I meant. Her face scrunched into lines of discontent. She looked like a pug denied a treat.

'He won't be caught in anything. He's got more sense, that boy. It's you who's the one that gets into scrapes because you've not got the common sense you were born with. Always losing stuff… like your school bag.'

For just about the first time since I'd had a rebellious teenage afternoon, I snapped at her. 'I once lost my school bag on the bus, and that was because Jandra James and Kenis Watts hid it – it turned up the next day anyway. It was hardly careless, and *it wasn't even my fault.*'

Brendon looked down at me from the top of the gate, and shook his head very slightly. He was right, this wasn't the time or the place for a family argument, with the smoke scraping its way towards us in overfilled pillows of black. The gold glimmer of the fire was clearly visible now, an etched line along the crest of the hill.

'It's burning uphill on the other side.' Brendon looked back.

'That should slow it down.' I said.

He shook his head again. 'Fire burns faster uphill.'

'Well that's just not bloody fair, is it?' Tass jumped down on the far side of the gate and stood in the scrubby field. 'What do we do?'

'Spread out, shout, but stay this side. Don't get anywhere near the fire – there's not so much in the way of trees this side so hopefully it will burn down before it gets here. And the fire brigade must be dealing with it from the other side. Wind's in our favour. We can make sure he's not stuck anywhere near the danger zone. Why would he not have just come back when he realised what was happening?' Brendon scanned the heathland, one hand over his eyes again, like a captain looking for a safe shore.

'Like I said, he wanted to take pictures. Maybe he might have decided to try to get some pictures of the fire?' Tass directed the question at me, I didn't know why, I hadn't even been there.

'Dyl's not… I mean, neither of us have a huge sense of self-preservation,' I said cautiously. 'We're not… we seem to be missing that gene.'

'OK. Let's just go up this field then. You think he won't have gone much further?' Brendon jumped down next to Tass and I followed them, reluctantly, with a look at my mother that could probably have split metal.

'Well, like Leah said, he could have gone to try to get pictures of the fire. But surely…? I mean, I'm from Bromsgrove and even I know that you don't run towards a fire.'

'Right. We scan this field. If you even so much as see the fire come over the brow, get out. It moves faster than you can run.' Brendon started to walk, keeping to the hedgeline, across the field. It widened out past the gateway into a gently sloping hillside populated with tufts of bracken and grass that had been beaten brown by the sun. A sandy track ran up to the top of the hill, the sand scuffed and skirled by wind and feet and the grass turned into ankle level bushes with sapling trees thrusting their way through like zombie fingers clawing for the sky.

Tass started up the track, they and Brendon were calling for Dylan and I felt dislocated, left behind. Surely my brother, daft as he might be, wouldn't be standing in the middle of a moorland with a clearly visible fire burning towards him? He was a general idiot, but even with our chaotic upbringing, he'd acquired more sense than that.

OK. So if I'd been Dylan, and I'd been up here taking pictures... I swung round. The whole of Steepleton Bay was laid out beneath me. The village was tucked into the fold of the cliff, but the rest of the view was postcard-like, the gentle arms of the bay curled protectively around the harbour and the beach. The harbour wall jutted like a rib into the water, and I could just see the spot at which the *Southern Cross* would be bobbing at her mooring, between the big, expensive, hired boats of the Londonistas.

Yes, this was a perfect spot for taking pictures. And Dylan might have walked up towards the top of the hill to get an even wider shot... I began edging my way upwards, one eye on the smoke. The fire was coming from our left, where the heathland sloped sharply downwards towards the bottom of the next valley and when I got higher up I could see the faint blue strobe of a fire engine light and hear distant shouts. That edge was covered, as the fire fighters struggled to stop the flames spreading any further that way toward the next village.

From the top of the hill it was easier to see what was going on. The glowing edge of flame was eating its way along a ridge, curling around the next hilltop. Behind it, the already burned landscape lay like tangled black knitting, all growth burned away to leave stalks and stems and branches, parched and charred. Smoke ran a little ahead of the fire line, trickling down into a thin ditch which delineated the top of the rise we stood on. It looked beautiful, wild and yet somehow safe at the same time, just a little trickle of fire teasing its way along the edge of another trackway now, as though it was being led along.

'Leah! He's not up here. We need to go back!' Brendon called across. We'd unconsciously formed a straight line, scanning along to the hilltop, Tass stood between us, the part of their face that wasn't covered by beard had dirty smudges on it.

'The fire is miles away. We should carry on looking,' I responded.

'We can't.' Brendon pointed. 'The fire might jump that gulley, and we won't be able to outrun it. This is as far as it's safe to go.' A small smile flickered across his face. 'Trust me, I'm an Australian.'

'A sentence never likely to be repeated,' Tass grinned. 'Let's go back, Leah. He's not up here. We've checked it out. Maybe he walked down a different way and we missed him? Maybe he's in the house now wondering where we all are?'

'But like you said, if he'd gone down, his phone would have been in signal.' A gust of wind blew the smell of smoke across the gulley at us and I coughed.

'We need to move.' Brendon's head came up. 'The wind is changing direction and we're going to be in the middle of that if we don't.' He pointed.

Over the top of the hill came the galloping flame. What looked like an innocent line of burning was being fanned by the wind and had risen up to a shoulder-height of flame.

'Move!' Brendon grabbed my hand.

Suddenly there was a sound overhead. The half screech, half chuckle with a hint of mew. I looked up. 'It's Roger.'

'What's that bloody wazza doing now?' Brendon half crouched. 'Has he come to check out whether we're dead yet?'

'No, he…' I watched the big bird swoop and then hang in the air. 'He didn't come up here with us.'

'Birds don't like fire.' Brendon gave my hand a tug. 'I thought we were safe.'

'He's been hanging around Dylan,' Tass said thoughtfully. 'Dyl's been feeding him. I don't know what it is with your family and big bloody birds, Leah. Were you raised by buzzards or something?'

'So then, why is he here?' I carried on watching the seagull. He was circling, not over us but further down the gulley.

'Someone probably dropped a sandwich,' Brendon tugged me again and looked back over his shoulder. 'We have to move.' His tone was urgent and his urgency was backed with the smoke increasing in the air around us.

'But what if he followed Dylan up here? What if…?'

'It's a fucking seagull, not Lassie.' Brendon was backing up, pulling my wrist as he went. 'Leah, we need to get off this heath.'

Beside me, Tass was hesitating too. 'But if he is there…'

The smoke was starting to make my eyes sting. It smelled of old things, wild things; gave me a creeping fear I wasn't sure I could name. And it was moving fast. Over the brow of the hill now, leaping towards us.

'All right!' Brendon let go of me. 'But we need to hurry. Tass, you get back to Jackie and move that car. We'll find our own way back. GO!'

Roger circled, dipping his head down to watch us. I could see his beady yellow eye, like a glowing ember in the sky as he swooped – wings angled to catch the new breeze – and I ran. Slipping and sliding down the slope, the grass cooked under the sun and as hard and shiny as nylon. I slithered down into the narrow trough between the two slopes, catching at bracken stalks to slow my descent and snagging my feet on little stumps as I went.

Behind me I could hear Brendon coming too, his breath catching, and a steady stream of very Antipodean swearing accompanying him. Overhead, Roger dived, swooped and was gone with a throat clearing sound of rusty bagpipes, leaving Brendon and I suddenly up to our ankles in the boggy remnants of a stream, hands covered in bracken cuts, and with smoke obscuring our vision.

'He's here!' I caught sight of a booted foot, jutting beneath greenery and followed it up the jeaned leg to the T-shirted form of my brother. 'Dyl…'

I wasn't sure then if the tears in my eyes were from the smoke or from fear. Dylan lay, curled around himself, half way to the edge of the gulley, whimpering. He didn't even raise himself when he heard my voice, just pulled his head down tighter into his arms.

A battering of the undergrowth and Brendon was there beside me. 'Dylan? What's up, man?'

'Can we save the small talk and get him out of here?' I scuttled along the ditch to stop beside my brother.

Dylan now managed a weak smile. 'That's my sister,' he said. 'Cutting to the chase.'

'The chase is approaching rapidly,' Brendon flicked his head up. 'So. Precise story, please. Anything broken?'

'I'd taken my pics, saw the smoke and heard the sirens. Came this way to take try to get some really good shots and was too busy watching the fire action to see this bloody great hole. Think I might have busted my ankle or summat. Hurts like a bastard with a pointy stick. And… hey, is that Roger?'

We all looked up to the edge of the gulley. Roger was strutting up and down, paddling his big yellow feet and doing 'distressed seagull' for all he was worth.

'That's how we found you. Roger was circling overhead, didn't you hear us calling?'

'Nah, can't hear anything from down here.' Dylan uncurled a little. 'I was feeding Roger my sandwiches earlier, but I thought he'd buggered off.'

Brendon, keeping one eye on Roger, edged up the side of the gulley. 'Hate to rush you,' he said, 'but if that fire gets any closer we'll be having roasted seagull for tea and don't tempt me on that one. Can you get your foot out, Dylan?'

Dylan looked ruefully at his leg, jammed firmly between the rocks. 'D'you not reckon if I could of, I would of?' he said, and his tone was quite reasonable for someone being asked a daft question.

'Could have,' I said, reflexively.

'No time for the grammar-nazis, thank you, Leah.' Brendon bent to the rocks and tried to move Dyl's leg, but the combination of a tight fit and a stream of invective from Dylan stopped him. 'Shit.'

'You're not going to do a forty-eight hours on me, are you? Leah, tell him he's not allowed to cut my leg off.' Dylan clutched at my arm. 'I mean, it went in, it must come out, it just hurts when I try…'

There was a strange smell in the air now and a grey mist of smoke floated down, filling the gulley until I could only see Dyl and Brendon.

'Fire's getting closer,' Brendon said, shortly.

'We can't leave Dylan.' I tried to move one of the rocks his leg was stuck between. It wobbled slightly, but wouldn't shift enough to give any clearance.

'There's no point anyway. You can't outrun fire. Even if we got him out now it would be on top of us before we were half way to the road.' Brendon closed his eyes. 'It's a bitch, fire,' he muttered. 'My parents lost everything in '09.' He opened his eyes again and looked at me. 'We had a farm in the southern Dandenongs, my parents got away but all the stock…' his voice trailed off.

'People don't die in bushfires in England though,' Dylan said firmly. 'I mean, this is England. You can drown easy enough – what with all the rain. But fire outdoors? That would be stupid.'

I could hear it now, the crackle of fire. Inexorable. Roger took off, wheeling into the sky without a second look.

'Traitorous bastard,' muttered Brendon. 'And you can die in fire anywhere, Dylan.'

Crack. Snap. I looked up. There was a lot of smoke now, curling over the lip of the gulley. 'What do we do?'

'You're not going to saw my leg off, are you?' Dylan's eyes were wide and black with fright.

'We need to get away,' I tried to make my voice sound reassuring, but it wobbled alarmingly. 'What do we *do*, Brendon?'

Dylan was pulling at his trapped leg, making little noises of pain with each tug. 'Come *on*,' he was muttering, 'come *on*.'

Brendon turned his attention to the boulders that had Dyl's leg jammed between them. 'Leah, you take that side. I'll take this and we'll kind of rock it. Dylan, you pull your leg the second you feel it go free, OK? One, two, *three*.'

We rocked the rock. After two shoves it gained momentum and forced enough of a gap that Dylan, grabbing his jeans leg between both hands and pulling, managed to free his leg, whilst letting loose with a tirade of swear words that I was fairly sure he hadn't picked up from family life.

'Well done,' Brendon leaned back. 'You're out.' Then he inched his way a few feet up to the edge of the gully, stuck his head up, then came back down. 'OK,' he said, but he looked as though he was thinking fast. 'We're stuck here. Fire's moving too fast and it's coming right for us.'

'You're not going to leave me?' Dylan stopped pulling his leg.

'Of course we're not going to leave you, doofus,' I patted his arm. 'At least— we're not, are we, Brendon?'

'Nope.' Brendon still had that 'deep in thought' look. 'No. Like I said, there's no getting out now, fire will overtake us anyway. And it's the heat that's the danger when you're outside, not the smoke.'

As if in answer, another curl of grey smoke wisped its way down to us.

'We need to get further down into the gulley.' Brendon pulled at me. 'Move!'

I grabbed out with both hands, reached for Dylan's jacket and dug both fists into the fabric. Then I allowed myself to slide. Dylan's weight above me, combined with Brendon's tugging at my shoulder managed to cause a kind of three-bodied slither that took us down the steeply sloping grass towards the little trickle of water at the bottom of the narrow gulley. When I looked up we were roofed over with smoke, a black, dense cloud of it.

'It's coming. Get your heads down, both of you.' And Brendon was there, over the top of both of us, all of us crouched together. His chest was against the back of my head, forcing it down into Dylan's shoulder, his body was curled around mine in a parody of spooning. Dyl was underneath both of us, face pressed into the layer of crushed bracken that lay between us and the water.

There was a roar, a noise like a train was passing close by, then a hot wind and smoke that made us all cough. A crack as a tree went down across the top of the tiny narrow ditch we lay in and a sudden heat that made me hold my breath.

Brendon had been pressed down on me for so long that I wondered if he was still alive. Wondered if any of us were still alive or whether this was some joke of an afterlife where we'd be doomed to remain in our death poses until eternity. Would we haunt Christmas Steepleton as little blackened, wizened creatures, hunched into…

…but beneath me, Dylan was breathing hard. 'You're squashing me, I can't breathe.'

'Stay down,' Brendon spoke into my back. 'Just a minute longer. Until I'm sure.'

'You're really heavy, Leah.'

Unless we were going to be ghosts that moaned about how uncomfortable and unfair death was, like a bunch of teenagers, I deduced we were probably still alive.

'Are you all right?' I asked, my mouth barely able to move as it had so much of Dylan being shoved into it.

'No. You need to bloody diet, you fat arse.'

'Not *you*, Dylan. Brendon?'

'I think…' The pressure lifted off me a little. 'Yes. Yes, I'm OK. We're all OK. The fire jumped the gully, it's too wet down here whereas the grass on the top will burn more easily. I've got a few holes in my T-shirt, but, yeah. We're all good.'

I burst into tears.

The little channel rang with the sound of male embarrassment. Brendon cautiously slithered off me and held out a hand to pull me free of Dylan. 'We're all right,' he repeated.

'But we might not have been,' I sniffed. 'We could have died.'

Brendon and Dylan exchanged a look.

'Well, yeah,' Dyl said. 'But we didn't. And there's no use crying over what didn't happen, cos that would be stupid. You might as well cry because you didn't win the lottery or you haven't got a Porsche.'

'I think Leah is crying out of relief,' Brendon said. His eyes were a little red-tinged too, but that could have been the smoke. It had filled the ditch and was taking its time in leaving. Up on the edge I could see the black of burned grasses and the gorse bushes which had hidden the lip of the gully from us until we were nearly on it, were now just dark stubs at nightmare angles. 'That was a close one.'

'How did you know the fire would go over the top of us?' Dylan seemed a bit awestruck at Brendon's fire-knowledge. 'Is it something you learn when you're Australian?'

'No, not really. Just been through a few fires in the outback.' Brendon pushed a hand through his hair. 'And I wasn't *sure* the fire wouldn't burn down here.'

'So we could have…?' I couldn't even finish the sentence.

'But we *didn't*. All right?' Again there was a catch in his voice, as though he was having to fight thinking about alternative futures.

All of a sudden a face appeared. It was heading up the canyon towards us, splashing through the little dribble of stream. It was wearing a helmet. 'Got 'em! They're down here!'

'Who the hell are you?' Brendon asked. 'It's getting a bit crowded down here. Who's next, the Geelong Aussie Rules team?'

The face, shortly afterwards followed by a body thrusting its way through the growth of bracken and ferns, ignored him. 'Three people, all alive!'

'Dylan's got an injured leg,' I pointed out, in a very reasonable voice, I felt.

'One injured! We need the ambulance!' Then, in a slightly more reasonable tone, 'Lyme Regis fire brigade. We got a message to look out for you up here.'

'Tass,' I said, relieved.

'Yeah. Don't you know how dangerous it is, coming up on a heathland when there's a fire?'

I elbowed Brendon in the ribs to stop him from replying to that.

Chapter Ten

It was dark when we got back to the house. Dylan had been checked out by the paramedics and his ankle had been pronounced sprained and wrenched but not broken. We'd all had every bit of treatment that the crews could muster to counter the effects of smoke inhalation and the ambulance dropped us back, with blood so oxygenated that it was practically fizzing.

'The fire stopped at the road,' Tass said. 'I was worried about the house for a bit, all the computers and everything, but it's fine. Just smells like a really bad barbecue. The farmer came and moved the cows though.'

I looked over into the dark, empty field. It didn't feel right without the little brown cows filling it up with their breathing noises and occasional jarring coughs, although the absence of bovine sounds meant that we could hear the sea at the bottom of the cliffs now.

'Funny, when you think about it. All that water down there, and up here on fire,' Tass said, philosophically.

I missed those cows. It felt like a huge hole in my life without their dark eyes and mooching figures, the sound of whisking tails and gentle belches. Like someone had taken something from me, something I wanted and needed.

The tears came, despite my desperate attempts to suppress them. *Crying is natural. It's allowed. Just because you've always been told it's pointless and that you won't get your own way by crying, doesn't mean it's not perfectly valid.* Big lumpy tears, fat and splashy poured down my face. There was a lump in my throat that felt as though it had formed from all those things I'd never been allowed to say, or cry at.

'Hey,' Brendon's voice was gentle. 'It's fine, we're all safe.'

'The… cows…' It was hard forcing words past that lump. Too much wanted to come with them.

'It's shock. Come on, let's go for a walk.' His hand was gentle too, although it was shaking a little. Clearly shock wasn't limited to me, or to fields of cows. We'd all had a narrow escape that was becoming more evident to us by the moment.

'I should stay here. Make sure Mum and Dyl are all right.' It felt as though there was a white-hot wire inside me, running from my brain to my stomach and tightening with every passing second. My head was pulling down to my chest and I wanted to curl up in a ball, hide in the darkness and weep for everything in the whole world.

'They're fine. Tass is here and they've even found your mum some cigarettes. Better make sure she doesn't drop any ash and start another fire!'

I could suddenly see that oncoming wall of flame and my tears fell faster.

'Too soon? Look, let's go and walk up to the cliff, it's a beautiful night and the air will do you good. Honest, shock is natural, it's just your body reacting to…' he stopped suddenly.

'To nearly dying? To facing mortality? To the fact that, if that fire hadn't jumped the gulley we'd be three charred corpses right now?'

'But we're alive, Leah. The worst didn't happen.'

Inner-Claire tapped on my forehead, but I didn't let her interrupt. I put the thoughts into my own words. 'Growing up… it was always about the worst. How we couldn't go out because something terrible would happen. How school was a waste of time because we'd never get to do what we wanted. How my degree – my doctorate – was pointless. Moving away, buying my house – it was all going to end in tears. Everything. Everything was going to be bad!'

I was aware I sounded like a spoiled five-year-old when I said that, and cleared my throat. 'Every single thing I did, I had to follow up with "that wasn't so bad, was it?" but she couldn't see it. It was always about what *might* have happened.'

We'd walked the length of the field now and stood on the edge of the slumped cliff. Even the landscape looked miserable and defeated, I thought. A reflection of me. This was how it was, and this was how it always would be, give or take a huge coastal storm and erosion. I didn't think a storm and some big waves would make much difference to my mother's mindset. Or mine, now. Too entrenched. Too *accustomed to being beaten down.*

'It's not your fault.' Brendon wasn't looking at me. He'd let go of my arm and was staring out at the sea, which barely moved under the night's weight.

'I know. I mean, logically I know that.' I wiped my face with the back of my hand. 'I know. And I know I can overcome it all, if I think logically. I try to, I really do.' It was suddenly important that he understood. 'I try to think of the positives so hard that I practically Pollyanna myself to death. But when things do start to slide – it's like I'm my mother all over again.'

I looked at his silhouette. The moon hadn't risen yet, but the sea seemed to give off its own light, plus the faint glow from

Steepleton off to our left made it look as though he had a kind of bioluminescence.

'Have you wondered,' he said, still focused on some spot out on the ocean, 'why I left Australia?'

'I…' I tailed off. I'd only casually wondered what had driven him half way round the world. I'd not really thought in detail.

'And don't say you're sorry for not thinking about it, please. There is not a reason in hell why you should have. I mean, I told you I came to find my great-grandad and you took that at face value, that's fine. No, really, that's good.'

'But you did say you ran away.' I hadn't *wanted* to ask, that was at the bottom of it. Hadn't wanted this nice, kind, good-natured man to reveal himself to be as shallow underneath as everyone else.

'And you didn't ask what from.'

'No.' And then, realising slowly. 'If you'd wanted me to know, you'd have told me. It wasn't for me to ask.'

An inclination of the head. 'Yes. But it was something… well. It didn't matter, not to you and me, not then. And now?' He lifted a hand and pushed it through his hair, as though he needed to do something physical and it was that or jump. 'I like being around you, Leah.'

'Yes, you said. You keep saying.'

'I left Australia because my girlfriend wanted to start a family.'

For a moment the words made no sense to me. 'Oh,' I said, to give my mind time to catch up.

'And I couldn't do it. I don't want children. I've never wanted children. There's just no way I can be the kind of dad my dad is. He's the most amazing man with so much patience – he was behind me doing whatever I wanted. Aussie Rules player or professional surfer. That man is just so calm and accepting. Kind of like the absolute opposite to your mum. But… yeah. That's not me. Not what I want from my life. I thought I'd told her that when we got together, but apparently she thought I'd change my mind once we had money and a house and all that.' He was talking faster now. As though the words had been there, waiting, queued up behind other stuff, just waiting for their turn. 'And, let's face it, it's not something you can compromise on, you can't have half a baby. So…' he spread his hands towards the sea, as though he was giving it back the idea. 'We split up. It was tough. And I came over here as my family clearly had a history of running away from things.' Another hand through the hair. 'And then, when you said you didn't want to have children – I thought, this is someone who *gets* it.'

'So you like me because *I* don't want children? Is that it?'

He half turned. 'No. I think I told you I liked you before that ever came up. But it's nice to know upfront, if y'see what I mean.'

'I'm not always very nice,' the words came out in a rush. 'That thing with Lewis… I *knew* it was wrong…'

'I once stole my sister's car,' he said. 'So, no position to be all judgemental and stuff. Plus, I'm pretty sure that Great-grandad is going to turn out to be a bigamist murderer.'

There was a flash of a grin in the darkness. It felt like a lightbulb going on, as though something switched in my head at that moment. Why *didn't* I talk about it? About my awful mistake? Because it would make me look bad? I chewed the inside of my lip for a moment. Not wanting to look bad was what had kept my mother indoors all these years, wasn't it? Not wanting people close, not wanting to admit to having children by men who didn't stick around. Getting pregnant whilst still eating school dinners. Not knowing how to bring those children up but being held back from asking for help by the fear?

'Leah, please tell me what you're thinking.' Brendon's voice was very level.

'I'm realising things,' I said. And my voice sounded different. Strange. Not like me at all. Maybe I *wasn't* quite 'me' at that moment. Maybe the shock was doing things to my brain. Maybe the near-death experience was making me think differently. 'My mother is afraid of doing things wrong.'

'She certainly puts up a good front,' Brendon seemed encouraged by my words.

'She's passed it on to me. I *can't* fail. I quite literally can't. So I've never tried anything that I might not be good at.'

'No attempts at the "round the world on a pogo" record then?' A definite laugh in his words and his smile gleamed through the dark.

'Exactly. I've stuck to what I know. And, OK, sometimes that's good. It's got me my PhD, professional reputation and all that, but it's made sure I never do anything that I don't already know I *can* do. I've never…' I stopped. Thinking of the one time I had done something wrong. Knowing that I was still dragging that behind me like an anchor. 'And that's keeping Dyl back too – he doesn't know how to get out, how to live a life without being told what to do. So he's stayed at home in the attic.'

'Like a really domesticated possum,' Brendon said.

'Yes, exactly.' I took a deep breath. 'I made one mistake. Just one, in my whole life.'

'Well, we've all—'

'No, a big one. A really big one. And I can't forget it.'

Brendon looked at me.

'Lewis.' I said his name and stopped. There was that image again, the crumpled, grey suit, the overlong hair. The tall, thin figure that I'd thought was everything I wanted. 'He was… clever, funny. Sexy. And I never thought I'd find that in a man. Never thought anyone could *be* like that. After Darric… well, I thought Darric was like everyone, that that was how relationships were.'

'You told me about Lewis,' Brendon said. 'That's a mistake. That's not a failure.'

The warm night air swooped around us. Buzzed in my ears, louder than the sound of the grasshoppers, louder than the sound of the gentle sea below.

'He was my best friend's *husband*! And she was lying there in that hospice, relying on him, relying on me and… what were we doing? Screwing each other in her house! Being there for her during the day and then going back and—' The memory of it made me blush into the dark.

'Yeah. That wasn't good.' Brendon touched my hair. 'But, you know what? You were both suffering. He was losing his wife, you were losing your friend. So maybe we can afford to cut you both a bit of slack.'

'You could be right. But it's making me wonder if he's still around.' I explained about the emails, about the little challenges – urging me to do things that made me just a little bit afraid.

'I stroked that dog on the beach and I didn't even *think* about the emails at the time, but the person sending them – OK, *Lewis* – somehow knew I'd done it. And it's someone who knows I'd worry if I hadn't. Do you think that means…?'

'Means that he's here? Watching you?' Brendon drew in a deep breath and stared out over the dark line of the horizon.

'Well, if he is then I'm bloody well going to find him. OK, like I said, pacifist and all, but I might be tempted to engage him in a Brit-Aussie slanging match, and I'm pretty sure I can win that.'

Despite the way he was keeping his back straight and his face averted, there was a levity in his tone that made my heart rise to meet it.

'And you're not disgusted by what I did?' I nearly whispered.

His voice was very closed in when he replied. 'Leah. Oh, Leah. You've been so well trained. You remind me of our old dog – once, when I got home, the puppy had been in the trash, pulled it all over the house. The old dog met me at the door with the biggest guilty look on her face, like it was her fault…' He took a deep breath. 'Look. You can't go through life not upsetting anyone. You're tiptoeing around, scared to say what you want and what you need—'

I interrupted him. 'But it's not about what I want or need!'

Another sigh. 'Sometimes it really is, y'know. Sometimes you're allowed to stand up and scream, "but what about ME!" Not when you're in the supermarket or something, cos that would be a bit crazy, but in private.' Now he turned round to face me. 'It really doesn't matter what I think about what you and Lewis did. You don't need my forgiveness, you need to forgive yourself and – dear Lord I sound like a self-help book here. Please tell me to shut up.'

There was a distant flash over to our left, far over the bays and hills that led towards the cities and towns of the real world.

'I think I can safely say,' and my voice shook a little bit, 'that I will never do *anything* like that again. I just wish I could…' And now my voice broke. I just didn't have the words for what I wanted to do. *To talk to Claire. To tell her what happened and why. To tell her how very sorry I was about it all, how stupid it all made me feel. That I fell for soft words and arms that hugged me, when I was more used to being told off or ignored. How any kind, gentle physical contact made me believe I was in love.*

'The best revenge is living well,' Brendon said. 'A very wise bloke told me that once. It was my dad, actually. Bit outnumbered by women in our house, it was just me and him and even the dogs were female. But, yeah. You can't really make it up to her, but you can live the rest of your life showing that you learned from it. You're never going to sleep with your best friend's husband again, are you? You kinda have to move on from it, stop dwelling on what you did.'

'Dwelling on things is what I *do!* Another flash in the distance, like the onset of a migraine, right at the edge of vision. 'It's sort of my raison d'être.'

Brendon's hand was warm on my shoulder again. 'No,' he said. 'It's your unique selling point.'

I moved a little closer. The weight of his arm and the feel of his body next to me was – yes – it was good. It was comforting. I could relax into it and give a little of the worry up. Not like with Lewis where it had felt good to have a man hold me, but the guilt had ridden on my shoulder like a devil the whole time, whispering into my ear that 'we shouldn't be doing this'. With Brendon, the devil was silent.

Another flash, and this time it was followed by a low grumble as though the land was getting annoyed.

'Weather's breaking. There's a storm coming,' Brendon said, giving me a look almost as fast as the lightning flashes.

'It's being metaphorical again, I think.' I raised my head and felt the weight of worry and grief slip from the back of my neck. I lifted my face towards Brendon. 'Can we try that kiss thing again, do you think?'

213

'Bonza!' He moved in very slowly as though afraid to startle me. 'Course we can. Might need a fair bit of practice really.'

I turned as his arms came around me. Our faces were very close now. He smelled of woodsmoke and of salt. Beneath us the sea twitched.

'Yes. Let's practice,' I whispered, and our lips touched.

This kiss went on until a crack of thunder overhead drove us apart.

'Think we angered the sea gods,' Brendon said, slightly breathlessly.

I laughed. 'No. It's just weather.'

A gust of wind blew across my cheek and swirled around us, as though wrapping us both in air. It carried the smell of rain and an edge of chill with it.

'Storm's coming,' Brendon observed. 'We should go inside. Don't want to get struck by lightning after all this.'

As if in answer, the sky flashed again, and this time the thunder's menacing roll was much closer. Overhead, the few gulls still flying in the dusk wheeled away in search of shelter, apart from one which swooped in low to the cliff face. Brendon ducked.

'It's got Omen written all over it, that bird,' he said.

'Come on, he saved Dylan's life! You've got to feel a bit warmer towards him now, surely.'

'Yeah, he saved your brother at no personal cost to himself. He wasn't going to risk so much as a singed feather, was he?'

We watched Roger, who seemed also to be watching us, as he hung just off the cliff as though nailed to the air.

'You called him "he",' I said.

'What?'

'You said "he", not "it". D'you know, I think you might actually be getting to like Roger?'

Brendon glanced up. 'Not "like", no. Grudging respect is as far as I'll go.'

The first drops of rain hit my skin. They were big, soft drops – almost warm.

'That's progress,' I said.

'We… er, we ought to get under cover.' The sky flickered like bad continuity, and the rain stopped being soft drops and became pellets. 'This is going to get—'

And then the deluge started. Blown in on a sudden rising wind which whipped the waves beneath us into a roar, so I couldn't tell where the noise was coming from. Thunder, pouring rain and the sea all combined into a noise that meant I couldn't hear Brendon's follow-up comment, I just went along with his pulling on my arm, and we ran. At first, towards the house, and then he seemed to change his mind and we dashed through the fast-forming puddles in the mossy yard, into the little shed.

'There might still be, y'know, a bit of an atmosphere in the house,' Brendon said, panting slightly. 'Thought we'd be better in here.'

'Mum will be all over Dylan and his bad ankle,' I squeezed water from my hair onto the tiled floor.

'Ah. But I gather from your tone she won't be putting his foot up on a cushion and bringing him hot tea?' Brendon flicked the light on and the single bare bulb flickered into a bleak kind of life. 'Look, sit here on my sleeping bag.'

'She'll be telling him how stupid he was to go up on the hill, probably with reference to every daft thing he's done since he was four. Well, every daft thing that she knows about, anyway,' I said, remembering a few occasions where our stories had holes you could have driven an earthmover through, in our attempts to keep Dylan out of trouble. 'Having an overprotective parent who doesn't actually do anything to protect you – well, it was complicated.'

'I can tell,' Brendon said, dryly.

I hugged my legs up to my chin and looked around the shed. 'You actually like it in here? You aren't, by any chance, a partly assembled push bike or a small horse, are you? Because those are the only things that I could see really being at home in here.'

Another lightning flash made the bulb flicker. Rain scrubbed the outside of the windows.

'It's OK,' he said gently. 'I'm not going to make you talk about your past. We've got time, y'know? It doesn't all have to be here and now, just let it come. I've seen enough to have a fair idea of how it was, but it's hard for me to relate.' He came and sat down next to me on the padded roll of the sleeping bag, and leaned his back against the bare stone wall. 'I *want* to understand.' He put his arm around me. 'I *will* understand. One day. But there's no hurry, Leah. No hurry at all.'

I felt a sudden twang that ran the length of me and my body rose into peaks and points all over. I was slightly surprised that my shirt hadn't started to steam. Brendon must have felt something change in the way I sat, because he half-turned and I raised myself up and kissed him again.

This was a different kiss to the one on the clifftop. With the background track of thunder and cascading rain, this one brought the heat to the foreground, as though I was a flame trying to start a fire, which flickered hesitantly for a second, and then caught.

'Are you sure about this?' His fingers were in my hair. 'I don't want—'

'Well, I *do*.' I rucked the bottom of his T-shirt so I could touch his skin. 'I really *do*.'

He breathed my name against my mouth, and then was kissing me again. I could feel his heart belting away in his chest as I ran my hands over his torso.

He had a tribal tattoo on one shoulder, which surprised me, and he seemed surprised by my body too. Surprised and appreciative at the way it responded to him, his gentle but thorough exploration that made me gasp delightedly. He wasn't like Darric and he wasn't like Lewis. He was caring and comfortable and kind as he made love to me, but with an edge of restraint, as though he didn't want to scare me. I was also different with him. Not the passive partner that Darric had wanted, nor the desperate, 'clinging-on-to-every-touch' person that Lewis had turned me into.

As I exploded with a passion I hadn't known was inside me, I finally felt as though I was truly *me*.

Afterward, with the rain lashing the door, the light bulb flickering and water coming through the cracked window to bead along ancestral cobwebs, I laughed.

'Well, that was a bit bloody mad,' Brendon said at last, when we were tucked up together in the sleeping bag. 'Not sure it was quite the right time and place, mind you.'

'Oh, it was *exactly* the right time and place,' I wriggled happily. The faint memories of how it had been before, with Darric, with Lewis, tried to crowd in, but I wouldn't let them. Brendon's uncomplicated grin and close warmth felt so normal, I didn't want to bring the misery of before into this.

'Yeah, well.' His smile widened as I watched. There was a new dimension to his face now that I had a new knowledge of his wide, beaming mouth's capabilities. His surfer hair was tangled because my fingers had dived into it, driven by passion more than once. It was as though sharing sex had reassembled his features and made them a touch more attractive but also more accessible. I was beginning to believe that Brendon really did like me. 'You're pretty hot yourself,' he said.

'No, I'm…' I stopped myself. 'It was amazing.' Yes.

'Yes.' Brendon kissed the top of my head. Stroked my hair, ran his fingers along my back, Gentle, gentle, with no expectation. And I fell into a sated sleep, squeezed up against him in the warmth of the down-filled bag, while the smell of damp earth and the sea filled the little shed.

* * *

We both woke with a jump. It was later, but not very much later, as it was still dark and the rain was still streaking the windows. The thunder was back to being a circular growl over the hills and the lightning had passed out over the sea and was illuminating the horizon with occasional coruscations.

'What?' I struggled to proper wakefulness as Brendon climbed out of the bag. The single bulb was still on and flared off his naked body, making me blink.

'Thought I heard something.' He pulled a shirt over his shoulders, which, from my point of view, wasn't really covering the points of interest, and went to the door. He put his ear against it.

'What did you hear?' I sat up. Water was coming under the door in little streams, paddled to mud in places. 'Someone coming?'

'More… a knocking.' And as he turned to look back at me, I heard it too. *Tap tap tap.* 'Could be water expanding the wood?'

I scraped my hair out of my eyes. 'Can you see anything out there?'

He shook his head. 'You OK if I open it?'

I was about to ask what sort of question was that, but then I realised that I was stark naked and in a sleeping bag. 'Go ahead, but if it's an armed lunatic, the problem is all yours.'

He grinned. 'I come from a country that wants to kill you. I'm good with dangerous creatures.' And, with his lower half carefully tucked behind the door, presumably in case the dangerous creature in question was my mother, he opened it a crack.

Then slammed it shut, spraying water inside the shed.

'Lunatic?' I asked. I was pulling on my own shirt now, and trying to work my legs into jeans that were still half damp.

'Worse.' He shuddered. 'It's that bird.'

The knocking had stopped and the only sound was the water cascading onto the cobbled yard surface. 'Why the hell would Roger be out there on a night like this?'

'Dunno. But it's way too Hitchcock for me.'

'Let me see.' I went past him and tugged the door open.

'No, don't open it! He might have friends! Armed friends!'

I ignored Brendon and looked down. Huddled in the meagre shelter of the tiled overhang, was Roger. Bedraggled wasn't the word, he looked as though he'd been through a wash cycle with a brick. His feathers were fluffed up, his head was down and his eyes were half closed. 'Roger? Are you all right?'

'If he answers, I'm running for home.'

I bent down. Roger tipped his head and looked at me. He didn't attempt to move out of the way, or even try to flap his wings, so I cupped my hands underneath him and picked him up. For such a large, menacing creature, he weighed almost nothing.

'He looks crook,' Brendon observed, still half behind the door. 'You'd better bring him in here.'

With the gull held against my chest, I turned back inside, half expecting him to suddenly take flight, but he just made a small mewing sound and huddled closer against me. His wicked beak was slightly gaping and his staring eye held an expression of slight desperation. Water rolled off his feathers in beads, but he still managed to look soaked through. I clutched him closer. 'What's wrong?'

'Bring him over to the light.' Brendon had put his jeans on now. I didn't blame him, I wouldn't have trusted that enormous beak anywhere close to my sensitive parts without a sturdy layer between them.

Under the meagre bulb, Roger looked smaller. His weightlessness and the overall fragility of his little body made me want to cry, despite the half-hearted attempt he made at snapping at my fingers when I changed my hold on him. His cold feet paddled against my arm but he made no real attempt to get down. 'Have you got anything we could feed him on?'

'Here, let's try this.' Brendon went to a tin and came over with a small slice of cake on one outstretched hand. 'If he bites me, we throw him out. Agreed?'

But Roger didn't bite. He didn't take the cake at all, just stared at it out of one eye slightly suspiciously, as though he thought Brendon might be trying to poison him.

'He's not eating, that's not good.' Brendon looked thoughtful. 'Can you turn him over?'

I looked doubtfully at Brendon, then dubiously at Roger. 'I don't think I've got enough hands. He's quite big.'

'Ah, come on.' And to my surprise, Brendon grabbed Roger and flipped him upside down in one movement that was so quick it looked like a special effect. Roger stared up at us both from between his own legs, but still made no attempt to struggle. 'Can you see anything? Any injury?'

'No, I... oh, wait a minute.' At the top of Roger's muscular thigh, I could just see a faint line. 'I think there's something wrong with his leg.'

Roger eyeballed me furiously, beak still agape.

'Maybe he's sprained something?' Brendon asked, hopefully.

'No, look.' I dug my fingers into feather and pulled. Roger scuffled, waving his feet and beak around at opposite ends, wings rising above it all. It was like dealing with a small and annoyed angel. 'It's one of those plastic things that they put round cans. Have you got a knife?'

'There's one in my bag.' Brendon looked over to the corner where his bag lay flopped on one side. 'I'll get it. Only I might want to be somewhere else when he can move properly again. Like Melbourne.' But he went and rooted around in the bag, returning to us with a small knife, which he weighed in his hand, looking at the bird. 'Have you got a decent hold?'

Roger waved his feet again, then seemed to understand we were trying to help him. He lay back with his head on my arm, watching Brendon carefully out of manic eyes as he bent down. I felt him run his finger along my hand to where it was hidden under Roger's feathers, tracing the way to where the plastic had pulled tight up against whatever it was that seagulls had that stood in for thighs. Then he started to cut the plastic. 'It's OK, I think he knows what we're doing.'

Brendon stopped sawing at the plastic for a moment and looked at the bird. 'I think he's fainted.'

'No, he's just lying quiet.' I could feel Roger's heartbeat, a brief scudding under the breastbone where he lay on my wrist. 'He feels so fragile.'

Brendon pulled and a piece of white plastic came away, falling to the floor with a rattle. 'That bird is built of sheet metal and hatred, don't be fooled.' He changed angle and started on another bit. 'He must have been fighting cans of Fosters or something.' Roger raised his head. 'And I'm watching you, mate. Any sign of that beak getting any nearer and you're out that door and I don't care if you've got an entire shopping bag jammed up your feathery backside, you'll be on your own.'

The head dropped again. Eyes like two amber beads fixed on me for a second and then went back to watching what Brendon was doing, as best he could, whilst upside down between my hands.

'Would you like me to take over?' I could see Brendon's cautious fingers feeling their way through feathers, as though he was afraid that they might suddenly sprout teeth.

A glance. Another one I couldn't read.

'I'm good.' And then a moment later, 'I'm seeing another side of you here, Leah.'

'I'm sorry.' I scrolled a mental checklist. I wasn't shouting. I was being helpful. What was wrong? 'I could turn him round, if that helps?'

Brendon laughed, which made Roger raise his head. The laugh must have had echoes of a roasting dish in it. 'Nah! I mean, you're more capable than you come across. Except when you're diving for the weed you try to look as though you're hiding all the time. Right now you're… actually, not sure what it is. I guess it's that you're not afraid. Usually you come over like someone who's scared of life.'

I stroked Roger's head with one finger. 'It doesn't scare me so much as it confuses the hell out of me. Everyone seems to know what they are doing, what *other people* are doing, and I don't. Like something's missing.'

The sudden warmth and firmness of his hand on my wrist surprised me and made me jump. Roger rolled an eye upwards. 'Look, Leah. Everyone feels like that, now and then. *Everyone.* We all misunderstand things or read people wrong; sometimes we all feel like life has a secret cheat code and everyone else has got it except us.'

I bent my head so he couldn't see my face. 'You're probably right,' I muttered. *This is what your mum always said. 'There's nothing special about you, Leah! You're just like everyone else, except you're too fond of showing off what you know, keener on reading books than watching the TV and finding out what everyone else knows. Not different, just self-obsessed.'* There was a hot stinging behind my eyes, but I wouldn't cry. I had thought that Brendon understood what it was like to be me – to live with this constant feeling of being a – but obviously he thought I was just trying to make myself seem special. 'I just think about myself too much.'

Between my hands, Roger struggled, flapping his legs against my arm and straining his head upwards. Brendon let go of me and went back to sawing through the plastic hobbles.

'I'm not telling you you're wrong, y'know,' he said. I wondered if he could see the tears threatening to fall. 'Course you're not. What you feel is as valid as what anyone else does. I'm just saying… OK, look. My sister – middle one – she was a bit of a tomboy growing up. She had horses in the paddock, all that. One day she told me to help her saddle up her horse cos she had to – I dunno – make a twelve hour phone call to her latest boyfriend, something like that. I'd never put a saddle on a horse before. Why should I? I played football! So I go out to this horse, and it stands there, and I put all the gear on it, and when my sister came out she nearly peed herself laughing. I'd got the bridle thing upside down, saddle half way off the horse's tail; I was trying to work out what to do with all the spare bits of straps I had left over. And all the while this horse is just standing there, things hanging in its eyes, saddle done up practically over its arse; did it give me any help? No it bloody didn't.'

Another burst of effort and he triumphantly pulled the shredded plastic away from Roger's feathers. 'To my sister, saddling a horse was second nature, she'd done it practically all her life. To me it was an exercise in logistics that I got wrong. Doesn't make me stupid, just means there's things I don't know how to do.' His eyes met mine and I tried to force any tears back down. 'Like you. OK, some of the things you don't know are a bit more front and centre than how to shove a bridle on a horse, but, yeah. Do you see?'

I swallowed hard. It felt a little as though I was swallowing feelings. Feelings I shouldn't have. 'Yes.'

There was a pause, during which Roger wobbled his head about, clearly wondering why he was still upside down.

'I'm getting the impression that I just kicked your puppy,' Brendon said at last, very quietly. 'Did I say something wrong?'

'No,' practically inaudible this time.

'Then you're going to have to help me out here, only I missed the term when we did "psychic communication" at school. I was probably surfing.' Although the words were a little pointed, his tone was very even and his voice held an undertone of laughter.

'I overthink things, you're right. I shouldn't.'

'Did I say that?' Now his voice had lost the laughter. 'Leah, you're like those chickens, y'know, the ones they used to keep in crates for the eggs? All their lives in this one little wire box so small they couldn't turn round.'

'Battery,' I said, slightly wearily. 'You mean I'm like a battery hen? I am *dying* to see how you turn this round.'

'Yeah!' There was a gleam in his eye. 'That's what I mean! One of those! You're like that. You were kept in this little box all your life – I mean, not a real box, that would be stupid and abuse and all that and your mum might be crazier than a possum in a pot, but she did what she could – and you've never had a chance to break out. Have you seen those hens? When they put them outside in the sunshine and they run back inside and hide because they've never felt the wind before? Give 'em a few weeks of open air and freedom and they're out there pecking away like they never knew anything else.' He gave me an almost tentative smile now. 'Once their feathers grow back, anyway.'

I just stared at him. I had to admit that the analogy was quite apt, and I admired the imagery, but… really? Was I like that?

He raised a hand, I think to brush my hair away from my face, but it coincided with Roger finally running out of patience. A sudden gathering between my fingers and there was an explosion of feathers, beak and feet in the shed, hurling itself between us like an over-anxious mother-in-law.

Brendon ducked. Roger, wings bashing against all surfaces, flopped and flapped towards the window. He finally arrived on the dusty ledge and perched there, clacking his beak in a threatening manner and stretching his legs as though to make sure that we'd done a thorough job on the plastic restraints.

'What's he doing?' Brendon was keeping his arms over his head. 'And I hope the answer is going to be "battering himself to death against his own reflection", it'd be a fitting end.'

I was almost surprised that it was still dark outside. It felt as though a lifetime's worth of experiences had happened since the storm started, but not even one night had passed.

'He's calmed down now,' I said. 'I think he felt a bit affronted that I was holding him upside down.'

Cautiously Brendon lowered his arms. He looked at Roger, whose feet had patterned the dust into leaf shapes. 'Can't we call a truce, mate? I just saved your legs.'

'Have you got any more of that cake? He might be in shock.' I had to stop myself from laughing at the sight of the bird and the Australian staring at one another.

'On my bag.' Brendon jerked his head. 'I don't want to move, I think I've got him subdued with the weight of my stare.'

Shaking my head at the pair of them, I fetched the previously rejected cake and held it out to Roger, who looked at it from each eye alternately, then pecked crossly at it.

'I think you're right,' I said.

'About the bird being a weirdo?'

'About me. I'm still not quite sure about the chicken thing, but, yes. So much of who I am is because of how I was brought up. But when it's all you know…' Memories of the small flat, the feeling of damp, the cold, the unwashed dishes and unswept floors… I pushed them away. 'I've made a start. I've moved out. I have a house. I'm divorcing Darric. But for *years* I thought she was right. I thought that was normal. I thought it was *me*…'

Roger pecked once or twice at the last crumbs on the stone ledge, then folded down onto his feet and sat like a realistic model, watching us.

'Well, now you know it's not. You're fine. You're *better* than fine.'

'But all this stuff with Lewis… the emails.'

Brendon looked at me thoughtfully, then reached out. Without thinking I walked into his arms and put my head on his shoulder.

'Maybe he is trying to tell you something.' I felt his words rather than heard them, reverberating through both our bodies. 'How do you feel about that?'

I thought again of the long body. Of the crumpled suits and the slow smile.

'He's a dick,' I said. 'I thought he craved comfort because he was grieving, but it wasn't really. He just saw me vulnerable and jumped in. He was the first person to ever show me affection, so I built it all up into some great, doomed love affair, when it was really just this practised seducer getting his kicks while his wife lay dying.'

Memory-Lewis ceased to be all charm and careless dressing. I began to remember now the slightly predatory chats over wine after he gave me a lift back from the hospital. I recognised them for what they were, checking me out. Seeing if I'd go for it. And I – stupid, naïve, desperate for love and warmth – I'd let it happen. Him sitting next to me on the sofa, prodding me into tears with 'when she's gone' talks about how we'd miss her. Little recollections about her foibles, her funny sayings, so that he could put his arms around me and we could sob together until…

Oh Claire. I'm so, so sorry.

I couldn't even imagine her reaction. There was a slightly irritated 'mew' from Roger, who had stood back up again and was tapping at the window pane with the tip of his beak. 'And I'm going to email him back and tell him to knock off all this "helping me get over my grief" crap,' I continued. 'He's just trying his luck again. Probably been dumped by whoever he took up with after me, and thinks I'm an easy mark. I *am* an easy mark! I don't read subtext unless it's footnotes in an academic journal!'

'It's nice to see you angry,' Brendon observed. He took half a step back and looked into my face. 'You do better when you're angry.'

'I wasn't allowed to be angry. I'm just learning. Anyway, I'm not angry now, just cross. It feels a bit like life has been one of those tangled-string puzzles, you know, when you have to follow one of the ends to find the prize? And I've been trying all the wrong ends and ending up with a bigger and bigger knot.'

'But you're starting to come unravelled?'

I narrowed my eyes. 'Be very careful what you say next.'

'No, no, it's good to see.'

We stood in our loose embrace for a while longer, until I shivered. 'I think I need some more clothes on.'

'Or we could go back to bed...' Brendon hovered a hand around my lower back for a moment, then moved it up between my shoulder blades. 'No, I take that back. I'm not sleeping with that crazed bird in here, I'd wake up to insane laughter and minus my kidneys. Come on, we'll sit down over here. We should keep an eye on the bird anyway, make sure nothing's been damaged.'

We slowly sat, arms still around one another, on the sleeping bag and I buried my chilly feet in its depths. Roger stayed hunkered down by the window as though he too was trying to sleep.

'It's going to take time,' I murmured sleepily. 'I've got a lifetime of conditioning to overcome.'

'Hey,' Brendon squeezed my shoulder gently. 'I've got time. Australia isn't going anywhere. I mean, yeah, tectonic plate movement and all but, not for a while. We've got time to see where this goes. We don't have to declare love and propose marriage, just say that we're interested and we like one another. I'm going to sell *Southern Cross* anyway, when this is done, but… yeah, Bristol sounds good. I'll get my own place, pick up some work. We don't have to rush it.'

'Mmmm.' I lowered my head onto his chest and fell asleep.

Chapter Eleven

I woke to daylight and feeling warm. I lay for a second, with my cheek on a gently moving chest, remembering what had happened the night before. Brendon had spent the remainder of the night with his arms around me. A total contrast to Darric, who complained that it was 'too hot' to sleep close to another person and, on the rare occasions we'd shared a bed, he'd hung on to the far side of the mattress as though he feared I had typhoid. And Lewis? Well, we'd never spent the *whole* night together. Now, here I was, with a man who actually wanted to be close to me. And it felt good.

My mother hadn't held me or cuddled me. I mean, she must have done in my early years but as soon as I was mobile I was 'too much of a handful' – or so she said. I relaxed back into Brendon's rhythmic breathing and wondered why she'd felt that way about her own child. Well, both her children really. I couldn't recall her cuddling Dylan much, although she'd put that down to him being a boy, which was absurd, sexist nonsense from someone who'd grown up in the seventies…

…and then it hit me. So hard that I practically jerked with the impact. *She hadn't grown up at all.*

'Mmmff?' Brendon moved, adjusting an arm. 'Before I open my eyes, where's the bird?'

'Still sitting by the window.'

'Not waiting to take my eyeballs out?'

'Not noticeably, no.' I stretched, trying to hold onto that thought that had come, trickling slowly through my recently woken brain like a dream. *She's never grown up.* 'Sorry, did I wake you up?'

He wriggled his shoulders. 'Nah, nothing to be sorry for. My arse feels like I sat on a funnel web, but I'm guessing it's probably just rocks. I may never walk again.'

I bit back the contrition that immediately begged me to apologise again and my internal Claire applauded. *Making progress! Wow.*

'I was just thinking…' I began. Over at the window Roger seemed to realise we were awake, and tapped his beak restlessly against the glass pane, as though he expected it to tilt like a cat flap. 'Something about my mother. Weird, really, that I didn't see it before.'

Brendon wriggled again. 'Please don't take this as a rejection of any kind, Leah, sweetheart,' he said slowly. 'It's not. I want to spend every night like this in future – OK, maybe without the bird – but I have *got* to move. I'm not pushing you away. Got that?'

I didn't know whether to be annoyed or touched. 'Yes, of course. Sorry.'

He looked at me and raised an eyebrow. 'You really don't need to apologise either.' Cautiously, as though he feared his legs would fall off, he stood up. 'Your mother?'

'Where?' I clutched the sleeping bag to me.

'This is going to be a long job.' He grinned then. 'You were saying, you'd realised something?'

'Sort of. I wonder if I was dreaming…?' I reached around my mind for the tattered edges of the thoughts that were shredding away with the daylight. There *had* been a dream, children on a beach… 'I was dreaming that my mother was a little girl and I was looking after her.'

Brendon didn't say anything.

'And, yes, now I come to think of it, it was fairly obvious, but it's hard, you know? When you're in it? Claire did say – well, never mind. She only met my mother a few times, so she wasn't really seeing things from all sides. But being here, in Dorset, seeing my mother out of her closed-in flat, her comfort zone and watching her trying to create a new one in the house, it's made me see what went on.'

Over at the window, Roger shifted, the matt gleam of his feathers caught the sun and shone a gunmetal grey.

'My mother is still fifteen,' I said, and my voice sounded distant as though it, too, was coming from the past. 'She never had the chance to grow up like most people do, sort of fumbling their way along through life. She was in care, she only ever had herself to rely on for security. She had to make a life before she'd had a chance to see how adult life went – a life where she was afraid to put her head above the parapet for fear of… something.'

'Losing you and Dylan, probably.' Brendon's voice was similarly quiet. 'She was afraid that asking for help would mean you'd be taken away.'

'She keeps the curtains drawn so nobody can see how badly she's managing. Never goes out for fear of seeing what she's missing. She's made her life this little cocoon and she thinks that's safe, and she's tried to make us think so too. But she was *wrong*! All that happened is that she brought us up to be afraid of everything she was afraid of!'

Roger knocked his beak on the window again. He seemed to be gaining energy from the sun, like a lizard.

'I think we might have to let the bird out.' Brendon didn't move. He cast an uncertain look towards the window. Roger stretched his wings and flapped, then threw his head back and let out a noise that made Brendon and I look at one another. 'I'm going in,' he said. 'If it all goes oggo, tell my family I loved them.'

Roger's mad little marble of an eye swivelled but he didn't attempt anything more rigorous than that. Brendon leaned across and flipped the window open. We were then treated to the sight of a large sea bird poking its way through a window. It was similar to watching a very old lady getting out of a car.

When Roger had finally flopped to the far side, stretched his wings and taken flight, Brendon let out a sigh. 'So you think your mum has never really grown up.'

I stared down at yesterday's clothes. They were still slightly damp and had creased into interesting patterns.

'She shut herself away,' I said. 'She's not matured past being fifteen because she hasn't been able to. Somehow, she's got trapped at the age she was when I was born.'

'Well, she managed to conceive your brother, so she's not exactly been nailing the front door shut,' he said, slightly acerbically. 'She must have gone out sometimes. And done things. Well, one thing in particular, for sure.'

'I think she's just never learned to cope with life.' I buttoned my shirt up properly. In last night's haste I'd done it up lopsided.

'You sure you're not just trying to find excuses for the way she is?' Brendon gave me a very direct look. 'You and Dylan, you're both kinda damaged. I'm not seeing much of a reason for her not to have gone out and got some help. I dunno what you've got over here, but she could have got *something*. A job?'

'I don't even think she's got a National Insurance number. She left school before she'd had any kind of careers advice and she ran away from care. She never really got to grips with paying bills properly or how bank accounts work or any of that. I did it all for her as soon as I was old enough. I think,' I said slowly, 'that she's really scared of the outside world.'

We looked out at the day, squeezing itself through the window in a similar way to Roger, only with fewer feathers. An acidic sun was slicing into the little yard between the shed and the house and reflecting off puddles that lay like little sky mirrors amid the cobbles.

'Ah, the outside world's not so bad,' Brendon said. 'Least your wildlife doesn't want you dead.'

'But when you were fifteen, weren't you confused?'

'Dunno. Not really, I don't think. I was just all about the surfing and the footie and my mates. Hanging out and drinking on the beach and – yeah, well, you probably don't need to know more than that. But then, I had a very different kind of family – we did little jobs around the place, earned money, got shown how to look after it. We thought we'd pretty much got a handle on life. I think most fifteen-year-olds think they know it all, it's just the old guys holding them back from… running the world, I guess.'

I imagined him then, tanned and lanky under the Australian sun.

'Yes, well, I'm not exactly a control group. I've been confused since day one. Fifteen wasn't much different.' Except that was the age I was when teachers had started to realise how 'different' I was. That I didn't have friends, didn't watch TV, didn't spend weekends shopping for clothes. I went to school, I went home and I looked after Dylan. And I studied. I thought that was normal. Hell, it was *my* normal. And then I remembered the girls who'd been at school with me. So sure, so certain. Yes, my mum probably *had* thought that she knew enough to get by.

Until she'd found that a screaming baby, no money and not really knowing where to go for help was just the beginning of a whole new set of problems.

Brendon ran his hands through his hair. It gave him an outdoors sort of look. With his brown skin and his surfer's streaks he looked as though he should have been outside in a field with his shirt off, doing something physical. I gave a little shiver of pleasure, remembering how physical he could be.

'OK then. Are you ready to do the walk of shame and go get a cup of tea?' He held a hand out. 'We ought to let them know that we're alive out here.'

We splashed across the steaming yard, where the water was evaporating in the stinging sunlight. I could hear the argument before we even set foot in the house.

'But I *want* the computer! You've got to get off it. It's my turn!' Dylan's voice had gone up an octave. He sounded like the peeved ten-year-old that used to run our house. I'd thought he'd been making progress. Dorset seemed to have shown him that there was so much more to life than a flat in Devizes and living behind an Xbox.

'I'm busy.' That was my mother, equally peevish.

I raised my eyebrows at Brendon as we quietly approached the open door, alert for missiles. 'My mother? On the computer? I always thought she thought it was some kind of very advanced shelving,' I whispered.

Dylan swung through the doorway, clearly in middle of a stroppy exit. Coming face to face with me, he paused. 'Tell her to get off the computer!'

Before… Ah. Before, I would have rushed to soothe everyone's feelings. But now…? Well, I wasn't going to overcome thirty-odd years of conditioning overnight, but I could bring my new insights to bear.

'Tell me what's going on,' I said, and Brendon and I carried on walking into the kitchen, so Dylan was forced to reverse. He performed a sort of doorstep rotation.

'Mum won't let me use the computer and I want to look up photography courses. Tass has said I can stay with them until I'm sorted.'

* * *

I didn't know what surprised me more, Dylan's attempt at forward planning or his easy use of Tass's preferred pronoun. And then there was the whole 'mum on the computer' thing to deal with, so I felt as though I'd stepped into Wonderland.

'Where's Tass?' It was all I could think of to say. The table was occupied with neatly stacked envelopes and prepped sample bottles, a collection of cups by the sink had been washed and tipped to drain and, in the middle of all this domesticity, sat my mother, as though none of it had anything to do with her which, to be truthful, it probably didn't.

She was staring at a screen and writing things down on a piece of paper beside her on the worktop, occasionally tapping ash from her cigarette onto a saucer. She looked a little bit like a vision of a journalist in a 1940s film, only with more tracksuit and less glamour.

'Tass is upstairs,' Dylan waved a hand at the kitchen, indicating I knew not what. '*Tell* her, Leah!'

'Mum,' I could feel the weakness in my voice, so I repeated myself with a bit more strength. 'Mum, I didn't know you could use a computer.'

She snorted and tapped ash into the saucer. 'Course I can. I goes up the library and uses theirs. I don't touch his.' She jerked her head towards Dylan. 'There's a really nice lady there that helps me, she taught me how to use it and what sites to go on for what I want.' She tapped a few more keys.

'So what *are* you doing on there?'

Now she looked up at me. I noticed that her eyebrows had been drawn on slightly crooked, that she'd got a patch of dry skin under one eye and there were the telltale fan lines around her upper lip that spoke of a smoking habit that went back decades. Suddenly I was seeing her as a real person, one with odd eyebrows and the wrinkles of a life of worry.

'Looking up *his* great-grandad,' she said, and the surprise was enough to knock me into a chair.

'What?'

Behind me, Brendon put the kettle on. We'd make a Brit out of him yet.

'Your bloke up there,' she jerked her head upwards, presumably indicating Tass and I was so deep in the throes of surprise that I didn't even correct her. '*He* reckons I'm a waste of space. Like I can't do nothing. But I've learned a bit over my time on this earth, and let me tell you, I ain't no useless piece of shit. I've got things I can do. I *know* things.' An indignant sniff. 'More'n you and him put together I reckon.'

I opened my mouth and then shut it again. My mother? Being proactive? Tass must have really got under her skin.

'I mean, he's supposed to be looking for his great-grandad. Well, I bet he's not even a member of the family websites, is he?' Tap tap went the ash. The smoke from her cigarette and my levels of surprise were reaching the ceiling.

'Well, I did do *some* research online,' Brendon said evenly. 'But I didn't know about him going under a different name then. And I didn't really know which sites to join. I didn't think it would be *that* hard to find him.' Mugs clattered. 'This country is bigger than I thought.'

'But I want the computer!' Dylan wailed again. 'You *never* go on the computer, Mum!'

'Well, I am now.' She practically snapped the words, and I was, again, surprised. Normally Dylan only had to wait for something for the length of time it took Mum to get on the phone and get me to bring it over – he was used to instant action. This was perhaps the first time she'd ever said 'no' to him. 'I'm getting somewhere and I'm not stopping now.'

Brendon and I looked at each other through the smoke. He was giving me a sideways sort of smile but I had the feeling that my eyeballs were about to fall out and roll along the floor. This behaviour was… well, it wasn't my mother. I watched her tap a couple more keys with her chipped nails.

'So how…?' My voice was so high with surprise that I sounded like Roger, and I cleared my throat. 'Why did you sign up to the family history websites then, Mum?'

A pause. Quiet, except for the burble of the computer fan and the gentle rustle of the static in her lounge suit.

'I was looking for my family,' she said and took a swig of something from the mug at her elbow. It was probably tea, although, in keeping with the '1940s journo' image she had going, it might have been gin. 'Thought I might be able to trace them. Had Mum's name and knew where I was born so I thought I might be able to find them…' The end fell off her cigarette. 'Well. It's what they calls a "learning curve".'

There was a silence in that kitchen that you could have bounced knives off. Dylan and Brendon were looking at me as though daring me to think of something to say next, but I had nothing. This was the first time our mother had ever spoken about her birth family.

'So, turns out it's easier to find death certificates than I thought.' She went back to the screen and tapped a few more keys. 'Mum's was drugs. Well, they says septicaemia, but she was twenty-seven, so I knows what that means.' Tap tap. I got the feeling she was distracting herself as much as typing. 'So, anyway. But I heard about this DNA stuff and how relatives can turn up, and I wondered if there were any more, like, if I had brothers or sisters. I sort of remember this older girl... So I joined all these ancestry groups and suchlike, so when your mate told me about him...' she jerked her head towards Brendon, '...looking for someone, well, I thought I might as well make use of them.'

My mouth was hanging open like a recently landed cod. 'You mean you got your DNA tested and *paid* to join these sites to try to find your family?'

A dismissive snort. 'Like I've got the money for that!' She stopped tapping keys and tapped her nose. 'There's ways, and that's all I'm saying. Haven't found no one yet, but I'm going to keep trying.'

Brendon put a mug of steaming tea in front of me.

'I think you'd better drink this,' he said quietly, his words almost drowned out by the click of the keyboard. 'Before something happens to your brain.'

Click click. And some notes, scribbled in her handwriting – which had always reminded me of a child's – words spelled phonetically. I stifled my astonishment with tea.

Dylan, who was clearly missing the point as firmly as ever, turned towards me again. 'But I *need* the computer!'

I didn't know why I should have expected anything else from him. He was reacting like he always did when thwarted in a desire, regressing to a five-year-old with a five-year-old's comprehension of a situation. I felt that uncomfortable thump in my chest at the acknowledgement that we'd both been damaged by our upbringing. I'd done my best with him, but he was my brother not my son, and I hadn't had the tools to correct our spoiled childhoods. I might – just *might* – be able to consciously overcome mine. But would Dylan ever be able to grow past his? All those years in the attic had stunted his brain – although that might have been the computer games.

'Look, use my laptop.' I found it on the table underneath the jiffy bags. 'Only don't touch *any* of these tabs, all right?'

'That your porn?' He gave me a grin. It threw me back to echoes of us as children, when I'd been the one to solve so many problems for him.

'You are disgusting. Now, just go and look up your photography courses or whatever. And no gaming!'

He seized the machine and clutched it to his chest. 'I'm going to find Tass. They're going to help me.'

A moment of panic. How would my largely feral brother cope with organised courses? With taking in new information, learning new stuff, maybe gaining qualifications? *Could* he? And then I gave him a grin back. Of *course* he could. He was as capable of change and growth as I was. Maybe we'd escaped in time.

'Go on then,' I said. But years and years of conditioning broke through and I was still compelled to call after him, 'But be careful! Don't break anything!'

Brendon had opened a window to let the smoke out, and the sunlight was thickening the air already as it crept in through the gap. My mum didn't seem to feel it, although her leisure suit must have been boiling her blood.

'There you go.' With an air of triumph, she wiggled the screen so that Brendon could see. 'I reckon that's your great-grandad, there.' She tapped the screen with a nail. I winced. 'Henry Gass. He went down with a fishing boat just off the harbour there, in 1953. There was a big storm.'

Now it was Brendon's turn to look astounded.

'How the hell did you do that?' The tea in his hand began to slop over the rim of the mug. 'I mean… *how?*'

There was an unfamiliar expression on her face. I'd seen expressions like it, when one of us had done something she'd told us not to and the inevitable had happened. Like the time she told Dylan not to swing on the curtain, and he'd carried on and brought the whole pole down, while she'd looked on from the sofa with an expression very close to this one. But this one held less 'told you so' and more of what could only be pride.

I'd never seen her proud before.

'I knows a thing or two about these sites,' she lit another cigarette. 'Got to know how to follow stuff back. Your great-grandad now—' she tapped the screen again, '—because he weren't going by his given name, it was messing up your search.'

'I haven't really had chance to check him out since I learned he'd gone under a different name. Everything Silas has been finding for me has been to do with previous generations of Gasses – not Great-grandad.'

'Happened a lot, 'specially after the war,' my mother said, laconically, even though she would have thought 'laconic' was a shade of nail varnish. 'There was people changing their names all over the place. Records got lost. Bombed out. All that. Your great-grandad went by Gabriel for the official stuff, which was how you managed to find anything about him, but when he went by Henry it would have been for stuff that weren't usually written down, like family stuff. Boat going down, that were a local thing, he sailed her as Henry, not Gabriel.' A triumphant gleam came into her eye. 'An' whoever registered him dying, they must've been in a state. Put Henry on the death certificate, which was why you couldn't find it. Told you. You've got to know what you're doing with these things.'

Brendon was reading the screen. 'Henry Gass. He was part of the crew of the *Mary-Anne*, which sank off Christmas Steepleton in February 1953, running for the safety of the harbour. All hands lost.' He sat suddenly. 'He didn't desert the family. No bigamy. No murder. He drowned.' His voice had gone a bit weak. 'Great-grandma was left with three tiny kiddos and no money – no wonder she forgot he wasn't born Henry when she registered him dead.'

'And no wonder she went to Australia for a new life.' I put my hand on his shoulder and he glanced up and caught my wrist.

'Families, eh?' he said. 'Feels weird. I mean, he's a few generations away, I would never have known him anyway, but – wow.'

'It's a bereavement, whenever it happens,' I was remembering my mother's words. 'Looking for my family.' So she'd been curious about them, despite never having mentioned one word about her past to us. All these years, whenever we'd asked, whenever there'd been homework involving our families and their past, she'd just said she 'couldn't remember'. I'd assumed that she'd been so young when she'd been removed that she really didn't know anything about them. But she had. She'd known her mother's name. And that faint memory of an older girl, maybe a sister? So, what *else* might she really remember, underneath it all?

I moved over and gave her a hug. It wasn't much of a hug, just a trace of contact around the shoulders, and she squirmed away like a cat being put in a dress. But I'd done it. I lacked the tools to go any further, to tell her that I was beginning to understand. *Fifteen. Probably socially awkward already, maybe even non-neurotypical. And taken advantage of by men, after a past I could only guess at. Trying to build a life for herself and her children when she was little more than a child herself.*

I had a headache. Probably caused by my princess complex imploding.

'I have to tell my mum,' Brendon still looked shell-shocked. 'She'll be happy.' He looked half way happy himself. Like someone who's got to the end of a particularly twisty thriller, to find that they had guessed the villain right all along, but had wavered around the middle of the book. Satisfied, at the end of a long ride. 'Yeah. This is fair dinkum, Jackie. Fair dinkum.'

Mum still looked proud. It lifted her face, made her look younger. Almost elated. And it hit me again that she'd not looked that proud when I achieved my degree, or my PhD and then, on another wave of understanding – *that wasn't her achievement. She didn't know how to be proud of me.*

'Leah!' Dylan was calling from upstairs, and clumping noises indicated that he and Tass were approaching.

'I bet the E has fallen off the keyboard again,' I said. 'Just work round it,' I called back, but the pair of them appeared in the kitchen, laptop held out like an offering.

'You've got an email,' Dylan said, slightly out of breath.

'I expect I've got lots.' My tone was slightly tart under the weight of professional guilt. I'd hardly been taking my job seriously in these last few days.

'This one is different.' Dyl put the laptop down on the table. 'It's *haunted*.' Over his shoulder Tass was shaking their head with an 'I have no idea what this person is talking about' expression.

'Haunted?' Brendon and I said together.

'Yeah. Look.' He flipped the screen up and clicked.

There was my email inbox. No password protection, because nobody ever used my laptop except me. Because nobody ever emailed me anything, except work. And some really boring spam.

'Oh god,' I said, and I'd come over as weak as Brendon must be feeling.

There at the top was a new email.
From Claire.

Hi Leah!

It's pretty much been a year since I went into the hospice. Not sure how long since I died because, well, obviously, I'm writing this beforehand, but it can't be long.

There's so much I want to say. So much. I hope the emails you've been getting have been giving you something to think about! Making you realise that you can step outside your normal life, do new things! Meet new people! You were always so afraid, Leah. Of anything new, of anything different. And I know it's not your fault. If even half of what you said about your family was accurate then I'm astonished you even made it as far as you did, PhD and all. You had it tough. And me dying, well, I can't help it (would if I could, trust me!) but I know it's going to screw you up again.

That's why I scheduled those emails. To make you think. Obviously I can't know if you've done any of the things I asked of you. But, because I know you and your sense of misplaced responsibility, I think you'll have done as many as you could. And I hope they've gone some tiny way towards helping you. Not just helping you to get over losing me (although I'm hoping that, by now, you've made big steps in that direction), but helping you to break out of your self-imposed shell.

Anyway. Morphine time again soon, so this had better be it, but I just wanted to tell you two things.

First, we never talked about it, but that big sadness I once mentioned in my life? The one I dismissed, told you it was nothing really and you, bless you, never asked about again. Remember? Well, I lost my only child – my daughter – at birth. Still can't talk about it to this day. Hoping I get to see her again on the other side – if there is another side! Anyway, to a small extent, you took her place. I'm so proud of you, Leah, of what you achieved. Thank you for giving me the chance to 'mother', even just a little.

And second. Ah, this is the biggie. Y'see, I know about you and Lewis. Oh, he didn't tell me, I found out by accident when he left his phone on, but don't worry. I know you and you'll be beating yourself up about it, but truly, don't. Just – well, obviously I don't know now, you might be blissfully happy together but – I know you and I know him, and I don't think he's really the man for you. But I know why it has happened. Funny how approaching death makes everything suddenly so clear. Weird. You both want a bit of comfort and you've found it in each other, for now. And I understand. I really, really do. And, for what it's worth and because I know you put store in these things – I forgive you. Not that forgiveness is really mine to give, but, ah, you know. Forgive yourself, that's what I really mean. Now, go and live your best life, sweetheart.
All my love
Claire x

And that was when I had to go and stand outside and look at the sky for a while.

* * *

I was standing at the edge of the cliff, staring out over the gentle sea, feeling the sun redoubling its efforts, almost as though it had let itself down with last night's storm. Overhead, a gull I strongly suspected to be Roger was circling in the updraught, head tilted and legs stretched; the air smelled of salt, warm cattle and crushed grass. How could it all be so peaceful when my heart was trying to drill its way out of my chest?

Too much life had happened in this place. My head was full.

For a second I looked down into the dizzying depths of the sea below the cliff and then up to the cloud-flecked blue of the sky. It was all so beautiful. Claire had had all this taken away from her by her illness; she would far rather have been here to stand on this grassy ledge next to me, but she couldn't be. I owed it to her to unpack my feelings, deal with them. OK, maybe it had all happened at once – Brendon and I, my mother, Dylan, all the stuff with Claire and Lewis, but – well – that was life, wasn't it? Apparently.

'Lee?' The shadow crept up alongside me. 'You all right?'

'I'm fine, Dyl.' Still I felt the urge to 'mother' him. 'Just thinking.'

'Only, it's all right. You and me, know what I'm saying?'

I didn't really have a clue, emotional fluency were just two long words as far as my brother was concerned, but he always seemed to think I could read his mind. My upbringing told me to nod, smile and agree, but instead I said, 'Not really.'

A cautious hand patted my shoulder.

'You're a great sister,' he patted again, then dropped his arm and, obviously having exhausted himself with this emotional outburst, continued, 'so, like, you reckon I could go live at Tass's and do photography and stuff?'

I took a deep breath of the blue air. 'Dylan, you're a thirty-two-year-old man. You can do anything you...' I thought about swearing. I wanted to burn the sky with a few epithets, but could still feel the echo of my mother's hand swiping me around the ear for 'language', '…anything you want to. I'll give you any help you need.'

'Thanks. London's where it's happening. Gotta be there, Tass says. And, I reckon I've played all the games now. Mates won't be happy but – they gotta move on. Get out of living at home with the family, do some stuff!' He shoved his hands in his pockets, deep in denial of the fact that he would have been more than happy to have carried on doing just that if he hadn't come here and realised there was more to life than an attic and an Xbox. 'Tass says I've got an eye for photography and they know people I can talk to and maybe get an apprenticeship or summat.'

There was a new straightness to his back, a new light in his eye. And, while I knew it wouldn't be as easy as he imagined, I knew he had to try. 'I think it sounds like a fabulous idea, Dyl.'

'So.' He fiddled his hands around inside his pockets. 'What do we do about Mum?'

A shadow loomed alongside us, and I looked up to see Brendon approaching, still with a slightly stunned look.

'I emailed home,' he said. 'Mind you, it's the middle of the night over there, so I'm not expecting a reply but – wow, bonza…'

And I knew, then. Knew that Brendon and I could have a shot at a life together. That his steady reliability was pretty much exactly what I needed in my life. He wasn't self-obsessed like Darric. Or self-serving like Lewis. He was himself and anything that came up between us we could talk about, without him shooting me down or ignoring my concerns. And Australia didn't sound that bad. I could stop overthinking it.

'I didn't know Mum could even *work* a computer,' I said.

'I don't think she's up to building a robot to talk to though,' Dylan's pockets bulged and rotated again. 'What will she do when I leave? We can't just leave her, Lee. In that flat an' all. On her own.'

We're talking about our mother as though she's an elderly cat, I thought. *But what can we do? A woman in her forties, who's got the entitled attitude of a teenager and the capacity for self-care of a toddler?*

'Caretaker,' I said, suddenly.

The two men looked at me quizzically. On Brendon's face, this manifested as a slight crease between his sun-bleached eyebrows and a twist to his mouth. It made him look a bit dishevelled and… and – I almost blushed to admit it to myself – quite sexy.

Dylan looked like a five-year-old who's dropped his pencil.

'They need a caretaker for this place.' I pointed back at the house behind us. 'Just someone to live in and tidy up after the students, make sure they know how the pump works and how to log in to the WiFi. It's not arduous.' I thought back to the bloke who'd driven me here in his van. 'In fact, I'm pretty sure you don't have to do more than just put off potential burglars during the times that students aren't here.'

We all did a sort of group-swivel to look more directly at the house.

'Who'd burgle that?' Dylan curled his lip. 'Reckon them cows is worth more than that house.'

'Yes, pretty much the only thing anyone's taking away from here is a new appreciation of running water and a decent phone signal.' Brendon backed him up.

'Well, anyway. We could always ask her. If we break it to her nice and gently. She'd have her own room, lots of company and, if the state of the place when I arrived is anything to go by, practically no housework. She can probably bully the students into clearing up.' I looked at the rambling building in its field.

'And her brand of "cheer up love, you'll be fine, make me a cup of tea and has anyone got a fag" caring will probably be exactly what a bunch of students need.'

'And she likes it here.' Dylan turned again to look out over the sea. Points of light glinted off rising wave tops. 'It's boring as fuck, if you ask me.'

Overhead Roger had seen Dylan and come to hang directly overhead, mewing little cries of joy. Or hunger. Dylan groped in his pocket again and threw something that looked as though it had once been a bit of bread into the sky. Roger caught it in his beak and hurtled down the cliff face to land on a rock and gulp down the bread. We all watched him.

'I like that bird,' Dylan said. 'Don't s'pose he'd like London much though.'

'London seagulls would mug him.' I carried on peering over the edge. 'Here he's a big bird in a small sky. Up in London, well, the gulls grow up beating rats into submission.'

Dylan shrugged and then, clearly having completed his mission to convince me that our mother was my problem, began to slouch back over the rapidly greening grass to the house.

Brendon put an arm around me. It felt natural now, not as though we were posing for Hallmark.

'So,' he said. 'You and me.'

You've only had two goes at men so far. Just because they were rubbish, doesn't mean they all are. Giving up on all of them on the strength of a couple of bad choices is what happens in bad books, not life. Like he said, you're allowed another go...

'The length of this pause isn't helping my ego,' Brendon cautiously tightened the hug. 'Anything you need to tell me?'

A gentle breeze blew against my cheek like a last message. 'No. Actually, yes.' I half-turned in his embrace. 'It's yes. You and me. Now I know that Claire knew about Lewis and me and forgave me, I feel… better.'

'Yeah, OK.' The breeze had caught in his hair. He looked like the sort of person you'd see on a poster for beach sports. 'I can see how that—'

'Like, how could I move on with that hanging over me?' I carried on. 'But she knew. All the time, she knew. And she never said anything when she could have. She could have told me to get out of her life for good. Or him, I suppose. And she…'

That last evening. Sitting by her bed, knowing that we were just waiting. Holding her hand as she dipped in and out of consciousness, tired and drawn from pain and procedures that sometimes helped and sometimes didn't.

Lewis had gone out of the room for some water, or tea, or something. Claire's eyes had flickered open for a moment. 'You don't need a man,' her voice a dry whisper. 'Leah. Be who you want to be. Fly free.'

They'd been her last words to me. And I'd thought it was approval of my solitary life she'd been giving. That she'd finally stopped trying to talk me into being more sociable and accepted that I was happy as I was, alone in the little house.

But now I realised. She'd been warning me off Lewis. Warning me off falling into being dependent on him and his peculiar brand of affection – using him to replace her. She really had wanted me to be free, free to love someone who was good for me.

'Claire would have liked you.'

'Well, I'd hope so. She sounds like a riot.'

Yes, Claire would have approved of Brendon. Surfer hair, broad shoulders, long vowels and all. She'd have loved him. She saw it all. And Lewis? She knew he wasn't the man for me. That we'd only been looking for comfort in one another, not an affair.

Claire knew.

And as we walked back in the brittle light, arms around each other, to break the news to my mother that we might have found her her first job in thirty years, I could hear Claire's approval as clearly as if we'd been sitting in that sunny kitchen still.

You're moving on, Leah. Finally growing up and learning to see people for what they are. Seeing the possibilities in them, rather than having expectations set in stone. Hey, it's just like life! Nothing is set in stone. Everything can change. Everything will *change and you can stop being scared of that now. What's done is done, and now you can get on with what comes next.*

In my head, I raised a glass of gin to memory-Claire, and I was almost sure I heard the tinkle of imaginary ice cubes and a hearty chuckle as she lifted her glass in response.

Acknowledgements

During the writing of this book I found myself briefly hospitalised, which was a frightening experience. So I'd like to dedicate this book to those ladies who shared a ward with me and helped keep my spirits up as we laughed and grumbled and generally got through hospital life. So, Kimberley Rooke, Daphne van Pul, Ayse Yesil and Rita Teresa Sanderson – this one is for you lot!

And an honourable mention – and thanks – goes to Ryan, for the Aussie slang!

Also Available

Christmas by the sea – that sounds romantic, right?

Tansy Merriweather is down on her luck. She's lost her business and her relationship, and instead of a glamorous London apartment, her home is now a campervan on a Dorset beach. And as if things couldn't get any worse, a scruffy dog called Brian with a taste for sardines has adopted her.

When Tansy's new-found friends at the café in the bay help her find a job as a location scout for a new TV show, things start looking up. However, when she finds herself babysitting the show's grouchy star, Davin O'Riordan, she's not sure she wants to stay around. But when Brian forges a touching romance with Davin's elegant whippet Seelie, Tansy begins to see another side to Davin.

As Christmas approaches, secrets emerge and Tansy and Davin discover a bond between them. But how will they cope with the storms headed their way – and can they save the café from closing?

Seasons by the Sea, Book 1

OUT NOW!

About the Author

Jane Lovering was, presumably, born, although everyone concerned denies all knowledge. However, there is evidence that her early years were spent in Devon (she can still talk like a pirate under the right conditions) and of her subsequent removal to Yorkshire under a sack and sedation.

She now lives in North Yorkshire, where she writes romantic comedies, one or two of which have won awards. Owing to a terrible outbreak of insanity she is now the minder of three cats and two terriers, one of which is a Patterdale and therefore as insane as Jane. Though smaller, and cuter, obviously.

Jane's likes include marshmallows, the smell of cucumbers and the understairs cupboard, words beginning with B, and Doctor Who. She writes with her laptop balanced on her knees whilst lying on her bed, and her children were brought up to believe that real food has a high carbon content. And a kind of amorphous shape. Not unlike Jane herself, come to think of it.

She had some hobbies once, but she can't remember what they were. Ask her to show you how many marshmallows she can fit in her mouth at once, though, that might give you a clue.

You can find Jane on Twitter at @janelovering, and visit her website at www.janelovering.co.uk.

Note from the Publisher

To receive updates on new releases in the Seasons by the Sea series – plus special offers and news of other humorous fiction series to make you smile – sign up now to the Farrago mailing list at farragobooks.com/sign-up.